WHEN THE ROAD COMES AROUND

BOOKS BY KATIE POWNER

The Sowing Season

A Flicker of Light

Where the Blue Sky Begins

The Wind Blows in Sleeping Grass

When the Road Comes Around

WHEN THE ROAD COMES AROUND

KATIE POWNER

BETHANYHOUSE

a division of Baker Publishing Group
Minneapolis, Minnesota

© 2025 by Katie Powner

Published by Bethany House Publishers
Minneapolis, Minnesota
BethanyHouse.com

Bethany House Publishers is a division of
Baker Publishing Group, Grand Rapids, Michigan

Printed in the United States of America

Library of Congress Cataloging-in-Publication Data
Names: Powner, Katie, author.
Title: When the road comes around / Katie Powner.
Description: Minneapolis, Minnesota : Bethany House, a division of Baker
    Publishing Group, 2025.
Identifiers: LCCN 2024059516 | ISBN 9780764245169 (paperback) | ISBN
    9780764245299 (casebound) | ISBN 9781493451005 (ebook)
Subjects: LCGFT: Christian fiction. | Novels.
Classification: LCC PS3616.O96 W53 2025 | DDC 813/.6—dc23/eng/20241213
LC record available at https://lccn.loc.gov/2024059516

Cover design by Studio Gearbox, Chris Gilbert
Cover image by John P. Kelly, Getty

Author is represented by WordServe Literary Group.

Baker Publishing Group publications use paper produced from sustainable forestry practices and postconsumer waste whenever possible.

25 26 27 28 29 30 31   7 6 5 4 3 2 1

To everyone in need of a little grace.

one

Tad Bungley had always hoped Sam's habit of disappearing would keep the kid safe from women like Maddie Pine. Women who knew how to get their sharp, painted fingernails into a guy and not let go until the moment it would cause the most damage. But as Maddie's red Mazda RX-7 wound its way up the dirt road to Come Around Ranch, Tad had a bad feeling.

Real bad.

"Sam?" Tad called into the barn, though Sam never responded out loud to his name. He just came. Or not. "Sam, you in here?"

Dust mites floated through sunbeams, and a kitten mewed. The kid was probably tucked away somewhere with Curly, the oldest mutt Tad had ever seen. But he should stop thinking of Sam as a kid. Sam was twenty, after all. Only four years younger than Tad, although somewhere along the line, his brain had stopped keeping up with this body.

Tad's brain had grown up like it was supposed to, though he wouldn't blame anyone for wondering after all the dumb stunts he'd pulled. Far as he could tell, the only real advantage his brain had over Sam's was he knew a set of dangerous fingernails when he saw one, and he had plenty of scratch marks to prove it.

Where the dirt road turned to gravel near the Wilsons' house, the Mazda crunched to a stop. Sam's parents, Dan and Anita Wilson, had hired Tad to work on the ranch, not mind their business, but Tad found himself marching briskly to intercept Maddie before she could walk up to his new employer's front door. Anita had the kind of heart that loved to take in strays and give second chances, and Tad had the kind that didn't trust Maddie as far as he could throw her.

She opened her car door and slid out in one fluid motion, flicking her long brown hair over her shoulder.

He stepped in front of her, squinting in the sun. "What are you doing here?"

Her face gave nothing away. "Thaddeus Bungley. Huh."

"It's Tad, and you know it. What do you mean *huh*?"

"The rumors were true."

His heart sank. Just what he needed. More people telling stories about him. "What rumors?"

"That the Wilsons were the only ones in the whole county who felt sorry enough for you to take you on."

He bristled. Okay, so maybe he himself was one of the strays in need of a second chance that Anita's kind heart had made room for, but that couldn't be the *only* reason the Wilsons had hired him. He was good with horses, decent at manual labor, and had always stuck up for Sam at school when other kids—including Maddie—were jerks. Surely all that counted for something. Plus, *his* intentions were pure. He needed a job and was willing to work hard. As for Maddie? Who knew what intentions might be lurking behind those fancy sunglasses.

"I don't put much stock in rumors," he grumbled. "Now,

back to my question. What are you doing here? We're all busy. The guest houses are booked from May to November. We've only got two weeks to get everything ready."

"I also heard your dad got in a fight with Scooter. And lost."

What he wouldn't give for a cigarette right about now. And what could she possibly know about his dad?

He tried his best to glower. "Maddie. What do you want?"

She turned up her nose. "Can't a girl get out of town for some fresh air and sunshine once in a while?"

He made a face. There was plenty of fresh air and sunshine *in* town. No need to come all the way out here.

Gravel shifted behind him, and he spun around. Sam was trekking toward them, walkie-talkie in hand and Curly at his side. The dog's grizzled face drooped like every step was a hardship.

Sam grinned at Maddie. "You came."

"Of course I did." She squeezed his shoulder. "How could I turn down an invitation from my favorite farmer?"

Tad scowled at the sudden sweetness in her voice. How dare she act like she hadn't tormented Sam all those years in school?

She turned to him. "Sam told me about his new kittens at church yesterday. I didn't see *you* there, by the way."

Tad grunted. He didn't know much about a lot, but he knew there was no way she'd come all the way out here just to see Sam's kittens. Or for the sunshine. He'd known her since fifth grade, when he'd been held back and had to get used to a whole new set of classmates. She was the one who started saying he'd "bungled it up" every time he messed up a project or bombed a test. She was the one who would bait Sam into some blunder and then act offended when everyone laughed at him.

How could someone as wretched as Maddie Pine and someone as caring as Anita Wilson go to the same church?

Maddie reached a hand toward Curly but stopped short of touching him. "What's your dog's name?"

"Curly."

She laughed. "But he's got the straightest fur I've ever seen."

Sam leaned forward earnestly and gave his best Billy Crystal impersonation. "He's like a saddlebag with eyes."

This time Tad laughed as a confused expression twisted Maddie's face. "It's from the movie *City Slickers*. Sam's favorite."

Tad had only worked at the ranch for a week, and already he'd heard Sam quote the entire movie at least twice.

Sam stuck his walkie-talkie in the back pocket of his jeans. He never went anywhere without it. "Want to come with us, Tad?"

"I wish I could, but I've got to keep working."

"Okay." Sam grabbed Maddie's hand and pulled. "Come on. They're in the barn."

Sam was strong and Maddie couldn't weigh more than a buck twenty. As the kid practically dragged her away, Curly gimping along behind them, Tad's heart sank a little deeper. As much as he wanted to keep a close eye on Maddie, what he'd told Sam was true. He had work to do. Dan had made it clear when he gave him the job that he expected Tad to keep himself busy. *"And if I ever catch wind of you smoking on C-A-R property . . ."* he'd said, and then let the words hang there ominously.

Tad returned his attention to the task he'd been starting when he first saw Maddie's red car—cleaning the guest house gutters. He'd already loaded the ladder, hose, and gloves in the back of the farm truck. As he walked past the barn, he heard Sam's laughter from somewhere inside and kicked himself. Why hadn't he taken the time to meet the new kittens? Sam had begged him repeatedly, *"Please, Tad, please, Tad, please."* He should've done it.

But Tad wasn't here to babysit Sam, much as he liked the kid. He was here to earn money for his own place so he could finally follow in his older brother's footsteps and move out of his dad's crap-hole shack. The sooner, the better. He couldn't help but keep an eye on Sam—the kid followed him like a baby duck half the time—but the ranch had to be Tad's priority. He had to make Dan happy and keep this job.

He hopped in the farm truck and drove toward the guest houses, thinking about Maddie and her stupid sunglasses and everything she'd said. The idea of his dad getting beat up by Scooter MacDonald sparked conflicting feelings in his gut. He didn't mind too much the thought of his dad, the infamous Bud Bungley, being put in his place. But man, he hated that Scooter guy. Scooter was a couple years older than Tad and the type who would throw a sack of puppies in the river just for fun.

When had this fight happened? His dad hadn't said anything. He'd been his usual surly self. Maddie had probably made that story up to get Tad's goat.

He pulled up to the first guest house and turned off the truck. Joke was on her. He didn't have a goat.

two

The big, blue Montana sky was turning gray as Tad finished the gutters on the last guest house. It wasn't much of a house. None of them were. Just small cabins with one bedroom, one bathroom, a kitchenette, and a sitting room with a stacked washer and dryer in the closet. No TV. No Wi-Fi. Yet schmucks from out of state paid hundreds of dollars a night to book one of these things a year in advance and encounter what the C-A-R website called "an authentic Montana ranch experience."

Well, he was happy to do his part, though he wasn't sure if the guests about to flock here from far and wide were going to be any easier to handle than the Herefords the Wilsons used to run. At least with cattle, you always knew what they wanted: something to eat, something to drink, somewhere to get out of the wind. With people, there was no telling.

At the truck, he took a swig from a bottle of Mountain Dew and saw Maddie's Mazda driving away. She'd been here this whole time? Didn't she have anything better to do? A job or something? He tossed the bottle back in the truck and wiped his mouth with his sleeve. She probably worked for her dad, the man whose face was on every For Sale sign, newspaper ad, and park bench in Grady. *Pining for a new home? Call Matthew Pine, Realtor.*

Speaking of schmucks. Matthew Pine walked around Grady like he owned it just because he had more money than everyone else, swooping in to buy up houses whenever people fell on hard times. It had never set right with Tad the way Matthew would shake his head and say *"What a shame"* the morning another place went into foreclosure and then make a deal with the bank before dinner the same day.

Two-faced. Like Maddie.

The three guest houses sat on a small hill overlooking the long, winding driveway, about fifty yards apart from one another. With the mountains in the distance, there was a great view even when clouds formed. Tad eyed the darkening sky with a grimace. Good thing he got those gutters finished. Rain was coming.

As Maddie's car disappeared around a bend, his fingers itched to pull the pack of Camels from the inside pocket of his coat. If he slipped around the corner of the house and hid the butt back in his pocket when he was finished, no one would ever know if he took a quick smoke break. Dan was down behind the barn in the round pen, working the horses, and last he saw Anita was in the house.

He leaned against the west side of the cabin and drew in a lungful of satisfying poison, his thoughts returning to Maddie. She was hot, he'd give her that, but her heart was stone cold. Sure, maybe he had some trust issues with women after his mother split when he was eight, but that wasn't why he harbored deep suspicions when it came to Maddie Pine.

A rumbling sound caught his attention, and he stiffened. Not thunder. It was Dan's four-wheeler. Shoot. He tossed his cigarette in the dirt and quickly ground it out with his boot. As he bent to pick it up, he could hear the four-wheeler come to a stop behind the farm truck. Tad shoved the butt in his inner coat pocket and coughed as he came around the corner of the cabin to meet Dan, resisting the urge to wave a hand in front of him to clear away the smell of smoke.

Dan stood beside the truck, arms crossed over his chest as if he knew exactly what Tad had been doing. As if he had seen through the walls of the cabin and straight into Tad's soul.

He gave Tad a long, hard look. "You about done up here?"

Tad swallowed. "Just finished."

"No gutters on the west side."

Tad tried to think of an excuse but couldn't. Quick thinking had never been easy for him. He settled for a change of subject. "Looks like it's going to rain. You want me to fill any of those potholes before I go?"

A load of gravel had been delivered that morning to be used to smooth out the driveway, which was riddled with potholes the size of Sam's dog. Since Dan worked four tens at the hardware store in town, Tuesday through Friday, he probably wouldn't be able to deal with the gravel until the weekend, unless he got it done tonight.

Dan hesitated, then shook his head. "Me and Sam'll do it. But Anita wanted me to tell you to stop by the house before you leave. I don't know what, but she's been baking something."

Tad perked up, his stomach already anticipating the buttery goodness of shortbread or chocolate chip cookies or almond bars. Anita's baked goods were well known to Tad. Even before he started working here, Anita would sometimes bring treats by the house for him and his dad, them technically being neighbors and all. *"Every time you take a bite, remember I'm praying for you,*" she'd say, and he couldn't even be annoyed about it because she was so nice.

Maybe it was a pie!

He tried to keep his lips from twitching into a smile. "Will do."

Dan uncrossed his arms, shifted on his feet, then crossed them again. "Look, Tad, I'm going to be straight with you. It was Anita's idea to bring you on, and I wasn't thrilled about it, but now that you're here I figure it's best for everyone if it works out, right?"

Tad tensed as he became aware of a prick of heat from the vicinity of his inner coat pocket. He stared dumbly back at Dan. "Yes? I mean, I want it to work out. Uh, Mr. Wilson. Sir."

He'd blown every other job he'd had the past five years, and he needed this one to take if he was ever going to get his own place.

"Then I've got to be able to trust you." Dan looked him in the eye. "When guests start arriving, I've got to know there aren't going to be any problems."

Tad looked away. Dan and his dad Bud were different as night and day on the outside. Dan was tall and lean and had gray specks in the light brown hair under his cowboy hat, while Bud was built like a bull, all muscle and rounded shoulders and aggression. Dark eyes, dark hair. But apparently they had one thing in common: a steadfast belief in Tad's ability to screw things up.

Okay, so maybe he didn't have the greatest track record when it came to employment, but anyone could've accidentally thrown the deposit bag from the gas station in the dumpster with the trash. And he never would've delivered that pallet of feed to the wrong ranch if he'd been given better directions.

"No problems." Tad shoved his hands in his pockets, heat spreading across his chest. "I won't let you down. Promise."

Tad thought maybe Dan would say something about where Tad could put his promises or how they weren't worth diddly-squat, but he didn't. That was another way Dan and Bud were different. Bud never missed a chance to tell Tad exactly how big of a loser he was.

Dan dipped his chin. "Okay, then. See you tomorrow."

He turned and climbed back on the four-wheeler. As he drove off, Tad tore open his coat, and a puff of smoke escaped. He fished out the smoldering butt and examined the small hole singed through his inner pocket, feeling like maybe there was a lesson there somewhere but not sure what it was.

⁕ ⁕ ⁕

Sam and Curly were waiting when Tad parked the farm truck next to the barn and got out.

"Maddie said my kittens are the cutest kittens she's ever seen."

Tad bit back a sigh. What did Maddie want with Sam, anyway? She'd never been his friend. Then again, she *could've* come here to see the kittens. What other reason was there? Even though he didn't trust Maddie, he didn't need to be so paranoid all the time.

"I told her she could have one when they get big enough," Sam continued. "I think she likes the white one with the black spot on its face. Do you think I should name it Spot?"

Tad shut the truck door. "You should probably let Maddie name it, if she's going to keep it."

Sam nodded solemnly. "She's nice."

Tad didn't have the heart to dispute that, so he turned and

walked toward the house. Sam followed a half step behind. He was a couple inches taller than Tad and at least twenty pounds heavier, but then, Tad had always been kind of scrawny. Which his father hated. From the corner of his eye, Tad saw Sam take a big swing at a rock with his foot and miss.

"Holy huckleberries." Sam laughed. "Did you see that, Tad?"

"I saw." He pointed to another rock.

Sam grinned and tried again. This time, his foot connected. "One, two, three, four, five, six."

Tad smiled. He'd learned that Sam liked to kick rocks as hard as he could and count until they came to a stop. "That was a good one."

"I'm going to help my dad move gravel."

"I heard."

"My dad said I'll be in charge of the shovel because he's feeling old."

Tad chuckled and glanced at the darkening sky. "I'm guessing you'll both be doing plenty of shoveling."

"Are you going to the house? Because my dad said my mom wants you to go to the house."

"Yeah, I'm going."

"Okay. Bye, Tad."

He spun around and headed back to the barn before Tad could even respond. That's how Sam was. When he was with you, he was really with you. When he wasn't, he wasn't.

Tad reached the house and slowed his pace, suddenly feeling like an intruder. He didn't belong here, did he? With people like this? People who went to church and stuck by one another and gave second chances. People who would never doubt Maddie's intentions for coming to the ranch. The house's welcoming warmth had an irresistible pull, however, and he took another step closer.

He knocked timidly on the front door. Anita opened it with a dish towel in her hand and a smile on her face.

"Tad, you get on in here. You don't need to knock."

He prickled inside. He wasn't going to just walk into their house like—

"We're all family around here." Anita ushered him toward the kitchen. "And we're all so happy to have you helping out."

Right. Except for Dan. But Tad figured it would be best not to bring that up.

"It smells good."

Anita's smile grew. "I made some maple pecan bread. I was going to send you home with two loaves, but I gave one to Maddie. She looked like she could use an extra hug, you know?"

His mind started to form the thought that Maddie didn't deserve a hug from a woman like Anita, but he stopped it. He was pretty sure he didn't deserve one either.

She held out a loaf wrapped in colorful fabric that had been rubbed with beeswax, and he took it. It was still warm. When was the last time he'd had something homemade like this, still warm from the oven? His dad had maybe warmed up a Pop-Tart for him once or twice when he was younger, but he had long ago quit making meals for Tad. *"When are you gonna grow a pair and stop mooching off your old man?"* he liked to ask.

Tad looked at the loaf in his hands. It was only bread, but his throat tightened. "Thank you."

Anita squeezed his hand. "See, it's like getting a hug. And every time you take a bite . . ."

One corner of Tad's mouth lifted. "I should remember you're praying for me. I know."

"Good. Bring that fabric back when you're done, and I can reuse it."

"All right."

Before he could get too comfortable or start doing something stupid like spilling his guts to Anita, he said good-bye and hurried out to his beater 1989 Ford Taurus. He'd bought it from a guy at his last job for two hundred bucks. Most of it was gray, but the rear driver's side door was maroon and rattled like a carnival ride at the county fair. As he did his best to navigate around the potholes down the long driveway, the smell of the maple pecan bread filled him with an undefinable longing.

He thought of his dad. The Wilsons had known Bud since they were growing up together in Grady. It was a small town. What had Bud been like then? As a kid in school?

Wait. Tad raised one side of his upper lip in a snarl.

Did Anita pray for Bud too?

three

It had been over an hour since Anita Wilson lowered the heat under the pot of minestrone soup and covered the corn bread with a tea towel, yet the guys hadn't come in for supper. They were still at it, trying to finish filling the potholes before the rain started. As she waited, she prayed the storm would hold off until they were through.

A cat rubbed against her ankles, and she glanced down. "Why do you suppose Dan didn't ask Tad to stay and help with the gravel, Sabina?"

The calico's crooked tail swished as she meowed in response.

"Well, yes, of course I would have insisted Tad stay for supper afterward."

Another meow.

"We'll have to keep praying that Dan will have a change of heart toward him, then, won't we?"

Sabina followed eagerly as Anita walked to the pantry for the bin of cat food and gave Sabina a scoop. Just because Anita had chosen to wait and eat with the guys whenever they managed to come in didn't mean the cat had to. Six-year-old Sabina was the only cat that lived in the house instead of the barn, because she'd been born with two deformed back legs. Anita had brought her inside when she was still a kitten, knowing the ranch posed many dangers for a cat that couldn't run. She'd named her after Sabina Wurmbrand, a strong woman of faith who had overcome unimaginable trials.

The cat shared little resemblance to her courageous namesake, hiding in fear at the slightest unexpected noise, but as Anita's rheumatoid arthritis had worsened over the past couple of years, causing her to feel much older than forty-eight, she had become more and more thankful for a household companion.

Anita left Sabina to eat in peace and looked out the kitchen window. Though imminent rain threatened over the ranch, in the distance a slice of the sun pierced through an opening in the clouds, sending brilliant rays of light in every direction as it set.

Beautiful. Though the world was home to many ugly things, God's creation was so beautiful it made her want to cry. How could anyone spend day after day with their head down and never once look up and see it?

Her thoughts returned to Tad. She understood Dan's reluctance to hire the boy. If his poor reputation around town wasn't enough, there was also Tad's father to consider. Anita's first love. But that was decades ago, and Bud had been a different person then. Before Holly destroyed him.

Anita didn't want to think about that.

When Dan had told her the man who'd helped them last summer had taken a job up in Bridger Canyon, she'd immediately understood why God had been bringing Tad to mind during her prayer time every day for weeks. Dan couldn't give up his job at the hardware store and the health insurance that came with it to do all the summer work himself. He would have to hire someone else. It was perfectly clear to her.

Dan had not seen it so clearly. She'd convinced him, though, like she always did, all the while pondering the fine line between stubbornness and conviction.

"Lord, am I bossy?"

A buzz caught her attention—a text message. She scanned around for her phone. Where had she set it down? She was always leaving it somewhere and forgetting about it, much to Dan's consternation.

After fifteen seconds, the phone buzzed again, as it would continue to do until she cleared the notification.

"Sabina, where did I put my phone?"

The cat didn't respond. Anita listened carefully and moved closer to the sound every fifteen seconds until she found the phone wedged between two couch cushions. The message was from her friend Diana.

Call me when you get a minute.

Anita squinted at the screen and dialed up her friend.

Diana answered right away. "Hey, Nikki went into labor. Jim and I are on our way to the hospital right now."

"Oh, that's wonderful." Anita smiled, even as a stab of longing pricked her heart. This would be Diana's third grandchild, and Anita was determined to be happy for her. Grandchildren were always a blessing, even if they would never be hers.

She took a breath. "What can I do to help?"

"Can you cover for me at the Coalition in the morning? I signed up for a shift because I didn't think the baby would come until next week. She went so late with her last one."

"Yes, I can do that. Nine to eleven?"

"Yep. Thanks so much, Anita. I've got to go, we're almost there. I'll text you when there's good news!"

"Okay, I'll be—" Anita's words were cut off as Diana hung up—"praying for Nikki."

She set the phone down on the counter. It seemed like someone she knew was welcoming a new grandbaby every other month these days. What would it be like to be a grandma?

She wouldn't wallow in *what-ifs*. She had a full life. And now she had the opportunity to spend extra time at the Coalition, the nonprofit outreach center for farmers and ranchers where she and Diana volunteered. The Coalition's mission was to offer mental health resources and support to the local agricultural community, and Anita had decided to become a volunteer when she'd learned that farmers and ranchers were nearly two times more likely to commit suicide than people in other occupations.

It was a difficult statistic to swallow. Hard to believe. Yet she and Dan had heard of three men in the past five years who had taken their lives, and she wanted to do what she could to help. She spent time at the Coalition at least twice a week and prayed for every single person she interacted with through the outreach.

Her heart squeezed. "Lord, thank You for this opportunity to serve."

The mudroom door opened, and the sound of boots and jackets being removed warmed Anita's heart even more. Was there ever a woman as fortunate as she? A hard-working, godly, and by-golly handsome husband and a kind and doting son who would never leave her as most women's sons did. Some people said Sam was touched in the head, but she knew that if he was touched by anything, it was angel wings.

She turned off the stovetop heat and pulled the milk jug from the fridge, ready to get supper on the table as quickly as possible. "You guys must be starving."

Sam entered the kitchen first, a grin on his face. "Mom! I shoveled way more gravel than Dad."

"That's great, honey. Did you get the job finished?"

Dan appeared, raking a hand through his thick, salt-and-pepper hair, which still held the unmistakable imprint of his hat. "Not quite, but we managed to fill the biggest ones."

A roll of thunder shook the house, followed by the sound of fat raindrops hitting the roof.

Anita smiled. "Just in time."

Sam's eyes widened. "Did God make the rain wait until we came in?"

Dan laughed. "Maybe so. Maybe He had pity on us poor souls."

While the guys washed up, Anita ladled soup into bowls and set out butter and honey for the corn bread. There was nothing better than soup and corn bread on a rainy day. She also poured warm water over a scoop of kibble in Curly's dish in the mudroom. He sat and waited patiently on his blanket next to the little table where they charged the walkie-talkies. The water softened the food so Curly's ancient teeth could chew it. At fifteen, he was almost a hundred in dog years. He and Sam had grown up together.

"Good boy." She gently rubbed his ear. "I'll save you some soup."

He had been a faithful and devoted friend to Sam. She wished he could live forever.

Once they were seated at the table and Dan had said grace, Sam began to wolf down his food.

"Slow down there, pal." Dan patted Sam's shoulder. "It's not going anywhere."

Sam replied with his mouth full. "I'm so hungry, I could eat a horse. No, what's something bigger than a horse? A whale!"

Anita snorted into her soup, loving, as always, his childlike enthusiasm, even though she knew he had no real concept of how immense a whale could be. That kind of uninhibited zeal for life was what made Sam *Sam*, and she wouldn't change him for anything. Though sometimes, in moments of weakness, she wished his body would've stayed eight years old along with his mind so people who didn't know him would be able to see that he was still a child. So they wouldn't assume her tall, strong son was as equipped to handle life as he appeared to be on the outside. Because he wasn't.

Sam's first bowl of soup disappeared in a flash, and Anita hopped up to refill it. "Did you check on the kittens before you came in?"

His forehead wrinkled. "No. Should I go back out?"

Dan shook his head. "I'm sure they're getting by just fine without you."

"Okay. Maddie likes the white one with the spot."

Anita set Sam's refilled bowl in front of him. "That one is very pretty."

"Maddie is pretty."

"Yes, she is." Anita thought of the way Maddie had taken the loaf of bread from her earlier, and her heart squeezed with compassion. Maddie and Tad were a lot alike. Both living in their fathers' shadows.

"Do you think she'll come back tomorrow?" Sam asked.

Anita exchanged a look with Dan as she sat back down in her chair. Sam had always been drawn to pretty girls. "She didn't say, but she's probably a very busy person. She won't have time to drive out here every day."

It was a twenty-minute drive to Come Around Ranch from where Maddie lived.

"Okay." Sam smeared a large pat of butter on his corn bread. "I'm glad Tad's coming tomorrow. He said I could go with him to town to pick up the mineral blocks."

Anita shifted. "I thought you were going to the grocery store with me tomorrow."

"Groceries are boring, Mom. I want to go with Tad."

An unfamiliar feeling prodded Anita's stomach. This was a change. Sam *always* went grocery shopping with her.

Dan leaned back from the table and gave Sam a fatherly look. "Your mother will need your help carrying the bags, pal. If you told her you were going to go—"

"No, no, it's fine." Anita raised a hand. "I'll manage. Carl will carry everything out for me."

"What about when you get home?"

"If I can't manage it, it can wait in the car until someone can unload it. Nothing's going to spoil."

"Are you sure?"

She found the concerned expression on Dan's face both endearing and frustrating. She knew he didn't like to see her struggle with tasks that used to be easy. She didn't like it either. But rheumatoid arthritis—RA—was part of her life now, and she was a ranch wife, after all. She wasn't going to break. Besides, Dan was always the one saying Sam needed to do more things on his own, away from her, so he could learn to be independent.

She didn't see any way he was ever going to be able to leave the ranch, though. No one understood him like she did.

She forced a smile. "It'll be fine."

"All right." Dan turned to Sam. "But you better unload the groceries as soon as you get a chance."

"I will."

"We don't want the ice cream to melt in the car."

Anita huffed. "What makes you think I'm getting ice cream?"

Dan grinned at her. "Because you love me."

"Hmph." She pretended to sulk. "I guess I can add it to the list."

Sam sat up straighter. "Oreos too?"

Her lips twitched. "Don't push your luck."

Between the two of them, Dan and Sam could polish off a package of Oreos in one sitting, even if there was a whole batch of homemade cookies sitting right there on the kitchen counter.

Dan carried his bowl over to the stove for another serving. "Soup's really good. Thank you."

Sam nodded vigorously. "Yeah, thanks, Mom."

And in a blink, the little bit of irritation that had been growing in Anita's chest was gone. This was what she lived for. For both the men in her life to come home safely at the end of every day, no matter how much dirt they trekked in with them. To do whatever she could for her family. To feed them. To pray for them. To never let the Lord forget how much they meant to her.

Even when her joints hurt too much to do anything but slide a frozen pizza into the oven, she could always pray. No matter how much her knees protested, she could always kneel.

She was a blessed woman. And she had everything she'd ever need in life right here at this kitchen table. Nothing was going to change that.

four

Mud. It had been raining for three days and everywhere Tad looked, he saw mud. The driveway up to Come Around Ranch was a mess, despite the filled-in potholes. The footpaths around the barn were miry muck. Snowpack that had been holding on for dear life in the shady places under trees and the north sides of boulders and buildings had melted, forming little streams as it made its way to lower ground.

Ugh. Tad's boots sank into the ground when he stepped into the round pen. He couldn't work the horses in this. It was too risky. That temperamental quarter horse TJ was hard enough to get along with when the ground was dry.

"I think we need to change our plans." He looked over his shoulder at Sam to find the kid only inches away, breathing down his neck.

Sam took a step back. "But Bob wants to run."

Bob was Sam's favorite horse, a raggedy eighteen-year-old palomino with one white sock and bald patches all over her body.

"She's going to have to wait another day. Why'd you give her a boy's name, anyway?"

Sam shrugged. "It's not her real name."

"What's her real name?"

"Belle of the Ball. She had that one when we got her. But that's too long, so I call her Bob."

Tad chuckled to himself. It made perfect Sam-sense, and somehow it figured that the ugliest horse he'd ever seen was named Belle of the Ball.

Sam leaned his arms on the top of the gate and looked out over the round pen. "What are we going to do now?"

"I'm going to dig a trench away from the fence. To drain the water."

"Can I help?"

"Sure."

He should've done it yesterday, but the rain had tapered off and the sun had come out and he'd been tricked into believing the weather had turned. He should've known better.

"When it rains in *City Slickers*, Mitch has to dodge a tree branch that gets struck by lightning and rescue a baby calf from the river." Sam pushed off the gate. "I like that part."

They retrieved shovels from the barn, where Curly had stationed himself in the doorway to keep an eye on Sam without having to get wet. He was older than dirt, but not dumber than rocks. Sam stopped to visit with the mutt for a minute before following Tad around to the south end of the round pen. Every time Tad saw Sam talk to Curly that way, he felt something in his gut he couldn't quite name.

Sam swung his shovel through the air like a lightsaber. "It's been raining a lot. That's probably why Maddie hasn't come back yet."

Tad frowned. "She might not ever come back, Sam."

The kid held the shovel over his head. "Maddie's my friend."

Tad focused on the ground. He'd believed that once too.

That Maddie was his friend. She'd started being nice to him their senior year, and he'd thought maybe she wasn't as bad as he'd always thought. She talked to him in the hallway between classes and showed him how to do the math homework he couldn't figure out. When she'd asked if he wanted to meet under the bleachers during lunch, he'd been quick to agree. When she'd asked if he'd bring pot to the rendezvous, a warning bell had gone off in his brain, but she'd touched his arm and smiled, and his teenage hormones had easily overruled the warning.

Finding a joint to share with Maddie that day had been easy. Explaining to the principal when they got caught that it had been Maddie's idea had been impossible. Maddie had cried and said that Tad had threatened her. That she'd been too scared to say no, even though she had been the one begging, only five minutes before, for "just one more turn."

He'd gotten five days of in-school suspension and a phone call from Matthew Pine describing how his dad would lose his property if Tad ever went near Maddie again. She'd gotten off scot-free.

No one had ever believed the truth, not even his father.

Especially not his father.

Tad glanced at Sam. "I don't want you to get your hopes up, okay?"

Sam smiled and shrugged, his hopes clearly up as high as they could go, and Tad sighed. "See that grassy area down there?" He pointed. "That's where I want the water to go."

"Okay."

The grass was mostly brown, but bits of green had started to appear this week, coaxed by the sun and rain. As Tad marked off a starting point with his shovel and started to dig, his stomach grumbled. He'd finished off Anita's maple pecan bread yesterday, so breakfast this morning had been a day-old donut and cup of coffee from the gas station. The gas station was out of his way when driving to the ranch, but Bud didn't keep much that resembled groceries in the house. Tad had survived for years on Mountain Dew, Oberto pepperoni sticks, and Camels.

"Tad, do you think it's going to rain all day?"

He grunted as his shovel struck the wet, rocky dirt. "I don't know."

"It's too bad horses can't hold umbrellas."

"That wouldn't make a difference. The mud is dangerous for their feet. You know that."

"Too bad they can't wear boots."

Tad couldn't hold back a small smile. "Yeah. That would be something."

As he stopped shoveling for a moment to picture it, he noticed Anita walking toward them wearing an oversized green raincoat with the hood up. He leaned his shovel against the fence and jogged to meet her, not wanting her to spend any more time in the rain than necessary.

"I got a call from Mrs. Duncan down the road." The misty rain collected on top of her hood and dripped down the sides. "You know the ditch that runs along the last part of the driveway?"

Tad nodded as Sam appeared beside him, eager to listen in, always wanting to be part of everything Tad was doing.

"She said it's clogged with debris and starting to flood onto the road. Can you go down and check it out?"

"Sure."

Sam bobbed his head. "Me too. Hi, Mom."

Tad put a hand on the kid's shoulder. "No, I need you to

finish the trench. Keep following the line I started toward that patch of grass I showed you. Keep it about this wide."

He held his hands out in front of him six inches apart to demonstrate.

Sam made a face. "But—"

"No buts. The horses are counting on you to help them. That's your job right now."

Sam held up his shovel with a look of fresh resolve. "Okay. I'll help them. Bye, Mom."

He turned and sloshed back to the round pen, stomping in puddles as he went.

Anita watched her son go for a moment before giving Tad a warm look. "A lot of people act like he can't understand anything. They talk to him like he's deaf. But not you."

Tad lifted one shoulder. Sam had never seemed all that different to him. "I think Sam understands just about everything."

"I do too." She turned to go back to the house, then stopped. "Be sure to come in and see me before you leave today. I made way too much chicken and rice casserole last night, so I put some in a container for you."

Tad's stomach practically roared at this news, but he hesitated. He didn't want to take advantage, and he cringed inside at the thought of what his dad might say if Tad brought home dinner he hadn't paid for.

Tad shook his head. "Thanks, but you don't need to—"

"I won't hear it." Anita raised one hand. "Please, nothing would make me happier."

He hesitated for a moment longer, but his stomach vetoed all his objections. Why argue with the boss? He was supposed to do whatever Dan and Anita told him to do, right?

"Okay."

She gave him a satisfied smile and hurried back to the house.

By the time Tad was standing on the side of the road staring at the overflowing ditch and pondering his options, the rain had let up again. That didn't stop water from thundering down the ditch from higher ground, bringing sticks and leaves and torn-up plastic bags with it. A battered Gatorade bottle rested precariously on top of a mass of tangled grass that looked like seaweed. It was a miracle any water was getting through the culvert, but a steady stream was coming out the other side.

"Need any help, son?"

A white truck with the words *Jefferson County Police* on the side had pulled up, and a large man older than Tad's dad was leaning out the window.

Shoot. Chief Stubbs. Good thing Tad hadn't been standing here smoking because the chief would've tattled to Dan for sure.

When Tad didn't answer right away, Chief Stubbs continued. "Did the Wilsons put you up to this?"

There was a hint of humor in his voice, and Tad tried to swallow the anxiety he felt whenever he glimpsed a law enforcement vehicle, especially this one. There was no need to freak out. He wasn't doing anything wrong.

At the moment.

"Yes, sir. Anita asked me to take care of it."

"I heard they hired you on. I was glad to hear it."

Tad tried to hide his surprise. Most of his previous encounters with the chief had consisted of Tad hanging his head and muttering to himself while the chief said something along the lines of *"I don't want to catch you doing this ever again, you hear me?"* Somehow, whether Tad was throwing empty bottles at the train with his buddies or tipping cows, he always got caught. It wasn't fair.

"I figure if anyone can make an honest man out of you, it's the Wilsons." Chief Stubbs's expression was hard to read, but his tone was pretty clear. "Good people. Known 'em for years. I'm sure you'll do right by 'em."

Tad shifted on his feet. "Uh. Yeah."

"I'm sure they'll never have any reason to regret their decision, will they?"

Tad's anxiety returned in full force. Dan already regretted it. "No, sir."

Chief Stubbs put the truck in park and hopped out. "Okay, then, let's see what we can do about this debris."

Tad looked around. *We?* As in, him and the chief? He would rather the man move on and bother someone else. There were probably plenty of other farms with flooding issues. If not that, surely there was a crime happening somewhere in the county right about now that he should be dealing with. But Chief Stubbs reached into the bed of his truck and pulled out a rake.

The chief drove around with a rake? What else did he have back there?

"You don't happen to know anything about a bunch of hooligans drag racing on Buck Road last night, do you?" Chief Stubbs reached his long arms out over the ditch and scraped away a big clump of muck. "No headlights? Around eleven thirty?"

Tad concentrated on the dirty water rushing past as his ears began to burn. See? He couldn't get away with anything.

◆ ❧ ◗

Tad was tired by the time he got home. He wasn't used to working so hard, but it felt good. Maybe he would finally grow some muscles like his dad. The man was built like an old-school boxer.

He was annoyed to see his dad's truck parked in front of the house. Usually, he was glad if Bud got home from work first. That way, he couldn't accuse Tad of being lazy if he walked in and found Tad sitting on the couch. Today, though, Tad had hoped to beat him in the door so he could eat his dinner in peace for once.

Why hadn't he eaten Anita's casserole before he left the ranch? He could've parked at the end of the drive, under the wooden ranch entrance, and scarfed it down in his car. He wished he would've thought of that sooner. He'd been smart enough to keep the maple pecan bread in his Ford. Maybe he should start keeping a fork in there. Not that he wanted to assume Anita would keep feeding him or anything, but he sure as shooting hoped she did. All the way home, he'd been tortured by the glorious smell of the chicken and rice.

He scooped the container off the seat and carried it reluctantly into the house. Bud was sitting on the ratty couch, drinking his usual Rainier beer and watching the news. He turned his head to give Tad a curt and indifferent nod, then looked closer and muted the volume on the TV when he noticed the container in Tad's hands.

"What you got there?"

Tad sighed. "Just some leftover food Anita gave me."

Bud frowned. "They think you're a dog or something? Throwing you their scraps?"

"You know it's not like that."

"I know they think they're better than us."

It would be pointless to argue. Tad held up the food. "You want some?"

Bud sneered. "Like hell. I'm gonna go to town and eat at Webb's later." He turned back to the TV.

Tad took it as a sign the conversation was over and slunk into the kitchen, blowing out a breath. He wasn't going to let his dad ruin this meal for him. The food wasn't scraps the Wilsons were ready to throw out.

Was it?

After nuking the casserole in the microwave for a minute and a half, Tad sat down at the table to eat. It was creamy and delicious, but it gave him the same sort of feeling he got whenever he saw Sam talking to Curly in that special way of his. The same sort of longing. Whatever that feeling was, he didn't like it.

He was starving, and he ate quite a bit before realizing he should save some for tomorrow. As he was putting the lid back on the container, Bud strode into the kitchen.

"Look at that fancy grub. I would say hanging around those Wilsons is gonna make you soft, but I don't think you can get any softer'n you already are."

Tad blinked. Apparently, the conversation was *not* over. He kept his head down and didn't respond.

"Do they think we can't afford our own food or something? Is that it?" Bud glared past Tad as if talking to someone else. His voice lowered. "They think I can't feed my own son?"

Tad tensed, unsure where this was coming from. "No, Dad. Anita was just being nice."

Bud began to pace. "You'd think they'd have enough to worry about with that dopey kid of theirs. Why're they so worried about other people?"

The hair on the back of Tad's neck rose. He pressed his palms into the table and stared his dad down. "He's not a dope."

Bud stilled at the hard edge in Tad's voice. Tad usually let his dad rant without comment because it was easier that way, but he wasn't about to let words spoken against Sam pass without a challenge.

Bud huffed. "Well, he ain't no genius."

"Like you would know, Dad."

Bud's expression hardened, and an angry glint appeared in his eye. "I think you're forgetting who you're talking to, boy. Whose house you're sitting in."

Tad tried to hold his father's gaze as his stomach twisted into a bowline knot. He didn't want to fight. Their confrontations rarely became physical, but he always came out on the losing end regardless. All his muscles tightened as tension filled the room.

A loud noise pierced the air, and he flinched. "Take the Low Road" played from the table where his phone was sitting. Who would be calling him? Nobody ever called, except Dan when he'd offered Tad the job. Maybe something was going on at the ranch. Maybe the flooding had gotten worse.

Tad tore his eyes away from his dad and glanced at his phone. Jenna? What the heck? He hadn't heard from her in almost a year, and he wasn't about to open up that can of worms again. He quickly reached over and silenced the call. Jenna could leave a message. And he would gladly ignore it.

He turned his attention back to his father. He was still staring Tad down, expecting an answer. Tad growled on the inside, tired of the standoff, then threw up his hands. "Sorry, Dad, but I don't like people talking about Sam like that. He's smarter than both of us combined."

Bud snorted. "Not smart enough to be suspicious."

Tad narrowed his eyes. "What's that supposed to mean?"

"Nothing."

"Have you ever even talked to him?"

Bud didn't answer, but Tad saw something shift in his eyes. With a sigh, Tad pushed away from the table and tossed the remaining food into the fridge. "I'm going to town."

He didn't look back. Just stomped out the front door he'd come in less than thirty minutes ago. He hadn't planned to go to town. Didn't want to. But being in the same place as his dad for even one more minute was suddenly not an option.

When he was sitting in his car, he checked his phone. One missed call. No message. Pfft. It had probably been a drunk dial. Jenna had never been able to handle her booze. He put the Ford in drive and tore down the dirt road, leaving a spray of mud behind him.

"I'm flyin' high when I take the low road . . ." He sang off-key as loud as he could and aimed his middle finger behind him at his father.

five

Anita stood in Cabin C's kitchenette on the last Friday of April and studied her surroundings. Everything was in place. The cupboards were stocked, the linens were fresh, the countertop sparkled. It had taken her all week to work her way through the cabins, preparing them with a vigorous spring cleaning, but it had been pleasant work. She loved creating a welcoming environment for their guests.

Their first guests of the busy season would arrive tomorrow from New Mexico. She hoped they would bring warm enough clothes, although no one ever did at the end of April. They always assumed it was well into springtime and past the point of freezing temperatures—it was almost May, after all—no matter how directly the website stressed that inclement weather was possible year-round here. She always made sure there were extra coats and blankets in the closet.

Anita stood in the doorway of the bedroom and gripped the frame. "Lord, I pray for Mr. and Mrs. Cunningham. Let their time here be filled with peace and rest, let them feel Your presence. I pray our hospitality will make them feel loved and point them to the fellowship and belonging that can only be found in You."

It was her custom to pray for every guest before they arrived. She left the bedroom, entered the tiny living room, and stood next to the window.

"I ask that every time they look out at the world You made, they will think of You. Every time they see the sun rising or a hawk flying, their hearts will be drawn to You."

She paused, watching a trio of deer cross the field on the other side of the drive. They walked slowly, without fear. "And, Lord, about Tad . . ."

The cabin door flew open. "Mom, guess what?"

Sam barreled into the small space, filling it with an air of excitement.

Anita put her hands on his shoulders. "Slow down. What is it?"

"Maddie's here!"

"Oh?" Anita kept her tone neutral, but inside she weighed Sam's words with caution. She'd been hoping for another chance to spend time with the girl—Maddie seemed like she could use a friend—but she was wary of Sam's evident delight. He'd always struggled to navigate relationships, especially with his peers. Especially with girls. She didn't want him to get hurt.

"She's here to see the kittens. I'm going to show her."

"Where is she now?"

"Talking to Tad. I said I'd be right back. I said I had to tell you. I told Curly to stay so he wouldn't have to climb the hill."

"You could've used your walkie-talkie." She pointed to the device hooked onto his belt. Hers was in her coat pocket. "That's what it's for, remember?"

Sam looked down at his belt, then back up at her with a grin. "I was too excited to remember."

Anita sighed. They'd purchased their first set of walkie-talkies when Sam was little so she could let him know when it was time to come in for lunch. They'd been cheap little things that needed new batteries every week.

When he got older, they'd tried giving him a flip phone instead, but he hated the thing and kept losing it—maybe on purpose. He had his heart set on walkie-talkies. So they'd purchased two new sets of heavy-duty, rechargeable ones. Long-range sets that worked up to five miles away. She and Sam and Dan each took one from the charging stand in the mudroom whenever they left the house.

Sam never failed to slide one in his pocket before going outside, but he often failed to respond to her calls. *"Did you hear me?"* she'd ask later, when they were back at the house, and he'd always say, *"Yes."*

She nodded toward the barn. "You better head back down. You don't want to keep her waiting."

"Okay."

He was gone in a flash, leaving the door wide open. She shook her head. He was going to be devastated once Maddie's kitten was old enough to go home with her and she no longer had a reason to come by. He loved it when people visited the ranch.

Dan was always saying it would be good for Sam to get a job doing something like bagging groceries at Zippy's Market so he could be around people more. He said it would make Sam happy. But wasn't he happy here?

She couldn't bring herself to encourage her son to be subjected to the kind of scrutiny employment would bring. Everyone in town would be watching his every move. Judging how well he could—or couldn't—do his job. Talking about him behind his back and probably sometimes to his face. People could be so cruel. And they didn't understand his limitations.

No. He was better off here. Maybe he was lonely sometimes, but at least he was safe and protected.

He never complained.

She left the cabin and closed the door behind her. She could see Curly wagging his tail as Sam reached the barn. Maddie turned and said something to Sam, but Anita couldn't hear the words from this far away or read the expression on the girl's face.

She looked up at the vast blue sky, unencumbered by clouds. "Lord, does Maddie need me?"

There was no clear answer in her spirit, but it would cost her nothing to invite Maddie in for a cup of tea when she was finished in the barn. Anita had mentored several young ladies before, girls she'd met at church. It came naturally to her, despite never having had a daughter.

As she watched from the hill, Sam and Maddie disappeared into the barn, and Tad stood outside looking after them. He didn't move. What was he thinking about? He'd been doing a good job so far. Dan had found no reason to criticize his work. But for some reason Tad always gave the impression he could spook at any time, like General, the high-strung bay gelding they used to have before they sold off most of their herd to help fund the cabins.

Her thoughts turned to Tad's father, and she pressed her lips into a line as Tad finally tore his gaze from the barn and strode off toward the round pen. What had Bud thought when Tad took this job? He'd grown increasingly unhappy with her each time she'd brought food over after Holly left. He'd eventually told her to mind her own business and leave him and his two boys alone. That they could take care of themselves. Anita had only wanted to help.

"Please let Bud's heart be opened to love again." He'd hate it if he knew she was praying for him, but she leaned into it. "Help him find new purpose for his life and stop wasting himself on anger and alcohol. Help him see that his bitterness over everything he's lost is keeping him from appreciating what he has left."

She started down the hill carefully, her knees sore. A chilly breeze picked up and blew her thick, wild mane of hair away from her face. "And, Lord, about Tad . . ."

◆ ～ ◆

Anita had been watching from the living room window for half an hour before Maddie came out of the barn, Sam on her heels, and Curly on his. The girl was stylish and walked like she knew exactly what she wanted out of life, just like her mother. Teresa Pine had always walked like that, even as a little girl.

Anita hurried out of the house to meet Maddie at her car, a fancy-looking red thing splattered with mud from the drive-way. "Hello, dear, how are you?"

Maddie looked up. "Oh, hi. Good. We were playing with the kittens, weren't we, Sam?"

Sam nodded vigorously. "Princess is feisty."

Anita's eyebrows rose. "Princess?"

"That's what Maddie named the white one."

"Ah."

Maddie appeared a little sheepish, her self-assurance slip-ping ever so slightly. "She's so pretty, and she acts kind of spoiled, so I thought . . ."

"It's the perfect name." Anita smiled. "Good choice. I'm glad you could come out and see her. How are your parents?"

Maddie shrugged. "Fine, I guess."

"And your grandpa Dale? I heard he had to have another surgery, is that right?"

"Yeah. On his back again."

Anita had actually heard about the back trouble and the surgery from Dale at the Coalition the other day, when he'd stopped in for coffee. She wasn't about to mention that, however. People were skittish about having any connection to the Coalition or the kind of support it offered, and all the staff and volunteers knew their work and interactions had to remain confidential. No one would ever speak to them again if word started getting around about who was stopping in and for what.

She took a step closer to Maddie. "Do you have to rush off, or can you stay for a cup of tea? I don't get to spend time with other women very often. I'm surrounded by men out here."

"Even Curly is a boy," Sam confirmed, his hand resting on the dog's head.

Anita smiled. "See?"

Maddie shifted on her feet. "I'm not sure . . ."

"It would be great fun for me if you could come in and visit." Anita sensed Maddie's hesitation and touched her shoulder. "Or I can make coffee, if you prefer."

Maddie looked over at the house, and Anita could sense the girl's inner conflict. Was she worried about intruding? No, that wasn't it. Did she think Anita was going to interrogate her? Possibly. Or perhaps she thought Anita had ulterior motives. As the only child of Grady's wealthiest family, Maddie probably had to be wary of people who might try to use her to get close to her parents. Matthew and Teresa Pine had a lot of influence around town. Had ties to almost every business and organization.

Anita had no such hopes or expectations. She merely recognized a young woman adrift when she saw one, no matter how confidently Maddie walked, and she felt she might have something to offer her.

"Thanks, Mrs. Wilson." Something flashed across Maddie's face, then was gone. "But I've got other plans."

She opened the driver's side door of her car and said, "See you, Sam," over her shoulder as she climbed in.

Anita started to say, "Maybe some other time," but Maddie shut the door, and quick as a wink, she was zooming away. Sam ran as fast as he could to where the driveway looped west and passed by the barn so he could wave as Maddie drove by.

Maddie honked twice, and Anita took a deep breath. She'd never succeeded in befriending Teresa Pine either. It felt like the Pines lived in a different world. They had a huge lodge-style house on a hill overlooking Grady and a vacation home near Canyon Ferry Lake. They went skiing at the Yellowstone Club and celebrated Christmas at the governor's mansion. People in town sometimes whispered that the Pines had made their money from shady business dealings, but Anita didn't believe that. Didn't want to. She did wonder, however, what Maddie's childhood had been like.

If the young woman came back another day, if she gave Anita half a chance to connect with her, Anita would try again.

six

I like Maddie's hair because it's shiny and it smells good. It's the same color as Bob's hair and I want to touch it to see if it feels the same but I'm pretty sure that would be crossing a boundary. Mom used to talk about boundaries all the time when we used to talk all the time and she said boundaries are like invisible fences.

My teacher Mr. Bill from church has an invisible fence at his house and I guess his dogs can see it because they never ever cross the fence and I wish I could see boundaries too. Then it would be a lot easier to know where they are.

I like showing Maddie my kittens and watching her pet them. Her hands are a lot smaller than mine and her nails have pink on them and sometimes when she's holding the white kitten up close and cuddling it to her face she looks sad. I don't know why someone who is pretty and has hair that smells good would be sad but I'm kind of sad now too because Maddie is gone.

I check to make sure no one is looking and then Curly and me hurry behind the patch of junipers except Curly doesn't actually hurry because he's too old. We sit behind the junipers for a long time because no one can see us. I like it when no one knows where we are and I like it when I don't have to wonder if I'm doing the right thing.

Maddie said she'll come back to see Princess soon. *Soon* is a confusing word. I know dinner will be soon, but I know Maddie won't be back before that so I don't know what kind of soon she meant. She said that I'm easy to talk to and she asked me a lot of questions about the ranch because I know everything about it and I don't know why she wanted to know if I ever go over the hill but I told her sometimes I do. Mom's questions usually make me feel like my forehead is tight and my tongue is slow but when Maddie asks me questions I look at her hair and talk fast.

I want to leave the junipers and go exploring but Curly is asleep and I'm afraid if I leave him here and he wakes up without me he'll be sad. My walkie-talkie crackles and Mom asks me what I'm doing. I say I'm just sitting here but she doesn't hear me so I say it louder but she doesn't hear me and I remember I'm supposed to push the button when I talk but I think Mom's gone now so I put my hand on Curly's head and watch the birds pick up grass in their beaks and fly away to make a nest.

I wish I could fly away but I don't know how to make a nest and I don't know where I would go and Mom says the safest place for me to be is on the ranch. Mr. Bill says the safest place to be is in God's will but I think maybe the ranch is God's will and that's what Mom meant because nobody loves me as much as Mom except for Jesus and I know they both want me to be safe.

seven

Tad had no idea how Dan could stay calm as Mr. Cunningham waved his arms around and shouted.

"Monday afternoon, you said. 'Monday afternoon would be the perfect time for your trail ride, Mr. Cunningham.' That's what you said."

Dan nodded. "I'm very sorry that we have to change the schedule. I thought the other guests would be here by now."

Tad glanced back at the driveway. Still no sign of Mr. and Mrs. Procter, who were supposed to arrive two hours ago.

Mr. Cunningham's face was a deep shade of red. "I can't possibly understand how that has anything to do with my wife and me. As you can clearly see, *we* are not delayed. I see no reason why *we* cannot proceed with our trail ride as planned."

Dan blinked at the finger in his face until Mr. Cunningham grudgingly removed it. "I realize this is unfortunate, but now that it's gotten this late and there's a chance of rain, I don't feel comfortable—"

"This is outrageous." Mr. Cunningham held clenched fists to his sides. "Your comfort is not my concern."

"But your safety is mine."

Tad discreetly studied Dan's face. No hint of anger. Tad

knew what his dad's approach would be in this situation, and it would not be anything resembling reasonable and courteous.

Mrs. Cunningham tugged on her husband's arm. "Now, Harry, hold on a minute, I don't want to ride in the rain. My hair is so sensitive." She gestured at Dan. "I'm sure this man can take us out tomorrow instead, right?"

She raised her eyebrows at Dan, and Dan gave a sigh that Tad only heard because he was standing so close. "Unfortunately, I'm not available tomorrow. But . . ."

He turned toward Tad, and Tad gulped. Uh-oh. That was not part of the plan. Tad was supposed to assist Dan on at least two trail rides before leading one himself. He'd been on trail rides before, of course, but he'd never led one on his own. He'd never been responsible for other people.

Dan's expression was hard to read as he continued. "Tad here is available tomorrow, and if the weather holds and the Procters agree . . ."

"There, see." Mrs. Cunningham patted her husband's elbow. "It's all settled."

"I don't give a hoot whether the Procters agree or not, Nancy and I want to go on a trail ride as promised."

Tad knew there had been no such promise. The C-A-R website was clear that none of the ranch experiences could be guaranteed, and he'd overheard Dan remind the Cunninghams of that fact upon their arrival.

He saw Sam near the barn out of the corner of his eye and hoped the kid would stay away. Mr. Cunningham didn't seem like the type who would be patient with someone like Sam.

Dan glanced over his shoulder to see what Tad was looking at and pressed his lips together, probably thinking the same thing. "Again, I'm very sorry. We'll schedule the ride for tomorrow after lunch and hope we don't get too much rain this evening, all right?"

Mr. Cunningham grumbled, but the missus steered him toward the corral. "That sounds fine, doesn't it, Harry? Let's go look at the horses. I want to choose which one I'm going to ride."

Tad gulped again. The guests didn't get to choose their mounts. It was up to the trail boss to match horse and rider based on a variety of factors, such as size, temperament, and riding experience. Would that job fall to him tomorrow? Would he have to be the one to tell Mrs. Cunningham she couldn't ride her chosen horse and face the wrath of Harry?

"I know this isn't what we had planned." Dan rubbed his chin as the Cunninghams walked away. "Do you think you're up for it?"

Tad hesitated, his shoulders tense. "Uh . . ."

"I'll assign the horses and let everyone know before I leave for work tomorrow. It wouldn't be fair to put that on you."

Tad relaxed a tiny bit. "Okay. Thanks."

"Even if it rains a little tonight, I think you'll be fine as long as you stick to the north trail. Better drainage."

"What if it rains tomorrow afternoon?"

Dan gave a half smile. "Then we'll have to hope Mrs. Cunningham cancels the ride herself so you won't have to do it. Her hair is sensitive, you know."

Tad couldn't help but laugh, though it felt kind of forced.

Dan leaned against the fence. "I've seen you with the horses, you'll be fine. Just remember to go easy. The guests paid good money to be here, and they want to have fun."

"What do I do if they're not having fun?"

Dan raised one shoulder. "I usually stick with the strategy of distraction. If they start to complain, point out the mountains or the wildlife or something. Get them to look around. You got any good horse stories?"

Tad thought for a second. "This one time, me and some buddies had this huge bonfire going by this field, and there was a mare, and we could tell she was in heat because—"

"Whoa there." Dan held up a hand. "Does this story involve alcohol?"

"Um. Yeah."

"Would it make Mrs. Cunningham blush?"

Tad cringed. "Probably."

"Then let's stick to pointing out wildlife, okay?"

Tad could feel his face heat up. "Okay."

Dan jerked his chin toward the corral. "I should probably go try and convince Mrs. Cunningham to ride Sandy tomorrow."

Tad nodded, grateful for the change of subject. Sandy was the gentlest of the horses. Actually, she was a mule, but "stubborn as a mule" didn't apply to her. She was docile and friendly. Mules often got a bad rap.

"What about Mr. Cunningham?"

Dan rubbed his chin. "I think TJ would be the best choice for him, don't you?"

Tad's eyes widened. TJ was short for Thomas Jefferson, and he was a muscular quarter horse with a beautiful black coat and a bad attitude. One of the only quarter horses Tad had ever heard described as mean, though Tad suspected everyone had misjudged TJ. Maybe the horse hadn't found someone who understood him yet. Or maybe he really was a grouchy old menace. Even people in town said he was nothing but trouble.

Hmph. Same thing they said about Tad.

In any case, Tad had assumed the trail boss would always ride TJ because he couldn't be trusted with guests.

He scratched the back of his neck. "Uh . . ."

"I'm kidding." Dan slapped Tad's back and grinned. "Probably Bob."

Tad let out his breath. "Yeah, that would be good."

Bob was steady and responsive—like most quarter horses except TJ—but she was feisty enough to not let someone like Mr. Cunningham intimidate her.

"How'd you end up with a horse like TJ, anyway?" he asked.

"Well, you know we used to have a dozen. Most of them were rescues or re-homing situations that Anita couldn't say no to. She always sees the good in everyone, even ornery horses. Anyway, TJ had been passed around to several places before Anita found out about him."

"Why didn't you sell him with the others?"

Tad knew the Wilsons had sold some of their horses when they sold their cattle, only keeping five for the purpose of offering trail rides to guests. It seemed to Tad that they'd kept the least desirable of the bunch.

"Anita was afraid he'd be mistreated. A headstrong horse like that is at high risk of getting whipped if owned by the wrong person. She says he has a good heart."

Tad's collarbone still hurt where TJ had headbutted him the other day, but he had to admit if anyone could recognize a good heart, it would be Anita. "And the others? Why'd you keep Bob and Prince and Sandy and Tinkerbell? How did you choose?"

"Easy." Dan adjusted his cowboy hat and shook his head. "No one else wanted them."

eight

Tuesday morning was Anita's favorite time to volunteer at the Coalition. On other days, her job consisted mainly of paperwork, answering phone calls, responding to emails, and assisting the rare farmer who actually showed up in person. About six months ago, however, the Coalition had initiated Coffee Break, an open-house style gathering on Tuesday mornings. They had sent invitations to every agricultural worker in a hundred-mile radius, offering free coffee and donuts from nine to eleven.

The first three weeks passed without a single taker. Then, much to Anita's delight, a few of the area producers had started showing up, followed by a few more. Farmers could never turn down free stuff. The Coalition's location near the hardware store didn't hurt either.

Some of the men—and the occasional woman—merely grabbed their coffee and donuts and hightailed it out the door, but some of them hung around, swapping stories and giving one another a hard time. Anita's job was to keep the refreshments flowing and to listen. Last week she'd heard John Starr mention a water rights dispute and was able to pass along the name of a lawyer who specialized in Montana water law.

Few things stressed out farmers and ranchers more than water. And helping them cope with stress constructively was what the Coalition was all about.

She smiled when Diana hurried through the Coalition door at quarter to nine. "You're just in time to help me set up the table."

Diana shed her coat and flung her purse down on a chair. "Sorry I'm late. I stopped by Nikki's on the way."

Anita stood on one end of the long folding table and waited for her friend to lift the other end. "How's Hudson doing?"

Diana's newest grandson was about two weeks old now. Anita hadn't met him yet, but Diana had shown her dozens of pictures. He had a bald head and a button nose.

"Nikki said she thought he had a fever last night, but everything was fine today. I was holding him and lost track of time."

Together they picked up the table and carried it across the room. As they unfolded its legs and stood it up, Anita chased away feelings of jealousy with an admonition to herself. She was a blessed woman. It would be extremely petty of her to begrudge her friend the joy of holding a baby.

But oh, how she would love to hold a baby!

"Well, I'm glad you're here now. I'm hoping for a good turnout today."

They quickly laid down a tablecloth and set out coffee carafes, mugs, donuts, and napkins. Anita pulled creamer and half-and-half from the mini fridge while Diana grabbed a sugar bowl and plastic spoons.

"How's everything at the ranch?" Diana asked.

"Good. Our first guests of the season arrived this weekend." They had occasional guests between December and April, but

May through November had proven to be their main cabin season. "I love meeting people from all over the country."

"And things are still working out with the Richardsons?"

"So far, so good."

That had been the hardest part of deciding to convert their cattle ranch: selling the majority of their land to their northwestern neighbors, the Richardsons. It had been Dan's biggest hang-up when she'd first suggested the idea of a guest ranch, and she couldn't blame him. The land had been in the Wilson family since Dan's great-grandpa moved to Montana in 1929. She didn't want to lose it either. But it had been getting harder and harder to manage, and Sam was never going to be able to take it over.

She'd prayed for months that if it was God's will, Dan would come around to the idea. When he did, her prayers turned toward asking God to put it in the Richardsons' hearts to allow the Wilsons to continue using some of the acreage for their trail rides. When they too came around, she'd thanked the Lord and suggested they give what had always been called Wilson Herefords a new name.

Come Around Ranch.

The whole thing had seemed overwhelming at first. Building the cabins, designing a website, filling out insurance paperwork. It hadn't been easy, but this would be their fourth summer as a guest ranch, and they hadn't gone bankrupt yet.

Diana helped Anita set out folding chairs. "Everyone thought you guys were crazy."

"I thought we were crazy too. But I couldn't think of any other way we could keep our house. I couldn't stand the thought of moving Sam to town."

"How's he getting along with the new guy?"

Anita checked the time. Three minutes after nine. "Him and Tad were friends in school. They make a good team, and Sam likes having someone his age around. The guy we had last summer was sixty-two."

A small pinch of guilt twisted her heart. Dan often suggested things Sam could do to spend more time around his peers, but Anita usually resisted. She didn't trust other people to treat Sam the way he needed. She didn't want him to get hurt. Was it so wrong to want to protect her child?

Her thoughts were interrupted as two men arrived, talking loudly about barley futures. Sam didn't have a worry in the world, not like these men fighting every day to keep their farms going. She hoped she could offer a small amount of encouragement.

"Hi, Craig. Hi, Vernon." Her smile was oversized and genuine. "We're glad you're here."

◆ ◆ ◆

Anita's intuition told her something was wrong. It was almost eleven o'clock, yet Vernon DeVries was still hanging around. Craig had left long ago, and only two of the dozen or so men who had come by remained. Vernon had visited with each person, had asked after their animals and fields, their families and their ditches, but now he sat alone in a folding chair, staring into the cup of coffee clutched in his wizened hands.

She eased into the chair next to him. "How are you, Vernon? You feeling all right?"

He glanced at her with deep-set, rheumy eyes. "Sure, sure. Can't complain."

"How are things shaping up at your place for the summer? You planted yet?"

"No, no. Not yet. The boys've been arguing over when." His voice held a note of regret, or possibly sorrow. "Two more weeks, maybe."

The boys weren't boys, of course. Vernon's two sons were both middle-aged.

Anita resisted the urge to give Vernon's bony knee a reassuring pat. "I'm sure they know what they're doing."

"Sure, sure." He hung his head and mumbled, "Just wish I did."

She had a feeling he wasn't talking about planting. Seed potatoes could be a burden, but that clearly wasn't the burden weighing him down. "I only know of your two sons. Do you have any other children?"

"I got a daughter in Billings. She drives over once in a while, but she's not too interested in the farm. It's the boys who care about it."

"I suppose that's why they argue about the planting. Because they both care so much."

Vernon bobbed his head slowly. "They argue about everything. Every little decision. I don't know what's going to happen when . . ."

His voice dropped off, but Anita could easily guess the words he didn't say. *When I'm gone.* It was a common concern for farmers, right up there with access to water: *What will happen to my farm when I pass away?* Many a farming family had been torn apart by greed, lack of a will, or misunderstanding upon the passing of a patriarch.

She guessed Vernon to be in his late seventies, though decades of hard labor out in the unforgiving elements had caused him to look older. She wanted to say he had nothing to worry about. That he had plenty of good years left. But there was a tremor in his hand, and his weathered skin hung off his bones like a bloodhound's ears.

"We've got these pamphlets about estate planning for farmers," she said. "Would you like me to get one for you?"

The pamphlets were one of many resources the Coalition had on hand. Surveys conducted by the Cooperative Extension Service had shown agricultural producers were more likely to accept help and advice from online classes and printed resources than in-person counselors or support groups. Therefore, the Coalition had a pamphlet for just about everything.

"I suppose I could look at it." Vernon's watery eyes followed the other two farmers as they made their way to the door and gave him a wave. Vernon raised a hand in return and waited until the door had closed before looking at Anita. "Don't know what good a pamphlet's going to do, but sure, sure."

As Diana began cleaning up the coffee table, Anita walked over to the wall where a plastic rack displayed close to twenty pamphlets. Many of them had to do with finances or retirement. Some covered legislative issues related to agriculture. Her heart twinged as she looked them over. How were they going to get more people to read them? And would reading them do any good? So many people were already in crisis. Already on the precipice of losing everything.

It took a lot of courage to be a farmer.

She found the pamphlet she was looking for and brought it to Vernon. He shoved it in the pocket of his denim jacket and rose to his feet with a heavy sigh.

"Thanks. I guess I better be going."

"I hope I'll see you again next week."

"Sure, sure." He hobbled toward the door. Diana held out

the last remaining donut as he passed, and he took it with a small smile. "Might as well."

Anita watched him go with a sense of unease. How many Vernons were out there, worrying about the future? Wondering if all their efforts were for nothing? Questioning how much longer they could hold on?

She'd already believed the work the Coalition was doing was important. Now she couldn't help but wonder if it was enough.

nine

Tad sniffed the air Tuesday afternoon. Did it smell like rain? Maybe it was going to rain. Should he postpone the trail ride?

He studied the sky. Nope. No chance of precipitation. A few wispy clouds here and there, but otherwise clear. There was no getting out of this.

Something bumped against his leg, and he looked down to find Curly staring up at him with cloudy eyes. He patted the dog's head and scanned around. Sam had to be nearby.

Ah, there he was jogging toward him.

"Tad, can I go riding with you today?"

"Hey, Sam." He shook his head. "I'm going to need all five horses, sorry. Maybe next time."

Sam wrinkled his nose. "Huckleberries. What if me and Curly drive the four-wheeler? Then can we come? I'll be real careful."

There were strict rules regarding Sam and the Honda four-wheeler. Dan had told Tad all about it on his first day of work. First, Sam couldn't go anywhere on the four-wheeler without his walkie-talkie. That wasn't a problem since Sam never went *anywhere* without his walkie-talkie.

Second, Sam couldn't go faster than fifteen miles per hour.

The Honda had the capacity to top out around thirty-five miles per hour, but Dan had said, *"If I ever catch wind that Sam was going that fast . . ."* He hadn't finished his threat, but his meaning was clear. Apparently, there were a lot of things Dan never wanted to catch wind of.

Third, Sam had to ask. After he took off on the Honda once without telling anyone, Anita nearly had a panic attack, and Dan made Sam promise never to do that again.

Tad gave Sam a punch in the shoulder. "I think you're going to have to stay behind this time. The four-wheeler might scare the horses. I don't want anyone to get thrown."

Sam pouted.

"And there are some pretty muddy spots," Tad added. "You don't want to get stuck."

"But I want to go with you. I won't get stuck."

"Like I said, maybe next time."

Sam kicked a rock and mumbled to himself. "One, two, three, four."

"Sorry, man." The last thing Tad needed was one more person to worry about on the trail.

Sam spun around and trudged toward the barn with his shoulders slumped. Curly followed close behind, limping more than usual. Tad thought about calling after the kid, but what could he say?

He turned his attention to the gear hanging from the fence. The Wilsons had decided their trail rides would offer as much of the full experience as possible, so he'd been directed to prepare all the gear but then guide the guests in saddling their own horses. *"They want to feel like real cowboys,"* Dan had said. *"Like in* City Slickers," Sam had added.

At one thirty, Tad had the horses in the round pen, and

they were raring to go, energized by the sun and the smell of spring. Tad took a deep breath and tried to calm his nerves. The Procters had arrived five hours late yesterday after hitting a deer on the highway with their rental car. Despite being a little shaken up, they had eagerly agreed to a trail ride with the Cunninghams today. And now Tad was about to be solely responsible for their safety. And their . . . fun.

The Cunninghams arrived first, wearing brand-new matching boots, jeans, and plaid pearl-snap shirts. Mr. Cunningham wore a cowboy hat, but Mrs. Cunningham's head was bare, presumably due to the sensitive nature of her hair. Neither of them was likely to be happy when Tad reminded them helmets were required for all riders.

Mr. Cunningham looked around with a frown. "Don't tell me we have to wait on those people again."

Tad tried to imitate the calm way Dan had dealt with this guy. "I'm sure they'll be here any minute."

He hoped that was true. Then a jangling sound caught his attention and drew his eye to Mr. Cunningham's boots. His eyes widened.

"Um, sir, are those spurs?"

Mr. Cunningham stood a little taller. "Custom-made in New Mexico. Nancy got them for my birthday."

Looking closer, Tad could see they were high quality and shiny. They also looked sharp.

Tad shifted on his feet. "Your horse is a good listener. She's trained. You're not going to need those."

Mrs. Cunningham clasped her hands together. "But they look so nice, don't you think? So *authentic*."

Drawn by the voices, Sam forgot he was supposed to be pouting and strolled out of the barn. "Whoa, cool spurs!"

Curly found a sunny spot to lie down, unimpressed.

Tad could feel sweat forming in his armpits. What kind of idiot thought they would need spurs on a guest ranch trail ride? "Bob won't like it if you kick her with those. She might freak out."

Mr. Cunningham made a face. "I don't want to ride a horse named Bob. I already told the other guy that."

"Her real name is Belle of the Ball."

"Then why don't you call her that?"

"Now, Harry, Dan explained all this already." Mrs. Cunningham fussed with her hair. "I'm sure you can call her Belle if you want to."

"Howdy-ho-oh."

Everyone turned toward the overly enthusiastic greeting to see the Procters approaching the round pen, grinning and waving. They were dressed in brightly colored shorts and T-shirts, as well as tennis shoes that were already covered in mud.

Mr. Cunningham snorted and whispered loudly in his wife's ear. "Greenhorns."

Tad stifled a sigh. "Okay, everyone's here. We better get started."

"Finally," Mr. Cunningham said.

Tad ignored him and focused on the task at hand. He didn't want to screw this up. Didn't want to let his boss down. Dan was trusting him to do this job.

Tad signaled to Sam that he could help him, then led the group through the process of saddling their horses. Brush, pad, saddle, straps. TJ may have appeared indifferent as Tad demonstrated every step of the process on him, but Tad wasn't fooled. The slight twitching in TJ's shoulder muscles and the turned-back ears told him the horse was on edge.

Tad leaned close and whispered, "I'm not thrilled about this either, but we gotta do our job, okay?"

TJ huffed but allowed Tad to continue. Tad was glad Anita was volunteering at the Coalition today so he didn't have to feel like she was watching his every move from the house. Mrs. Cunningham took the longest to finish saddling up because she kept stopping to take pictures on her phone, and Sam kept asking to see the photo.

The final step was the bridle. Mrs. Procter had squealed several times during the saddling process and squealed again when Tinkerbell's muzzle tickled her bare forearm as she tried to get the snaffle bit in the creature's mouth.

"She's so soft," she said. "She's like a fuzzy bunny."

Tinkerbell was a Shetland pony with three white socks. Despite being advanced in age, she was strong enough to carry any of them. Mrs. Procter was the shortest, though, and wouldn't have to worry about her legs being too long for the stirrups, which is why she'd been assigned Tinkerbell.

Sam helped Mrs. Procter insert the bit correctly. "Tink is the fuzziest one, that's for sure." He rubbed Tinkerbell's neck. "You shoulda seen her with her full winter coat on."

Mrs. Procter leaned close to the pony and talked in a funny voice with her lips pursed. "I bet you were be-ooo-tiful. Yes, you were. So pretty, yes, you were."

"No, she wasn't." Sam laughed. "Her winter coat is messy."

Tinkerbell nickered. Tad checked the sky, checked the time, and took another deep breath at the same time TJ did. This was taking forever. If it got too late, the horses would start feeling anxious about heading home for dinner and might become unmanageable. He couldn't let that happen.

"All right, guys, we better get going."

Sam stuck out his bottom lip. "I want to go too."

Tad gave him a look. "Sam."

"Oh, huckleberries." Sam kicked a rock and mumbled to himself. "One, two, three, four, five."

In some ways, it would be nice to have Sam along for support. He was an expert on equines, especially these five. He knew exactly how tight a girth strap should be and how to get a horse to listen. But Tad had his hands full as it was, and there was nothing that could be done.

Tad looked at the guests, each standing by their horse—or mule or pony. He looked back at TJ, and the horse gave him a look as if to say, *Let's see what you got, hotshot.*

Tad pressed his lips into a tight line. Here went nothing.

ten

Aside from an almost wintry breeze that left his fingers cold and stiff and wishing for gloves, Tad was pleased with how the trail ride had gone so far. The few patches of mud they'd encountered had been easily avoided, and when he'd pointed out a bald eagle, all four guests had *oohed* and *aahed* and Mrs. Cunningham had pulled out her phone to capture the moment. Dan had been right.

Tad nodded. Being trail boss wasn't so hard after all.

Smiling to himself, he continued on in the lead until something ahead in the dirt caught his attention. His smile wavered. A cigarette butt? It couldn't be one of his. He didn't remember smoking up here. He wouldn't be so careless, would he?

His thoughts were interrupted when he heard Bob snort behind him. He glanced over his shoulder. She'd been tense the whole ride due to Mr. Cunningham's spurs, which jangled with every step, and now she was letting her unease be known.

Mr. Cunningham scowled. "She doesn't like me."

Mrs. Cunningham piped up. "Don't be silly, dear. Horses don't have feelings."

"Are we heading back soon?" Mr. Procter called from the back of the line. "We're freezing."

Mr. Cunningham turned around in his saddle and waved an irritated fist at the Procters. "That's what you get for dressing like you're going to the beach." He turned back around and grumbled under his breath. "Idiots."

Tad gripped his reins tighter. The trail ride was supposed to last two hours. He'd never thought to ask Dan what he should do if the guests wanted to head back early. Would he get in trouble if he cut the ride short?

"Look." Mrs. Cunningham gasped and gestured dramatically toward the open field on their left. "Baby deer."

A doe and two fawns stood in tall grass a couple hundred yards away, staring at them. Tad was surprised Mrs. Cunningham had spotted them.

She continued gesturing. "We need to stop so I can get a picture."

Tad rolled his eyes but pulled TJ to a halt. TJ gave his opinion by stomping his feet.

"Are we going back?" Mr. Procter asked.

Mr. Cunningham huffed. "We'll go back when the trail boss says it's time to go back."

"They're too far away. I can't get a good picture." Mrs. Cunningham squinted at her screen. "I told you we should've upgraded our phones before the trip."

Mr. Cunningham huffed. "Not this again."

Bob shifted uneasily under the man, and Tad began to feel nervous. The last thing he wanted was for the horses to start getting antsy. They needed to either keep moving or head back.

"What's that noise?" Mrs. Procter asked.

Mr. Procter frowned. "I hear it too."

Tad listened but didn't hear anything except Dan's voice in

his head saying he didn't want there to be any problems when the guests came. Saying it hadn't been his idea to hire Tad. Then Dan's voice morphed into his father's, asking *"When are you going to stop mooching off your old man?"*

He couldn't take any risks with this ride. "All right, folks, I think we should go back."

"Finally," Mr. Procter said.

"I haven't gotten my picture yet." Mrs. Cunningham tapped her phone frantically. "They're all blurry."

"Oh for heaven's sake, let me see." Mr. Cunningham tried to move Bob closer to Sandy. "Give me the phone."

He reached but wasn't close enough. He leaned over in his saddle, causing his spurs to scrape against Bob's side. She protested.

Tad winced. "You're hurting her."

"I thought we were going back," Mr. Procter called, his lips appearing a little blue.

Mrs. Procter looked around. "There's that noise again."

This time, Tad heard it. The unmistakable sound of the Honda four-wheeler.

Oh no. No, no, no.

With his reins, he asked TJ to make a tight turn on the narrow path and the horse obeyed. "Mr. Cunningham, you need to move Bob away—"

"Tad," a familiar voice shouted. "Tad, wait for me!"

Tad stiffened. Time froze. He knew he should do something, but before he could think through the options, Sam crested a hill on the four-wheeler, a huge smile on his face. Bob spooked and lurched wildly into Sandy, jostling Mrs. Cunningham, who was not holding on to anything except her phone. As Tad watched in horror, she lost her balance and slid off the saddle, hitting the ground with the sickening sound of Tad's hopes and dreams being yanked out from under him.

"My arm," she shrieked.

The Procters looked on with their mouths hanging open as Tad dismounted and ran to Mrs. Cunningham's side. "Are you okay?" he asked, while the words *please be okay, please be okay* played over and over in his mind.

She looked up at him with wide eyes that were quickly filling with tears. "M-m-my arm."

In a flash, Mr. Cunningham was beside them, his finger in Tad's face. "I'll be talking to my lawyer about this."

Sam brought the four-wheeler to a stop near TJ and hopped off. "Guess what, Tad? I found a robin's nest."

◆ ◦ ◗

Tad and his father sat side by side at the bar, not speaking. Their elbows almost touched as they stared straight ahead and nursed their beers. Bud hadn't questioned it when Tad said he was going to tag along to Webb's, but he must be wondering. Tad didn't usually drink during the week when he had a job.

If he still had a job.

An unfriendly voice came from behind him. "Hey, Bungley, I heard you really bungled up a trail ride today."

Tad flinched. Why'd Scooter MacDonald have to be here tonight? And how had he found out about that already?

Bud looked over at Tad with a scowl, and Tad wished he could sink into the floor. He hadn't mentioned anything about what happened today to his dad.

It had been a dumb idea to come here.

Scooter continued his verbal assault. "I never understood

why the C-A-R hired you in the first place. Didn't they know you bungle everything up?"

Tad could feel his dad tensing up beside him. He better get rid of this guy before there was trouble. Again.

"I don't know what you heard, but it wasn't a big deal."

That wasn't true, of course. It was a really big deal. But it could've been worse. At least Mrs. Cunningham had only sprained her wrist and bruised her knee. Mr. Cunningham had threatened to sue, however. Ugh. Him and those stupid spurs. Tad had tried to leave Sam out of it when explaining the incident to Dan and Anita, but Mr. Cunningham had thrown Sam under the bus somewhere in the middle of his high-pitched, red-faced tirade.

"No big deal?" Scooter taunted. "I heard they might lose the ranch because of you."

Tad blanched. Lose the ranch? No, that wouldn't happen. The guests had to sign waivers to ride the horses, and no bones had been broken. Dan had not been happy about the situation, but he hadn't yelled at Tad. He'd taken responsibility for the whole thing. No matter what Mr. Cunningham said, there was no way he would win if he took the ranch to court. Right?

Yet a sliver of doubt poked at Tad like a shard of wood under a fingernail. Not only about a potential lawsuit, but also something else. That cigarette butt he'd seen on the side of the path . . . Where had it come from? Maybe he *had* left one up there last week when he was trimming back the brush. Why couldn't he do anything right?

His inner turmoil must have shown on his face, because Bud gave him a look of wide-eyed disgust.

"What's he talkin' about, boy?"

Scooter wouldn't let up. "It took you a year to pay back the gas station. How long's it going to take to pay back an entire ranch?"

Tad wanted to say something clever, but nothing clever ever came to mind when he needed it. He shrugged and made a move that was supposed to mean *mind your own business and leave me alone*, but the message must not have been clear. Or maybe it was too clear.

Scooter stepped closer. "Don't turn your back on me when I'm talking to you, Bungley."

Tad could feel his father's disgust toward him grow when he didn't immediately spin around and tell Scooter to back off. That's what Bud would've done. That's what Bud wanted Tad to do. Tad suddenly wished he was drinking something stronger than beer.

Scooter shoved Tad's shoulder. "How does it feel to be the biggest screwup in town?"

Tad stared down at his hands. It felt like being kicked in the chest by a horse, that's how it felt. Much as Bud probably wanted him to get upset over what Scooter had said, Tad had no response. There was no defense he could make, either with his words or his fists. But Bud rose to his feet and faced Scooter.

Ah crap.

Bud stuck out his chest. "Why don't you get your red neck out of here before something happens to you."

Everyone in the bar was looking now. Tad was frozen. Once again, he knew he should stand up or say something—do *something*—and once again he couldn't move. Humiliation buzzed through his veins, setting his blood on fire. Out of the corner of his eye, he saw Maddie Pine sitting with some guy, watching, and his face burned. Great. It figured *she* would be here to witness this.

It felt like forever as Bud and Scooter stared each other down. Tad had never heard exactly what transpired the last time these two faced off. He only knew that if they got in another fight, there would be no winner.

A familiar voice broke through the tension. "Hey, boys, is there a problem here?"

Tad's body finally unfroze, and he let out a long breath. He'd never been so glad to see Chief Stubbs in his whole life, and man, had he lucked out that it wasn't Deputy Beaumont the Bonehead instead. He slowly turned around.

Scooter took a step away from Bud with poison in his eyes. "Nope. No problem, Stubby."

"You're already on thin ice after last weekend, Scooter." The chief wasn't in uniform, but his voice held plenty of authority without it. He hooked his thumbs in his belt loops. "I think it's time for you to go home."

Tad had no idea what happened last weekend, but Scooter suddenly looked awful nervous. With a long string of muttered cuss words in tow, he split for the parking lot, throwing one dark look back over his shoulder before he was out of sight.

The chief wasn't done. "You too, Bud." He jerked his thumb at the door. "Party's over."

Bud's face gave nothing away. He slowly turned back to the bar, drained the rest of his beer, and slammed it down. Looking straight ahead with a grim expression, he shook his head, and Tad had no doubt that was meant for him. Then, without ever glancing in Tad's direction, Bud strode out into the night.

And just like that, Tad was walking home.

eleven

Anita knelt in front of the couch in the living room as the first rays of sun leapt from behind the mountains Friday morning. She clasped her hands together tightly and bowed her head.

"Thank you, Lord, for the peaceful resolution with the Cunninghams. Give us wisdom in teaching Sam how important it is to follow the rules, even when he doesn't like it. And while we're talking about Sam, I know dogs can't live forever, but if You could please sustain Curly's life just a little longer? I don't want the poor thing to suffer, but Sam is going to be so lost without him."

The sound of someone bumbling around in the kitchen interrupted her thoughts.

"Amen."

She slowly, painfully pushed off the couch and stood. In the kitchen, she found Dan in front of the fridge, holding the door open with one hand. She walked up and hugged him from behind, leaning her cheek against his back.

"Good morning."

He put his free hand on her arm. "Good morning. Do we have any of those mini quiches left?"

"Sam ate them all." That boy was a bottomless pit. "I can make pancakes. Or cook up some oatmeal."

"That's okay, I've got to leave soon. I'll have coffee and toast."

Anita let go of her husband and reached for the fruit bowl. "And a banana."

One side of his mouth lifted. "And a banana."

"You'll be home around six thirty?"

He nodded. "Closer to seven, but I should be here before the fishermen."

A group of men from Chicago had booked all three cabins for a weekend of fishing. They were going to get beautiful weather, according to the forecast. The Cunninghams and Procters were checking out this morning by ten, and she would be spending the rest of the day cleaning their cabins for new guests. Thank goodness the third cabin had sat empty this week. It would be hard enough getting two ready in time.

"Don't let Tad or Sam off the hook today." Dan poured his coffee and kissed the top of her head. "If I catch wind they were fooling around while you cleaned those cabins by yourself . . ."

He let the words hang there, as was his habit. She smiled to herself at how they were both thinking about the cabins. Twenty-five years of marriage could not wear away every point of contention and method of miscommunication, but it could sure make two minds feel like one sometimes.

"Don't worry. I promise to crack the whip. They won't get a moment's rest."

"Ha."

They both knew she was not a whip-cracker. They also both knew she had no choice but to rely on Tad and Sam to do the heavy lifting. Especially since she had baking to do. Fresh baked goods were part of the deal when someone booked a cabin. Today she was planning blueberry muffins and bacon cheddar scones.

"Is Tad still working extra hard trying to make up for the riding incident?" she asked.

"Far as I can tell. And in town I heard . . ."

Anita frowned. "Heard what?"

"People are blaming him." Dan buttered a piece of toast. "They're saying he bungled it up."

"That's terrible. You need to set the record straight, Dan. If anything, it was Sam's fault."

"I tried, but lies always spread faster and farther than the truth. You know that."

She sighed. Yes, she knew. "Well, I'm sure you're doing your best. One more thing to talk to the Lord about, I guess."

She would add it to her already very long list.

"This is the kind of thing I was afraid of. With Tad." Dan gave her a look as he peeled his banana. "I'm worried it's always going to be something with him."

Anita couldn't hold back a slightly undignified huff. "He wasn't the one wearing spurs."

"But why didn't he tell Mr. Cunningham to take them off? And how did he not notice Sam coming up the hill on the Honda?"

"You can't blame—"

"I need him to be responsible. I don't know if I can trust him."

Anita turned on the burner under the kettle. She preferred tea to coffee in the morning. Then she pulled her favorite mug from the cupboard and turned back to Dan.

"You can trust him. I know he's rough around the edges, but he's a good kid. And he's so good with Sam. What happened Tuesday could've happened to anyone."

"I caught him smoking the other day. Behind Cabin C."

Anita wrinkled her nose. "You saw him?"

"Well . . ." Dan rubbed the back of his neck. "I didn't actually see it, but—"

"Dan." Anita put her hands on her hips as the water in the kettle began to simmer. "You know better than to jump to conclusions."

"I smelled it, plain as day. And his face looked guilty."

"You didn't ask him?"

Dan hung his head. "No. I didn't want him to lie to me, and I didn't want to fire him his first week on the job."

Anita leaned toward her husband and kissed his cheek. "You're a good man, Dan Wilson. I love you."

⬧ ⬧ ⬧

The early morning chill was long gone, and the afternoon sun washed the ranch in bright, hopeful gold. From the porch, Anita breathed deep of the spring air, relishing the smell of it. No matter how long she lived here, she never grew tired of the days growing longer and the lilac buds appearing and the fields turning green. If she believed in magic, she would say that's what spring in Montana was. Instead, she called it glory.

Through the screen door, she heard the loud, insistent dryer tone that meant the linens were ready to be driven up the hill to the cabins. Her short reprieve was over.

She pressed the button on the side of her walkie-talkie. "Sam. Come in, Sam."

No matter how many times she talked to her son about answering the walkie-talkie, he still only responded to about half of her calls. He usually came to the house, though, even if he didn't answer. She just had to wait.

"Sam, come in. Sam, where are you?"

To her surprise, when she let go of the talk button, the walkie-talkie gave a sputter of static and then spoke.

"Sam's with me, Mrs. Wilson. Is the laundry ready?"

Tad. Oh, but did she have a soft spot for that boy. She still remembered what he looked like when he was little and how he couldn't make the *l* sound. *"Hewwo,"* he would say, when she would drop by to see Holly. *"Wook at this!"*

She pressed the button. "Yes, the last load just finished."

"We'll be right there."

Her hands ached as she set the walkie-talkie down and pushed herself out of the wooden rocking chair that had been passed down to Dan from his grandfather. She made her way to the laundry room and was debating whether to pull the linens out of the dryer herself or wait for the boys when Sam came crashing into the house, sputtering and breathing hard.

He was jubilant. "We raced, Mom. And I won."

Tad came in behind him, coughing. "You got a head start." He grinned. "Cheater."

Sam's eyes shined. "Did not."

"Did too."

"Did not."

"All right, all right, you're both winners in my book." Anita pointed at the dryer. "Now pull those sheets out, please."

Sam picked up the big wicker basket in his long arms, and Tad bent over to retrieve the bedding from the depths of the dryer. Anita smiled to herself. See? She could crack the whip.

Sam turned toward the front of the house suddenly, almost dumping the basket. "What was that?"

She tilted her head. "I didn't hear anything."

"Someone's at the door."

"I'll go check." She walked to the door, limping slightly. Her left knee was giving her trouble today. Through the living room window, she saw an unfamiliar car parked in front of the house. Sam had been right. He had the hearing of a hawk. Had the fishermen arrived early?

She opened the door and found a thin young woman in a T-shirt and jeans, picking the skin of her elbow nervously. Definitely not one of the men from Chicago. Anita's spirit was on high alert as she noted the marks on the girl's arms and agitation in her eyes.

Anita gave her a welcoming smile. "Hello. What can I do for you?"

The girl looked about Tad's age. She wore bright red rain boots and shifted on her feet as she looked back at her car, which she had left running. "Uh . . . I . . ."

"Do you need help?" Anita opened the door wider. This girl wouldn't be the first person to show up at their door needing assistance, and a feeling in Anita's heart told her something was wrong. "Would you like to come in?"

The girl looked back at her car again, then shook her head. "No, I—uh, is Tad here?"

"Oh." Anita's eyebrows rose. "You're looking for Tad?"

Tad was coming around the corner to her left as she spoke, and he stopped short when he heard his name.

Sam bumped into him from behind with the basket. "Who is it?"

Tad glanced out the window, then came up alongside Anita. "Jenna, what are you doing here?"

The girl—Jenna—looked back at her car a third time. "I need to talk to you."

Tad's expression revealed irritation. "I'm working."

"Yep." Sam bobbed his head and held up the basket. "We're working."

Jenna's eyes swept over Sam then fixed on Anita, pleading with her.

"It's all right." Anita nodded at Tad. "Sam and I can get a snack while you two talk."

Whatever this girl needed must be important for her to come all the way out here. The cabin beds could wait a few more minutes.

Tad didn't move, so Anita nudged him toward the door. "Go ahead. We'll be in the kitchen."

He walked out looking kind of dazed, and she shut the door.

"Can I have one of those muffins for a snack?" Sam asked.

In the kitchen, Anita gave Sam a muffin and peeked out the window. Tad and Jenna were standing on the far side of her car, so Anita could only see their heads and the top of Tad's shoulders. Jenna seemed to be waving her arms around, and Tad seemed to be frozen in place. She didn't want to be nosy, but she was sure curious what they were speaking about.

Anita had often talked to God about Tad over the years. After Holly left, she'd felt a strong conviction that it was her duty to see to it the boy was covered in prayer. At first, she'd prayed that his grief over his mother wouldn't be too great and that Bud would not take his own grief out on his two boys, especially Tad, who was six years younger than his brother.

As Tad got older, she prayed the Lord would keep him far away from drugs, alcohol, and compromising situations with young ladies. On Friday nights, she would pray that if Tad was somewhere he shouldn't be, the Holy Spirit would hound him with uneasiness until he got himself out of there. She wanted to protect him, and she didn't want him living with regrets.

Sam asked if he could have another muffin, and she nodded distractedly as she continued to watch Tad and Jenna outside. Jenna opened the passenger door of her car and started pulling things out. It looked like she was setting them on the ground. What had she brought for Tad? What was going on?

Tad was still standing there frozen, looking lost, when Jenna got into her car and slammed the door. She paused for a moment, then put the car in drive and pulled forward, revealing a pile of stuff left behind. As her car bumped down the driveway, Anita squinted to study the pile. A couple of black garbage bags, stuffed full and about to tip over. A long, narrow cardboard box. A teddy bear wearing a pink dress. And—Anita gasped and leaned closer to the window. She blinked twice.

An infant car seat.

twelve

Tad had a dream once that he was swimming in Harrison Lake and started to drown. He tried to call for his mother, but no sound would come out.

Standing in the Wilsons' driveway as Jenna drove away felt a lot like that.

He watched until the car was out of sight, but she didn't turn around. Didn't even tap the brakes. He held his breath and slowly turned toward everything she had left behind. Two bags of blankets and clothes. A folded-up bassinet shoved into a duct-taped box. A teddy bear.

And his daughter.

She was sleeping. Only her face and one fist pressed to her cheek were visible above a frilly blanket. Tad didn't let out his breath until his lungs screamed for mercy. Then he swallowed hard and wondered how he would know if he was having a heart attack.

Footsteps on the gravel made him tense up. He had only vaguely been aware of the sound of the front door opening and closing.

"Tad?"

Anita's voice reached him, but he couldn't speak, still stuck in a drowning dream.

She touched his arm. "Tad, are you okay?"

He opened and closed his mouth twice before he was able to get his throat to work correctly. "Charlie."

"What?"

"Her name is Charlotte, but Jenna calls her Charlie."

Anita looked at the sleeping baby and pressed her hands to her chest. "She's beautiful." Her voice was soft. "She has your nose."

A sense of relief flooded his body that Anita understood without having to be told. Because how could he tell her? How could he explain something he didn't yet understand himself?

He nodded dumbly.

She took his hand and placed it on the car seat handle, holding it there until he gripped it. "Let's go inside."

He straightened, lifting the car seat off the ground. It was heavier than he expected. Anita signaled to Sam, and he hurried over and scooped up the bags and the box.

Anita gently picked up the teddy bear and tucked it under her arm.

"Come on." She spoke to him as if he were a child. "Follow me."

Somehow, he made it inside the house. Somehow, Anita prodded him onto the couch and unbuckled the baby—His baby. *Charlotte.*—and laid her in his arms. And somehow, he held on.

Sam pushed the box and bags into the corner of the room and sidled up close to Tad. "That's a baby."

Tad looked at the baby's face. It scrunched into a pout, then smoothed out again.

"She's tiny," Sam continued. "But not as tiny as Princess."

Anita clasped her hands in her lap and gave Sam a serious look. "Sam, honey, I need you to take the sheets up to the cabins, okay?"

"But I want to see the baby."

"First I need you to finish your job."

"Tad's supposed to help me."

Tad flinched at the sound of his name and shook his head, trying to clear it. "Yes. Help. I—"

"He'll help you in a minute." Anita pointed her chin at the laundry basket on the floor by the door. "Please bring the sheets up the hill for me."

Sam looked like he might argue, but something on his mom's face must have stopped him, because he sighed and grabbed the basket. After he'd gone, Anita sat quietly for a moment, then scooted closer on the couch.

"She really is a beautiful baby. Charlie, you said?"

"Jenna said." Tad's heart squeezed. Jenna had said a lot of things. About how Charlotte had been born three months ago and how Tad was her father and how Jenna needed him to take her for a little while. How she was going through a hard time and "dealing with some stuff," whatever that meant.

What she hadn't said was why she'd never told Tad he had a child. His mind kept going back to the night she'd called and he hadn't answered.

He'd only been with Jenna a couple times. For some reason, whenever things were going in that direction with a girl, Tad would get a strange feeling in his heart. Almost like there was something trying to stop him. Sitting there next to Anita, he couldn't help but wonder if her prayers had anything to do with that.

He looked down at the baby in his arms. "What do I do?"

Anita's voice was careful. "Did Jenna say when she'd be back?"

He shook his head.

"Did she tell you anything about Charlie's feeding schedule?"

Tad's shoulders slumped. "Yeah, but I can't remember. She said there's bottles in the bag."

"That's all right." Anita peered at Charlie's face. "It shouldn't be too hard to figure out. She'll tell us when she's hungry."

Something broke inside him. "I can't do this. You take her." He held the baby out toward Anita, feeling the desperation on his face. He had no idea what to do with a baby. He'd always thought Jenna was a little crazy, and this proved it. She had to be nuts. He never should've gotten involved with her.

For a second, it looked like Anita was going to take Charlie from him like he wanted, and a strange mixture of hope and panic flooded through him. Then Anita tucked her hands under her legs.

"I'll show you how to make her bottle and change her diaper and get her dressed. But she belongs with you."

"I can't."

"I'll help you. We'll help. It's going to be okay."

Okay? Nothing about this was okay. He couldn't even handle being responsible for another adult for a couple hours on a trail ride. How could he possibly be responsible for someone this small? How could Jenna do this to him?

Why hadn't she told him?

His throat tightened. What would he have done if she had?

His mother's face flashed through his mind, and he drew Charlie a little closer to his chest. He tried not to look at her, but his eyes were drawn again and again to her little face. Anita was right about her nose. She was so . . . so . . .

With a squeak and a stretch, Charlie woke up. Her mouth formed a tiny O as she yawned, her fists raised above her head, her thick black hair rubbing against his arm. Then her dark blue eyes found his and widened as if she'd been searching for him, and she smiled.

And the Tad he had always been no longer was.

• • •

Tad's eyes flew open in the dark, and he sat up with a grunt. What was that noise? Like someone was in the room with him. The sound came again, and reality struck him like a sideswipe from a grizzly.

Charlie.

He bolted from his bed and was beside her bassinet in an instant. He never even knew what a bassinet was until today. He gripped the side and tried to mimic the way Anita had talked to the baby earlier.

"Shh. Hey, hey, shh."

A wail twice the size of its source cut through the night, and Tad's heart hammered. *"I don't want to hear a peep out of that thing,"* his dad had said when Tad had brought Charlie home. Right after looking at him like he'd lost his mind and right before storming out of the house, grumbling under his breath.

"Shh, Charlie. You gotta be quiet."

His words were like fuel thrown on a fire. Her volume increased. Bud was going to pitch a fit if Tad didn't do something fast.

He reached into the bassinet and picked Charlie up the way

Anita had shown him. Her back was wet. What on earth? It took him a second to realize she was soaked in pee.

"You gotta be kidding me."

She continued to cry, and a sinking feeling in his gut told him there was only one way to get her to stop. He tucked her awkwardly against his chest, and her crying immediately dropped off to a whimper. Pee soaked through his T-shirt, and he looked around the room. Where had he put her extra pajama things with the feet?

He sniffed. Oh no. It wasn't just pee. He made a face.

"Charlie," he whispered. "What did you do?"

Checking the time, he realized he would need to make a bottle while they were up. It had been four hours since her last one. But he had to change her first. He turned the lamp by his bed on low and stumbled around the room, gathering supplies. A dry one of those pajamas. A container of wipes. A whatsit-thing with the snaps at the bottom that Anita said to put on under the pajamas to ensure Charlie would be warm enough.

When he laid her on his bed, she started to cry again. Anita had prepared him for this. *"Babies like it when you sing to them,"* she'd said.

"I'm flyin' high when I take the low road," he sang. "Where all the cowboys and coyotes go."

She quieted, and he took off her pajama thing. Poop had leaked up her back and was—was it in the folds of her neck? This was insane. How was that possible? He gagged as he took off the whatsit-thing and found her diaper only half-attached. He must not have pulled the Velcro tabs tight enough earlier. Wait. He'd forgotten to grab another diaper.

The sudden desire for a smoke jabbed him in the ribs, so

strong it nearly stole his breath. But even he wasn't dumb enough to smoke in front of a baby. Plus, he needed both hands to deal with this . . . situation.

He turned to look around. The box of diapers he'd bought on his way home was across the room. Was she going to roll off if he left her on the bed? Anita had said something about that, but he couldn't remember. The page and a half of information and reminders she'd written down for him was in the kitchen. She'd told him he could call her anytime, day or night, but it was three in the morning.

He wouldn't take any chances. He picked Charlie up and held his breath against the smell as he hurried over, grabbed a diaper, and hurried back. Why hadn't he put a towel under her or something? There was poop all over his bed. More poop than he would've ever believed could come from such a small person. He gagged again.

"Charlie, why?"

Thirty-seven wipes later, Charlie was clean and dressed, and Tad's clothes were in a stinking pile on the floor with hers, along with the blanket from his bed. Was this going to happen every night? He shuddered. He would need to be more prepared next time.

If there was a next time. If he couldn't convince Anita that Charlie would be better off with her. He had no business taking care of a child.

He held the baby like a football as he stood in the kitchen in his underwear, trying to make a bottle with one hand. Is this what Jenna had been doing the past three months? Or had she—you know, breastfed or whatever. How did that even work?

And another thing. What if Jenna *hadn't* had "some stuff

to deal with"? Would she have ever told him about Charlie? Was that even legal?

Charlie grew warm and heavy on his arm. It ached from holding the position, and she slobbered all over it like she was trying to eat him.

"You must be hungry," he whispered. "I'm working on it."

He winced when he knocked over a glass reaching to turn off the water. The sound echoed through the house like a gunshot. He could only hope Bud had drunk enough earlier to put him in a deep sleep.

After dumping formula all over the counter twice, he finally had a bottle ready. He was not going to be able to afford that kind of mistake again. The cost of a can of formula was unreal. When would Charlie be able to drink real milk? When would she be able to eat food? There was so much he didn't know.

It didn't matter. This was only temporary. Right?

He eased onto the couch and slipped the bottle into Charlie's mouth. She went after it with gusto, sucking like it had been days. He leaned his head back against the couch. As the minutes ticked by and her little body warmed him, he fought to keep his eyes open. Exhaustion pressed down on him. He couldn't nod off now. He must stay awake.

Stay. Awake.

"Maybe if I talk out loud, that will help." He forced his head back upright with great effort and kept his voice low. "Tell me, Charlie, what is all this 'stuff' your mother has going on right now?"

Her eyes were closed, but her eager sucking continued.

"Oh, sure, you get to shut *your* eyes."

Her little noises filled the dark room. She was a feather, a stone, a chain in his arms. A free fall. An anchor.

He shook his head, trying to clear it, trying to keep the sleep away.

"What do you do during the day? When are you going to, like . . . walk?"

She reached up and curled her tiny hand around his pinkie.

thirteen

Tad looked at Anita, then down at Charlie. His heart wobbled like a newborn foal's first steps. It had been the longest three days of his life, home alone with a baby he had no idea what to do with. Trying to keep her happy, keep her quiet, keep his dad from having any excuse to do something stupid like kick him out of the house. The minutes had crawled by like the shadows slowly creeping across the yard.

He hadn't left the house except to smoke when Charlie was napping, breaks he'd cut short each time for fear she would wake up when he wasn't there. He'd called Anita with questions seven times. He'd barely slept. Hadn't even showered since Friday morning, and here it was, Tuesday. Disgusting.

A sudden bolt of panic hit him. Should he have given Charlie a bath? What if she smelled bad and Anita noticed? She hadn't written anything about baths on the note she sent home.

Anita gave him a gentle smile. "You can stop in to check on her anytime."

He'd been certain that he'd be desperate by now to put a little distance between him and the baby. That placing her in Anita's arms where she belonged would provide a sense of relief. But now that Anita stood there holding open her front door, waiting for him to hand over the car seat, the thought of leaving Charlie weighed on him.

"You're sure you don't mind watching her all day?"

Anita's smile grew. "I've been looking forward to this all weekend. It was all I could do to keep myself from driving over to your house to see her."

Tad looked away. He was glad she hadn't. Bud would've had a cow.

"This wasn't part of the deal when you hired me. You'll need to take babysitting fees out of my paycheck. Whatever you think is fair."

"Don't be ridiculous." Anita waved his words away. "I won't hear of it."

She gestured toward the house, a clear message that it was time, and he tentatively entered and set the car seat on the floor. "She had a bottle at seven."

Anita nodded.

He pointed at the elephant blanket covering Charlie's legs. "She likes this blanket, but I packed the one with the stars too, just in case."

"We're going to be fine."

Charlie stared up at him. What was he supposed to do? He had to work. Now, more than ever, he needed to make money. Needed to get his own place. "If she starts to—"

"Tad." Anita put her hand on his elbow. "Everything's going to be fine. I promise. I'll call you if anything comes up."

His heart squeezed. "If I'm out past the cabins, there won't be any reception."

She tapped her chin. "How about if I give you the extra walkie-talkie?"

He stood up a little straighter. Those walkie-talkies, they

seemed like they were kind of special to the Wilsons. A family thing. He'd used Sam's but never carried his own. "Really?"

"That fourth one just sits on the charger every day. You might as well use it."

"If you're sure . . ."

"I'll go get it."

He stood there with his arms hanging heavy at his sides as she hurried off. It was almost too much to think about, what she was doing for him.

He knelt beside the car seat. "I need you to be a good girl for Anita. No temper tantrums, no neck poops, okay?"

Charlie only blinked at him, but when he leaned closer, she made a gurgling sound. He touched her cheek. "Promise?"

She smiled.

♦ ▾ ♦

Tad held his breath as he wrapped a cotton roll around and around TJ's back right leg, hoping the horse would continue to tolerate his treatment. He'd already applied the SSD cream and Telfa pad, and so far, the horse had stood still.

TJ shifted his weight and blew a puff of air from his nose. "I know, buddy, I'm sorry. But you got yourself into this mess."

There had been no wounds on the horse when Tad performed his morning check, but now there was a shallow gash on TJ's leg. It was a mystery where the injury had come from, but Tad had his suspicions. TJ had a favorite place to stand by a large Rocky Mountain maple, and currently Bob—old Belle of the Ball herself—was camped out in that very spot.

"Girl trouble, am I right?" Tad held up a roll of Vetrap. "Now don't move. One more step to go."

Tad quickly finished the job, then laid a hand on TJ's neck. His glossy black coat was warm from the sun. Tad glanced over his shoulder before whispering, "Speaking of girls, I got a daughter. What do you think of that?"

TJ tossed his head but stayed put.

"Her name's Charlotte. She's got dark hair almost the same color as yours." Tad grinned. "Except prettier."

When TJ took no offense, Tad dared to move slowly in front of the horse and touch his nose. "I don't believe that you're nothing but trouble."

TJ held his gaze for a moment, as if trying to tell him something. Then he tossed his head again and moved out of Tad's reach. Tad let him go and ducked out of the round pen. Best not to push his luck.

As soon as he was clear of the fence, he pulled the walkie-talkie off his belt for the hundredth time that day, and for the hundredth time he immediately hooked it back on. What was wrong with him? Five days ago, he could go for hours without thinking of anything but the next task he needed to complete on the ranch. Now he couldn't go five minutes without wondering how Charlie was doing. Whether she was okay. But he didn't want to bother Anita. She was doing enough for him as it was.

With a shake of his head, he grabbed a grooming bucket from the barn. Maybe he could bribe Bob to move away from TJ's tree. She was long overdue for a good brushing, though he would need to be careful to avoid her sensitive bald spots or he might get nipped.

As he pulled a curry comb from the bucket, a muted rumbling sound caught his attention. He held up the comb to block the sun as he peered down the driveway and groaned.

"You gotta be kidding me."

Maddie again. What was her deal? She couldn't possibly be that interested in a bunch of kittens.

He tossed the comb back in the bucket and loped around the barn in time to see Maddie park her Mazda in the shade of a cottonwood tree. She climbed out and shot him a smirk.

"Hello, Thaddeus."

He rolled his eyes. She couldn't have come yesterday, when he wasn't here? "It's Tad."

"Is Sam around?"

Once again, Tad was glad for Sam's recurrent disappearing act. "Nope."

Maddie frowned. "Oh. Do you know when he'll be back?"

"Nope."

He'd gone off somewhere after lunch, and Tad wasn't worried. He did that sometimes. Tad was grateful for the good timing, sure that Maddie's visit would be cut short as a result of Sam's absence.

She ran her fingers through her hair. "Maybe I'll drop in to see Mrs. Wilson, then. In case he shows up soon."

Tad raised one shoulder, ready to say, "Suit yourself," but the words stuck in his throat. Charlie. Charlie was in there with Anita.

"Wait."

Maddie had already turned toward the house, and as she spun back around to face him, her eyes narrowed. "What?"

He rubbed the back of his neck. "I can show you where the kittens are."

She looked at him like he'd stepped in a pile of manure. "I know where they are."

Sweat beaded on his forehead. He couldn't let her see

Charlie. She would have all kinds of questions. She would
. . . what *would* she do?

"I think Anita's busy."

Maddie wrinkled her nose and took a step toward the house.
"She told me to stop in to visit next time I was here. She was
pretty adamant about it. So . . ."

She watched him, eyebrows raised. He opened his mouth,
but nothing came out. What could he say to stop her? What
could he do?

His mind was blank. Like every other time he needed it to
do something, it provided nothing.

Maddie wasn't one to wait around. When he continued to
stand there gaping like an idiot, she did that hair comb thing
again and strode to the house. He froze for a second as a hundred different scenarios played out in his imagination—none
of them good—before he forced his feet to move. He followed
Maddie at a distance, his heart pounding. How had he found
himself in this situation?

Jenna, that's how.

As he neared the house, he looked around for something
to do so it would appear as if he was working. He spotted
some weeds poking out of the gravel by the porch, so he bent
to pull them.

At Maddie's knock, Anita answered the door, holding Charlie. She grinned. "Why, Maddie, how lovely to see you."

Tad strained to watch them from the corner of his eye as
he stooped over a dandelion.

Maddie shifted. "Oh. Hi. Who's this?"

"This?" Anita glanced at Charlie. "Oh, this is, um . . ."

Anita's smile faltered as she looked past Maddie at Tad.
Their eyes locked. He could see in her face that she wasn't

sure what to do. She wouldn't lie for him—he knew that—but he sensed she was looking for his permission to reveal Charlie's identity.

He straightened and started to shake his head, hoping she would understand and tell Maddie something like "I'm baby-sitting for a friend" or "Baby? What baby? I don't see any baby." But he stopped himself. Steeled himself. Everyone was going to find out. He had to face the facts. Grady was too small of a town to keep anything a secret for long, and Maddie would never be satisfied until she had the whole story. There was only one thing to do.

"That's Charlotte," he called. Maddie turned around and looked at him with surprise.

He gripped the dandelion in his fist. "She's my daughter."

fourteen

Tad couldn't stand it any longer. Maddie had been in the house for almost an hour. She was probably holding Charlie right now. Talking baby talk to her. Booping her nose.

He growled as he stomped behind the barn and shook a cigarette from the pack in his jacket. Dan wouldn't be home for a couple of hours and Anita was clearly preoccupied with her guest, so nobody was paying any attention to him. He clicked on his lighter and glanced over his shoulder twice before touching the flame to the tip of the cigarette.

He took a long drag and held it. What were they talking about in there? About what a joke it was Tad thought he could take care of a baby? No doubt Maddie had all kinds of opinions about the situation. He'd seen the wheels turning in her mind earlier on the porch. Now she was in the house, trying her best to weasel information out of Anita.

"Dad says smoking is bad for you and gives your lungs the cancer."

Tad startled, which made him cough. He threw the cigarette on the ground and covered it with his boot. His eyes watered as he tried to hold back another cough and act normal. "Hey, Sam. Where've you been?"

Curly gave one half-hearted wag of his tail, and Sam stared at Tad's foot until Tad moved it and picked up the butt with a sigh. "Your dad's right. Smoking is bad."

"But you were smoking."

Tad blew out a breath. This was all Maddie's fault. "Yeah. I'm sorry. Let's keep that between us, okay?"

He couldn't afford for Dan to find out. Especially now.

"Between us? Like a secret?"

Tad's hands clenched. He didn't want to encourage Sam to keep secrets from his parents. Sam had probably never done anything sneaky in all his twenty years, at least not on purpose. But Tad thought of Charlie and how he needed to keep this job. He thought of how much it cost to buy formula and what it was going to take for him to move out of his dad's house. He had to think of his daughter.

He shoved down his reservations and forged ahead. "Like a promise. You promise not to tell anyone about this cigarette, and I promise not to smoke ever again." Tad swallowed hard and felt compelled to add, "At work."

Sam held up his hand. "A pinkie promise?"

"Sure."

Sam's eyes widened. "I've always wanted a pinkie promise."

He reached out his pinkie, and after a moment's hesitation, Tad hooked it with his own. He tried to tell himself it was no big deal, what he was asking of Sam. He would never smoke on C-A-R property again. He would leave his Camels at home from now on. It was no big deal.

The twisted feeling in his gut told him otherwise. But what choice did he have?

Sam knelt down and put his arm around his dog. "Curly is tired today. I carried him partway."

"From where? Where were you guys?"

"Hey, Sam."

Tad turned to find Maddie walking toward them, followed by Anita with Charlie in her arms. At the sight of his daughter, his heart did a strange squeezing thing that felt horrible and wonderful all at once.

Sam scrambled to his feet. "Hi, Maddie. You came."

Tad hurried toward Anita, his eyes fixed on Charlie. "It's not that warm out here, is she . . . ?"

Anita held her out toward Tad. "She's fine. It's plenty warm."

Tad reached for Charlie but hesitated. He was dirty. Covered in horsehair, dirt, and sawdust. He didn't even know what was under his fingernails, and he could feel Maddie watching him. Judging his every move. But Charlie started to make intent gurgling sounds in his direction, so he pulled off his coat, hung it on a fence post, and took her from Anita.

He tried to make a stern face as he peered down at his daughter. "You're bossy."

She waved a fist in the air.

"Do you want to see the kittens?" Sam asked.

Maddie gave him a teasing nudge with her elbow. "Of course. Why do you think I'm here, silly."

But Sam wasn't looking at her. He was looking at Charlie.

Tad looked too, and it seemed like she was listening. She made a noise that almost sounded like "uh-huh."

Sam's eyes widened. "She said yes! Come on, Charlie."

He spun around and marched toward the barn. It took him a minute, but Curly slowly stood, wobbled for a second, and followed. Tad looked at Anita and hesitated.

"Go ahead." She made a shooing motion. "Your work will keep."

"But I'm on the clock."

Technically, he had agreed to a weekly salary that covered him working Tuesday through Friday, plus any other hours that were needed, so he could always stay longer if something had to be done. But it felt weird to play with his daughter when he was supposed to be working.

"Come onnn," Sam called.

"Yeah, Tad." Maddie smirked at him. "Come onnn."

Anita put her hands on Tad's shoulders and turned him toward the barn, then gave him a gentle push. Sam was practically bouncing on his feet by the time everyone else caught up with him in the corner of the barn where his cat Peaches had laid her kittens. Curly had stretched out nearby.

Sam held a small, gray kitten in his hand. "This is Stormy." He held the kitten close to Charlie's face, and it meowed.

"He's the loudest. And here's Slick. He's the smoothest."

He held up a darker gray kitten. Tad adjusted to give Charlie a better view. She stared at the creature, unblinking.

"I think she likes Slick." Sam put Slick down and picked up the white one. "And this is Princess."

Maddie took Princess from Sam and cuddled her. "She's getting so big. How much longer, Sam?"

He thought for a second, his mouth moving silently as he counted to himself. "Three more weeks."

"Then she'll be old enough for me to take home?"

Sam nodded. Tad cringed inwardly. Three more weeks of Maddie coming by? Ugh. She was not the kind of person he wanted hanging around his daughter. The kind of person who manipulated others to get what she wanted and would lie to get out of trouble.

He gazed down at Charlie. What kind of woman would she be when she grew up? Like Maddie? Like Anita?

He stiffened. Or Jenna. Was Charlie destined to become like her mom? He tensed even more as a cold chill swept over him. What did he have to do to make sure she didn't grow up to be like *him*?

Curly lifted his head to check on everyone, then let out a huff before lowering it again.

Maddie looked at the dog. "How about Curly? How old is he?"

Sam got down on the ground beside Curly and leaned against the mutt. "He's almost sixteen, like I'm almost twenty-one. We have our birthdays together. Right, Mom?"

Anita smiled. "It's always nice to share a birthday with your best friend."

Maddie's eyebrows shot up. "You're turning twenty-one soon?"

"May thirty-first."

"Huh."

Tad didn't like the sound of that *huh*. What did she care about Sam's birthday?

Charlie began to fuss in his arms, and Sam sprang up from the ground with a frown. "What's the matter?"

"She's fine." Anita patted Sam's arm. "She's just getting hungry. It's about time for her bottle."

Anita reached for Charlie, and Tad reluctantly handed her over, shocked at the sudden feeling of emptiness that came over him.

Anita gently grasped Charlie's arm and moved it back and forth through the air to make it look like she was waving. "Say 'Bye-bye, Daddy.'"

Sam said something in response, and Maddie laughed, but Tad only heard them as a distant, muffled noise. Like voices moving through water.

Daddy. That was him.

Daddy.

fifteen

When Mom takes Charlie back to the house and Tad goes back to work I hope hope hope that Maddie will stay a little longer and she does. I sit down in the dirt and pet Stormy and Stormy makes little baby sounds and I like the way Maddie tucks Princess under her chin and whispers to her like I sometimes talk to Curly. Curly is laying next to Peaches who is Stormy's mom. In *City Slickers* when the cowboys are mean to Bonnie, the movie Curly lassos the tall cowboy and tells him he owes Bonnie an apology and that's what I would do if someone was mean to Maddie.

"Does Peaches have kittens every year?" Maddie asks.

I nod and tell her how Peaches has had four litters of kittens because she must like babies so much and I don't know why Maddie laughs about that but I like it when she laughs.

"I like babies too," she says, and I say "Me too" and I say I like Charlie.

"How long has Charlie been with Tad?" Maddie wants to know and I think about it.

"Jenna brought Charlie on Friday."

"Jenna? You mean Jenna Jackson?"

I shrug because I don't know if that's what I mean.

"Jenna brought her here?" Maddie asks.

I tell her yes and she brought all Charlie's stuff and I was so happy to meet Charlie but Tad didn't seem so happy.

"He didn't know Charlie was coming?"

"I don't know."

"Had he ever talked to you about Charlie before Friday?"

"No."

I know that's true because I would remember if he did because I'm good at remembering and also because Tad doesn't talk much about anything. I like to talk to him a lot but he doesn't say a lot back and that's fine. Dad says God put a whole lot of words inside some people and not as many inside others and there's nothing wrong with that.

Curly moves over and puts his head on my leg and I set Stormy down so I can pet Curly because Curly is my best friend and Stormy isn't. Curly is really old and the fur on his face is gray and he snores louder than he used to but he's the only one who knows all my secrets and I love him.

"I wish my dog was as calm as yours," Maddie says.

I tell her I didn't know she had a dog and she says his name is Jasper and he's six months old and he's really hyper and he's a golden retriever because golden retrievers are her favorite. I wonder if Princess and Jasper are going to get along but I don't wonder that out loud because I don't want Maddie to worry. I want her to be able to smile all the time and I know not all dogs and cats fight. Curly never fights with any cats.

"I wish every dog was like mine," I say.

Maddie has a big breath in and a big breath out like Mom does when her knees hurt really bad and Maddie's voice sounds different when she says, "I wish a lot of things, Sam."

And she says it kind of quiet.

"Dad says you can make a wish on a falling star."

"I haven't been spending much time looking at the stars lately. Maybe I should."

"Mom says it's fun to make wishes but if something's really important we should pray about it. Are your wishes really important?"

I wait for Maddie to answer and I wait and wait and then she turns her head away from me and says yes.

"I guess you should pray about them then, okay?"

"I don't think God would listen to me, Sam."

"Why not? He listens to everybody. You gotta do it if it's important."

She turns her head back and looks at me and I look at her and she kind of smiles but her eyes don't smile when she says okay.

I think I will pray for her wishes too in case she forgets.

sixteen

"Amen."

Anita slowly pushed herself up from where she'd been kneeling in front of the couch Friday morning. She should've prayed for strength for her body. It had been a while since it had protested this strongly against her movements. Her prayer had been reserved for something else, however. Or rather, someone else.

Charlie.

It had only been one week since she'd met the little girl, but already Anita couldn't imagine life without her. Watching her for Tad had come as naturally as breathing the past three days. All her mothering instincts had come rushing back the moment she'd first caught a glimpse of those tiny hands and wide eyes.

That didn't mean it had been easy. Working the little snaps and buttons on Charlie's clothes with her swollen fingers took extra time. Walking the floor to console the baby when she cried put extra strain on her knees. And Charlie couldn't even crawl yet. Caring for her would be a whole different story once she became mobile.

Would Anita's body be able to keep up when Charlie was

walking around the house? When she started to run? Would Anita be able to keep her safe?

She stretched carefully from side to side and shook her head. She was getting ahead of herself. She had no idea how long Charlie would need her. There was no reason to borrow trouble.

When Tad had picked Charlie up after work yesterday, Anita had asked if he'd talked to Jenna, and he'd said no. Jenna hadn't returned any of his calls or texts. It was hard to understand how she could leave Charlie like that, but Anita refused to think poorly of the girl. She was in no place to judge Jenna's situation.

Still, she couldn't help but wonder. What if she never came back?

Anita walked stiffly into the kitchen to find Dan reading yesterday's paper. He'd warmed up the leftover pancakes from two days ago and drowned them in homemade brown sugar syrup. These few moments of peace with her husband before the demands of the day began were something Anita cherished.

"Good morning." He peered at her over the local sports page. "How are your knees today?"

She shrugged. "Oh, you know. Same as usual."

He harumphed. "We've been married twenty-five years. I can tell when you're in pain."

"I'm fine."

She took an orange from the fruit bowl and focused on peeling it, but she could feel Dan's eyes on her. She knew what was coming. After twenty-five years, she could tell a few things too.

Dan folded the newspaper and set it aside. "You watching Charlie again today?"

She popped an orange slice in her mouth. "Yes."

He knew that already. He'd heard her and Sam go on and on about the baby for the past week, but because of his schedule, he hadn't yet met her in person.

"And our new guests arrive this afternoon?"

She didn't respond. He knew that already as well. He was taking the long way around to his point.

He moved his pancakes around his plate. "Sounds like it'll be a long day for you."

There it was.

"Yes, but I can handle it. Tad and Sam will help."

"And you're going to make donuts?"

She sighed. Maybe the donuts weren't a great idea. Time would be tight. "I might make banana bread instead."

"How are you going to do that while holding Charlie?"

She pulled out a chair and sat across from him. "I don't hold her every minute of the day, dear. It's going to be fine."

"Our guests expect their cabins to be ready when they arrive."

"Yes, I know." Her voice held an edge she hadn't planned on.

Dan raised his eyebrows in surprise. "I'm just saying—"

"I know what you're saying." She rubbed her temples. "I didn't mean to snap at you, but it's going to be fine. Everything will be ready in time."

"You've taken a lot on. Volunteering at the Coalition, being in charge of the cabins, and now watching Charlie? What's going to happen if you push yourself too hard and have a flare-up?"

Anita wanted to be angry and indignant, but Dan had a point. A severe flare-up would mean certain jobs would not get done, and everyone needed to be able to do their part around here if this whole guest ranch thing was going to keep working. Whether she liked it or not, she had to take into account her physical limitations or she would end up being no help at all.

"Sam and Tad will help me, like last Friday."

"Maybe I should stay home. I could take a sick day."

"Don't be silly." The edge was back in her voice. "We managed fine last summer without you ever missing work."

She knew Dan cared about her health and comfort, but she wasn't sure where all this was coming from. She'd never once failed to have the cabins cleaned, ready, and stocked with baked goods when guests arrived. She didn't plan to start now.

"We didn't have Tad last year," he replied. "And we certainly didn't have a baby in the house."

So this was about Tad. Dan had been set against him since she first suggested they bring him on.

"Tad hasn't done anything to deserve your distrust."

Dan gave her a look, and she knew that look, and she dreaded that look. "You mean aside from unknowingly fathering a child outside of marriage?"

His tone was gentle, but his words felt sharp.

"We all make mistakes, dear." She matched the gentleness of his voice. "You and I included. You've got to give him a chance."

She reached across the table and set her hand on his. He grasped it. "I don't like seeing you suffer. I wish . . ."

She pulled his hand toward her and kissed the back of it, then a knock sounded from the front of the house. Her heart did a little skip.

"Charlie's here."

She sprang from the table, the pain in her knees forgotten,

and grabbed one of the walkie-talkies from the mudroom before answering the door. The sight of Tad with a car seat in one hand and a diaper bag in the other made her smile.

He yawned. "Hi."

She waved him in. "Good morning. You're early."

He always looked so lost when he came to their house, even after nearly a month of working for them.

"I knew there was a lot to do today. I wanted to make sure we'd have enough time before the guests got here."

Anita beamed with satisfaction, hoping Dan had overheard. Heavy footsteps thudded above her, indicating Sam was up and on the move. Her few moments of morning quiet were over.

Tad set the car seat and diaper bag down and knelt to unbuckle a wide-awake Charlie. "She promised to be extra good today."

"She's extra good every day."

Dan appeared as Tad stood with Charlie in his arms. The men nodded at each other.

Tad carefully transferred Charlie into Anita's outstretched arms. "Her last bottle was at five thirty."

That explained the dark circles under his eyes. He probably hadn't gone back to sleep after that. She remembered those days, but only through the rosy haze of time that softened the memories.

She handed him the walkie-talkie. "Sam will be out soon."

"Okay." He kissed the top of Charlie's head, then hesitated. "It seemed like maybe she wanted more milk. Do you think she's getting enough?"

"I can add more to her bottles today and see if she takes it."

His eyes were fixed on the baby. "All right. Thanks."

Still he hesitated, but before she could ask if something was wrong, he tore his gaze away from his daughter and cleared his throat.

"I better get to it."

He shut the door behind him, and Anita turned to catch her husband staring at Charlie.

She shifted to give him a better look. "Do you want to hold her?"

Dan glanced at his watch and back at the baby. "I should probably get going. I've got to stop for gas on my way in."

"Oh." She noted Charlie's mismatched pink socks and smiled. "Okay, well—"

"Maybe for a quick minute." Dan stepped closer and lifted his hands. "I can always get gas on the way home."

⋆ ⋆ ⋆

"Pat-a-cake, pat-a-cake, baker's man." Anita sang softly and patted Charlie's hands. "Bake me a cake as fast as you can."

From the blanket laid out on the floor, Charlie cooed, and Anita's heart melted like butter on a biscuit. What a doll. What an absolute darling of a child.

"Pat it and prick it and mark it with a C. And pop it in the oven for Charlie and me."

Anita raised her hands and wiggled her fingers to finish the song with a flourish, and Charlie watched with wide eyes. From her place on the floor beside Charlie, Anita put her hands on her hips. "Is Miss Anita being silly?"

Charlie kicked her legs. Her expression reminded Anita of Tad, which made her think of Bud. How had he reacted when Tad brought Charlie home last Friday? He used to be fun-loving and freewheeling in their younger years. The kind of guy who was always up for anything. She imagined *that* Bud scooping Charlie up in his arms with a grin and saying, *"Looks like I'm a grandpa now."*

That Bud was long gone.

A high-pitched and persistent beep came from the kitchen, and Anita sighed. Break time was over. The banana bread was done.

"You stay right there, little miss." She wagged a finger at Charlie as she scrambled awkwardly up off the floor. "I'll be right back."

She hurried into the kitchen, grateful she'd given up on the idea of making donuts. Even the banana bread had almost proven to be too much. As she pulled two loaf pans from the oven, Charlie started to cry, and a knock sounded from the front door.

"Oh, dear. Hold on, everyone."

She slid the pans onto a cooling rack and jogged back to where she'd left Charlie. Because of the pain in her knees, she bent at the waist to pick up the baby, and her back objected. Another knock sounded as she carefully straightened.

She nuzzled Charlie's neck and kissed her cheek. "We're coming, aren't we?"

When she pulled open the door, she found a handsome young couple in stylish clothes checking their phones. Must be Cabin B's new occupants from Seattle. They looked up.

"Hello." Anita adjusted Charlie in her arms. "Welcome to Come Around Ranch."

"Hi." The young man tucked his phone in his pocket. "We're ready to check in. We're here for the key."

"Of course, you must be Ben and Skyla. Come on in." She stepped aside and they entered the house with curious expressions, examining the furniture, the coats hanging on the rack, the rustic decor. Anita tried to imagine what kind of sleek and modern studio apartment they might live in. There were probably no antlers on the wall.

"Smells good in here," Ben said.

"That's the banana bread. It just came out of the oven, but if you give me a minute, I can wrap it up for you to take to your cabin."

She'd meant to have the bread waiting for them on their counter before they arrived, but the day had gotten away from her. The floors of the cabins had been a muddy mess, and on top of that, Charlie had had two major blowouts.

Skyla wrinkled her nose. "Is it gluten free?"

Anita's heart sank. She'd completely forgotten to check the online dietary request form.

"I'm so sorry, it isn't. But I can make a gluten-free batch and have it to you by the morning. It's no trouble."

"No, that's okay." Skyla exchanged a look with Ben. "We don't typically eat carbs, anyway."

"Oh. I see."

Anita felt terrible about the bread. She prided herself on meeting the needs of every guest, and they often told her how much her efforts were appreciated. Most of their guests were kind and thankful, as a matter of fact, although not all.

Skyla peered at Charlie. "Is this your granddaughter?"

Anita's insides stilled. More than anything, she wanted to say yes, but being a grandma was a dream she knew could never be fulfilled. She had no claim on this baby.

Still, it was hard to say the words. "No, I'm watching her for a friend."

Skyla reached out to touch Charlie's hand. "She's cute."

Cute? Anita had to hold back a huff. She was the most beautiful and precious child in the history of children, that's what she was. Cute. Pfft.

"Let me get your key."

She took a deep breath as she snatched the key from the cubby in the mudroom. For heaven's sake, she needed to calm down. What kind of craziness might come out of her if she ever *did* have a grandchild?

seventeen

The Seattle couple was settled into Cabin B, and two little old ladies had checked in to Cabin C. Tad scanned the driveway for any sign of the people who had booked Cabin A, the only cabin that allowed more than two guests because it had a hide-a-bed couch. He saw nothing. If he hurried, maybe he could stop in to give Charlie a quick snuggle before they arrived.

Ha. Since when was the word *snuggle* part of his vocabulary?

"Hey, Tad, look at this."

Tad spun around to find Sam balancing on one foot on top of a large rock, his arms up in a sort of crane pose. Curly looked at him from the ground with a weary and resigned expression.

"Careful up there." The last thing they needed was for Sam to break his ankle.

Sam jumped down and landed next to Curly. "Can Charlie come see the kittens with me?"

"I don't think so."

"Why not?"

"I think your mom's busy."

"I can do it myself. Mom showed me how to hold her."

Tad's chest tightened. Sam was becoming like a brother to him, but the thought of Sam carrying Charlie around sent up a flare of panic. What if he dropped her? What if he set her down somewhere unsafe? A dozen nerve-wracking scenarios flashed through his mind.

"Maybe I can help you after the last group of guests checks in. We can do it together."

"Okay."

As if on cue, the sound of a loud engine cut through the early evening air. A silver Ford F-150 sped up the driveway. Tad grimaced as it bounced along the uneven dirt and then hit the parking area ten miles per hour too fast before coming to a stop in a spray of gravel. Curly eased up from his spot by the rock and moved closer to Sam, shooting the truck a wary look.

Sam's eyes lit up. "That's a cool truck."

It was nice, all right. Only a couple years old. Tad watched as all four doors opened at once and four guys about his age spilled out. He looked at his beater Ford Taurus with a frown, unable to imagine being able to afford a truck like that.

The driver approached Tad and Sam with a swagger and a fake country twang. "Howdy doody, dudes."

When the other guys laughed, Driver Guy laid it on real thick. "Do either of you'n cowpokes know where a fella can git the key for one of them there cabins up yonder?"

Tad resisted the urge to roll his eyes. What a punk. "Sure. I'll grab it from the house."

Sam tilted his head. "You talk funny."

Driver Guy dropped the fake accent. "You look funny."

"I do?" Sam patted his shirt and pants with a confused expression, searching for anything out of the ordinary.

Driver Guy snorted. "Where'd you get those clothes? Farmers 'R' Us?"

"No." Sam shrugged. "My mom got them at Big R."

Tad didn't like where this was headed. "Come on, Sam, let's go get the key."

Driver Guy glared at Tad. "Now hold on a minute, we're talking here." He moved toward Sam and mimicked his voice. "'My mom got them at Big R.' Does she fold your underwear too?"

The other three guys snickered, and Tad's neck muscles tightened. He jerked his chin toward the house. "Let's go, Sam."

To get to Tad, Sam had to walk around Driver Guy. As he did, Driver Guy turned so he would keep facing Sam.

"Time to go see your mommy," he said.

Tad caught Sam's eye. "Ignore him."

"No need to get offended." Driver Guy took a step backward with his hands raised in mock surrender. "I'm only fooling around."

Behind Driver Guy, Curly was slowly getting to his feet to follow Sam. As Driver Guy took another step backward, the heel of his foot connected with the dog. "What the—"

Curly tried to get out of the way but couldn't move fast enough. He yelped as Driver Guy stumbled over him and landed on his behind in the muddy gravel.

Driver Guy jumped to his feet with a loud curse and kicked at the dog. "Stupid mutt."

"Hey!" Sam ran to Curly's side.

Tad's hands clenched into fists.

"Forget the dog," Driver Guy fumed. "I'm the one who got mud all over my pants."

Sam frowned at him as he knelt beside Curly. "You kicked my dog."

"You need to teach him to stay out of the way."

Tad knew he should do something. Say something. Though

Sam was bigger and stronger than he was, Sam would never use his strength to defend himself. Tad opened his mouth, but nothing came out. When had he turned into such a coward?

"I don't like you." Sam's voice cracked as he glared at Driver Guy with tears welling up in his eyes. "You're mean."

"'You're mean,'" Driver Guy mocked. "Yeah, well, you're an idiot."

That did it. Blood roared in Tad's ears as he put himself between Sam and Driver Guy. "Take that back."

Driver Guy huffed. "Take it back? What is this, fifth grade? We just want the key to our cabin so we can unload our truck."

"Maybe it would be best if you didn't."

Driver Guy's face turned red. "Are you crazy? You can't kick us out."

"Yes, I can. I want you to leave. You're not getting a key."

Sam sniffled behind him. "Tad, you can't—"

"I don't take orders from the hired help." Driver Guy sputtered with rage. "I will destroy this place. No one will ever rent one of your stupid cabins again."

Tad couldn't think of any comebacks. He had no smart remarks to offer. He glanced back at Sam, whose hands were gently rubbing Curly's head, and folded his arms across his chest. "Okay."

Driver Guy narrowed his eyes and shook his head. "You're going to get fired for this. I'll make sure of it." He turned to his friends. "This place is a dump anyway. Let's go."

With enough cuss words to fill the back of the Ford, the four men climbed into the truck. The engine cranked, and they took off. With a final pat on Curly's head, Sam rose to his feet beside Tad, and they watched the truck jerk and jolt its way down the driveway.

"Holy huckleberries." Sam wiped his nose with his sleeve and looked at Tad with wide eyes. "Do *you* fold your underwear?"

✦ ✦ ✦

Tad was surprised to see Bud's truck parked out front when he finally got home. This late on a Friday night, Bud was usually at Webb's. Tad pressed his lips together. He didn't want to see his dad.

He released the latch and pulled the car seat from the back of the Taurus. Charlie was asleep, her head leaning to the side. One foot poked out from her elephant blanket. It was almost nine o'clock.

He'd waited until Dan got home from work so he could explain what happened, but he never got the chance. Before Dan could even step out of his vehicle, Sam began a dramatic re-enactment that made Tad out to be a big hero, which couldn't be further from the truth. He'd been rash and shortsighted. Tad cringed even now thinking about it.

"We'll have to refund their money," Dan had said, his tone indecipherable. *"Next time, call me before you make a decision like that."*

Tad hoped there would never be a next time.

Anita had insisted Tad stay for dinner. His stomach had been too tied up in knots to eat much. A nasty one-star review full of lies about the ranch had already been posted online by the time he was packing up Charlie's diaper bag to leave. He'd seen it on his phone but hadn't had the nerve to show the Wilsons.

He reached the door to Bud's house and muttered to himself. "Tad Bungley bungles it up again."

The TV was on inside, loud enough Tad worried it would

wake up Charlie, but she didn't even flinch. Bud sat on the couch, Rainier in hand. Tad had never developed a taste for it, but it was the only brand Bud would buy. Tad was surprised the store even kept it in stock, because he was pretty sure no one else in the whole county drank the stuff.

"Where you been?" Bud asked.

Tad set the car seat down. "Had to work late."

"I ran into Orin today." Bud's eyes never left the TV. "He asked me when you were planning to bring Charlie in."

Tad looked down at his daughter. As he'd expected, word about his new family situation had spread through town quickly. The man Bud knew as Orin, Tad knew as Dr. Trent. He'd been Tad's doctor growing up, though Tad hadn't been to his office in years. Why did Dr. Trent want to see Charlie?

"What for?"

Bud set his beer down and gave Tad an irritated look. "For a checkup. Unless she's already got a different doctor."

Tad's blood cooled a few degrees. He had no idea about that. Jenna hadn't said anything, and she still hadn't responded to any of his texts. But Charlie wasn't sick. Was she supposed to go to the doctor, anyway?

"What did you tell him?"

Bud muted the TV and gave Tad his full attention. "What do you think I told him? That you'd take care of it."

Though his blood was cold, Tad began to sweat. "When's she supposed to go in?"

"How would I know?" Bud studied Tad's face and frowned. "You telling me you had no plans to take her to the doctor?"

"I—uh, I hadn't thought about it yet."

He didn't even know her birth date. Jenna had only said she'd been born "about three months ago."

Bud's expression hardened. "And I bet you haven't thought about how you're going to pay for it either."

Tad swallowed. How much did it cost to take a baby to the doctor?

"Has she got insurance?" Bud asked.

Tad stared at his daughter's face helplessly, wanting this conversation to be over, but Bud wasn't done.

He pushed off the couch. "You never thought about any of this stuff? You thought you could bring a baby home one day, just like that?"

"I—"

"Don't expect me to help you."

"I haven't asked you for anything."

"You really are stupid, aren't you?" Bud drew closer, hesitating for a moment when he saw Charlie was sleeping. He lowered his voice, even as he stuck a finger in Tad's face. "You got no business raising a baby."

He marched out of the house, slamming the door behind him, and Tad didn't move. The roar of Bud's truck driving away and the small scrape of Charlie's delicate snore were the only sounds.

Bud was right. Tad hadn't thought everything through. He had no business raising a baby. He was not cut out for this. He'd been thinking it since the first day Charlie showed up. He'd almost asked Anita to take her a thousand times, so Charlie would be in good hands and his life could go back to normal.

But he was Charlie's father. No matter what Bud said, he would *not* be one of those parents who abandoned their child. And he would *not* leave his daughter wondering for the rest of her life what she had done to drive him away.

eighteen

Tad sat in Dr. Trent's waiting room Wednesday morning, clenching his jaw and jiggling his knee. What if Dr. Trent saw something that told him Charlie wasn't being well cared for? What if he asked questions Tad couldn't answer? Seeing Chief Stubbs drive by and wave at him as he walked into the office hadn't helped any. That man's attention made Tad nervous.

Charlie wriggled in his arms, and Tad relaxed his hold. "Sorry, was Daddy holding on too tight?"

A woman with a huge pregnant belly and two squirrelly kids were the only other people in the room. Tad hoped he could get out of here quickly and get to the ranch, even though Dan had assured him that whatever time he could make it in would be fine. He didn't want to give anyone any reason to doubt he was working as hard as he could, especially after the angry phone call Dan had received from Driver Guy's father about Tad.

He ran a finger over Charlie's cheek. If providing for her meant dealing with entitled jerks once in a while, he would do it. He would do . . . anything.

He'd left Jenna several voicemails over the weekend asking what he should do about taking Charlie to the doctor. Finally, Jenna had texted him Charlie's birth date, social security number, and a picture of her Medicaid card. When he'd texted back to ask Jenna where she was, however, there was no response.

He'd called Dr. Trent's office first thing Monday morning after discovering online that babies are supposed to get a checkup at four months and realizing Sunday marked Charlie's four-month birthday. He had no idea if Charlie had been to any previous checkups.

A middle-aged woman in flowery scrubs poked her head into the waiting room. "Charlotte?"

Tad jumped to his feet. "Here."

The nurse introduced herself as Cindy. Tad's heart pounded as he followed her to a small yellow room with pictures of animals on the walls. He should've taken Anita up on her offer to come with him to this appointment. He was way out of his element. But she was already doing more for him than he could ever repay.

By the time Cindy took a hundred measurements and asked a million questions Tad tried his best to answer, his nerves were fried. He was sure the nurse was judging him. And they hadn't even seen the doctor yet.

Cindy typed something into the computer and peered at Tad over her thick glasses. "Dr. Trent will be right with you."

She disappeared, and Tad caught Charlie's eye. "I don't think she likes me."

Charlie cooed.

"Well of course she likes *you*. How could anyone not like you?"

Minutes ticked by, and the room began to close in. Tad could hear muffled voices through the door occasionally as someone walked by, but otherwise the silence was thick and uncomfortable.

"Why don't they play music in here?" he whispered. "And why aren't there any clocks?"

Charlie had no more answers than he did. She waved an arm in the air. Several more minutes ticked by slowly before there was a knock on the door, and Dr. Trent entered.

He was a small man, but he had a big voice. "Thaddeus Bungley, it's good to see you."

He held out a hand, and Tad shook it. "Uh, thanks."

"And who is this sweet child?"

"Ch-Charlie. Charlotte."

"Your dad told me she was pretty, but I'd say she's about perfect, don't you think?"

Tad's brow furrowed. His dad said that? "Uh, yeah."

Dr. Trent slapped Tad's knee. "How've you been? You haven't been here in a long time. You taking care of yourself?"

"I'm good."

"Working at Come Around Ranch, I hear?"

"Yeah."

If the doctor was disappointed in Tad's underwhelming responses, he didn't show it. His face crinkled with a giant smile.

"That's great. Now, let's get down to business, shall we?"

Tad watched in fascination as Dr. Trent performed a physical examination like he'd been doing it since he could walk. How many of these had the man done over the years? When he finished, he eased himself onto a rolling stool and consulted the computer screen.

"Everything looks great. Charlotte's measurements are good. Her growth curve is normal. You've got her sleeping in a crib?"

"A bassinet."

Dr. Trent's head bobbed. "And you lay her on her back?"

"Yeah."

Anita had drilled that point home to him the day Charlie arrived. *"Babies should always sleep on their backs."* She hadn't explained why.

"Good. Now, let's go through a list of safety questions. Are there smoke alarms in the house?"

Tad hesitated. He'd never paid attention. "I'm not sure."

"Something to look into, then." Dr. Trent waited until Tad nodded before continuing. "Any firearms in the house?"

"My dad's old hunting rifle's out in the shed. We haven't used it in years."

"Is it secured?"

"Uh, it's not loaded."

Dr. Trent typed a note into the computer. "I'll have Cindy bring you the firearm safety handout. What about lead paint?"

Tad shifted. Lead paint? His heart began to slowly list back and forth and sink, like a bandana dropped in water. How many dangers were out there that he'd never even thought about? "I—I don't know."

"When was your house built? Is it older than 1978?"

Tad looked down at Charlie, who was starting to grow tired of her current situation. What kind of interrogation was this? "No, my dad built it in the nineties. When my older brother was born."

"Good. Don't have to worry about lead paint. Is it on well water or town water?"

"Well."

He made a note on the computer. "Charlotte may need a fluoride supplement when she's older then. Has the water ever been tested?"

Tad's heart continued to sink down, down. "I don't know."

"We don't have to worry about that yet." Dr. Trent squinted at the screen. "Does anyone in the household smoke?"

Tad's heart lay at the bottom of the river now, trapped by the weight of the water. "Uh, yeah. Me and my dad."

Dr. Trent's face took on a more serious appearance. "I'm sure you're aware of the dangers of second- and even third-hand smoke. What precautions are you taking?"

"I only smoke outside. I would never smoke in front of Charlie."

"That's good, but"—Dr. Trent leaned toward Tad and softened his tone—"are you interested in any smoking cessation resources?"

Charlie's forehead puckered in what Tad recognized as her pooping face. "Uh . . ."

Dr. Trent gently touched the top of Charlie's head. "She's going to need you around for a good long while. Quitting now could mean up to ten years of increased life expectancy."

Tad hadn't even considered what would happen to Charlie if something happened to him. He was twenty-four. Death was not on his radar.

His throat felt thick. Who would take care of Charlie if . . . ? His dad certainly wouldn't. Tad's blood began pumping faster as the thought of being separated from Charlie worked its way through his brain.

"Maybe I could try."

"Wonderful." Dr. Trent beamed. "I'll have Cindy bring you the packet when she comes back in to do the shots."

Tad barely had time to say "okay" before Dr. Trent was out the door, on to the next patient. Tad wiped a hand over his face. This whole being-a-dad thing was so much more frightening and complicated than he could've ever imagined.

Wait a minute.

Did he say *shots*?

The nurse, Cindy, pulled on a pair of latex gloves and studied Tad. "How did Charlotte do after her last round of shots?"

His stomach churned as he stared at the two needles sitting in a tray next to her. "I don't even know if she had any before."

"I checked the Montana state immunization database. She did." Cindy opened two Minnie Mouse Band-Aid wrappers, peeled the tabs off, and stuck the bandages to the side of the tray. Then she smiled at Charlie. "I bet you handled them like a perfect princess, didn't you?"

Charlie squirmed in his lap. Tad had changed her poopy diaper, but she still wasn't happy. She whimpered and rubbed her eyes. It was past time for her nap. It felt like they'd been here for hours.

"It's normal for babies to have a mild fever and discomfort after getting shots. You can give her 2.5mL of infant Tylenol if she needs it."

His mind raced through questions. Infants had their own Tylenol? Did they take it from a bottle? How would he know if she needed it? He didn't want to do this. He wanted to jump up and run Charlie out the door. But he also didn't want her to get measles or polio or whatever. He wouldn't be able to live with himself.

Cindy picked up a plastic squeezy thing about the size of Tad's thumb. "We'll do the easy one first."

She indicated that Tad should lay Charlie back, then she twisted off the top of the plastic and squeezed the drops into Charlie's mouth. She was talking the whole time, explaining something about what the drops were for, but Tad barely heard her as he braced himself for Charlie to cry.

She didn't. She opened and closed her mouth a few times and looked at him.

That wasn't so bad.

"Next, I'm going to need you to take off her pants," Cindy said.

Tad reluctantly removed Charlie's pink-and-white heart pants so she had only a diaper and onesie on. Cindy dabbed alcohol on a ball of cotton and wiped the outside of both of Charlie's thighs.

Tad swallowed. "You're going to stick them in her legs?"

Cindy nodded. "You'll need to hold her still."

He felt the blood drain from his face as Cindy picked up the first needle. That huge thing was going in his daughter's tiny little leg?

Cindy gestured toward Charlie's hands. "Secure her arms so she doesn't swat at it."

He didn't like it, but he wrapped his arm around her body with her arms tucked underneath. She fussed and tried to wriggle free, but he held fast, afraid she would lash out at the needle and puncture her hand. He had never imagined using force on her like this. It made him feel sick inside.

His chest tightened as Cindy grasped Charlie's left foot and pulled her leg straight. Charlie fought against her but was no match. Cindy raised the needle to Charlie's thigh.

Tad's heart dropped. "Wait—"

Too late. In a blink, Cindy jabbed the left leg and applied the prepared bandage. Charlie's body stiffened in shock, and after a delayed reaction, she let out a terrified cry that pierced all the way through Tad's skin and bones to his heart.

"It's okay." Tad choked on the words. "You're okay."

With smooth and practiced movements, Cindy jabbed the other leg. She secured the second bandage and took a step back. As she pulled off her gloves, Tad released Charlie's arms and caught a glimpse of her tear-streaked face. It registered agony and confusion. How could she understand what had happened to her? How could she understand why he had done nothing to stop it?

He'd never before known the burden of choosing pain for someone else for their own good. He'd never thought about how protecting someone could look like hurting them. As he tucked Charlie against his shoulder—her body trembling, her cries unsettling—she pressed into him for comfort, and he marveled at how she could still trust him. Still love him. Him, who was only just beginning to understand what love even was.

He gently dressed her and buckled her into the car seat. He walked woodenly to the lobby. And he carried her out to the car, tears streaming down his face.

nineteen

Anita rushed into the Coalition ten minutes after nine on Thursday. Typically, she was at least fifteen minutes early for her shift, but *someone*—she gave Charlie a tired smile—had been having a rough morning. The poor dear wasn't feeling very well after her shots yesterday.

Anita heaved the car seat into the room with a grunt. That thing was getting heavier every day. Toting Charlie back and forth from the Coalition had proven to be the hardest part about her new babysitting job so far. Gripping the handle of the car seat was painful and awkward, but it was nothing compared to dealing with the buckles.

She'd done her best to hide the pain and swelling in her fingers, but she'd never been able to hide anything from Dan.

After quickly getting the coffeepot going in case anyone stopped in, she knelt beside the car seat and began slowly working to remove Charlie. The baby fussed, and Anita spoke in a singsong voice. "Mister Dan is worried about us, isn't he? He's not sure if we belong together, but we do, don't we, sweetheart?"

Charlie squeaked as Anita picked her up and carefully stood. The weight of her in Anita's arms felt right. The noises she made sounded like everything falling into place. Of course they belonged together, and even more so in order that Charlie and Tad could stay together. There was no way Dan could argue with that.

"He'd be lost without you too, I think." She kissed Charlie's forehead. "I saw the way he was looking at you this morning."

Dan had only had a couple of minutes with Charlie before he had to leave for work, but he had hidden his face behind his hands to play peek-a-boo and made Charlie laugh. Dan had looked up in wonder. *"Did you hear that?"*

Anita saw many more games of peek-a-boo in their future.

She sat down at the desk the volunteers shared and laid Charlie on a blanket by her feet. There was a lot of work to do. Some of it was kind of boring, but she knew it was important. Hoping it would occupy Charlie for a little while, she held a soft toy near Charlie's arm until she grabbed it.

"Good job, sweetheart." Anita tickled Charlie's tummy. "You're such a big girl."

Charlie cooed in response, but it sounded a little strained. It would probably be a few days before she was back to a hundred percent. When he had dropped her off this morning, Tad had wondered if the baby needed to go back to the doctor, but Anita had assured him the way Charlie was acting and her slightly elevated temperature were all very normal.

Anita tried to focus on her work. She responded to a handful of emails and sorted the mail. When she answered the phone, Charlie started crying. Anita held the phone with her shoulder so she could use her hands to pick the baby up, but the crying wouldn't stop. She had to cut the call short, and as soon as she hung up, Charlie grew quiet.

"You're not fond of Miss Anita giving her attention to anyone else right now, are you?"

Charlie closed her eyes. Aha. That explained a lot. Anita stood and walked the floor. By her fifth pass around the room, Charlie was sound asleep. Anita's knee protested as she knelt to gently lay Charlie back on the blanket.

She stood with a sigh. Less than an hour left in her shift, and she'd hardly accomplished anything. Maybe she could stay a little late. No, that wouldn't work. She hadn't brought a bottle, because she'd fed Charlie before they left and had planned to be home in time for the next feeding. She'd just have to do what she could with the remaining time.

While she shifted in her chair, trying to decide what to work on next, the door opened. A gust of air swirled through the room as Vernon DeVries entered. It was turning blustery outside, as the weatherman had predicted. Thunderstorms and hail were expected this afternoon.

"Why hello, Vernon." Anita knew the older man couldn't hear very well after decades of running farm machinery, but she kept her voice soft so as not to wake the baby. "It's good to see you."

He appeared troubled, his brows knit together and his shoulders stooped. He raised a finger in greeting and turned to pour coffee into a Styrofoam cup. His worn and faded jeans sagged in the back. His hands were unsteady.

When he turned around, Anita pointed at the mini fridge. "There's half-and-half in there, if you're interested."

"I like it black." His watery eyes caught on Charlie and widened. "Whatcha got there?"

"Oh, she's my—um, she's Tad's daughter. The young man working for us this summer. I get to watch her while he does all the hard stuff."

One side of Vernon's mouth lifted. "Well, I'll be. I don't suppose he had to twist yer arm."

Anita smiled. "Not even a little. What can I do for you today?"

It had continued to be a rare occasion indeed that any farmers or ranchers ventured into the Coalition outside of the two-hour Coffee Break on Tuesdays. When they did, it was always out of concern for someone else. A friend or family member whose mental health they were secretly but gravely worried about. Never did they take home resources on depression, alcoholism, time management, or any other number of things for themselves.

Or so they said.

Vernon leaned against the desk and hesitated. He studied a poster on the wall labeled *Five Ways to Handle Stress* and cleared his throat. "I read that pamphlet."

Anita tried to sound nonchalant, though her insides gave a small jump of satisfaction. "Oh? What did you think?"

He still wouldn't look at her. He took a sip of coffee and raised one shoulder, looking conflicted. She'd known Vernon her whole life and didn't think she'd ever seen him so unsure.

Charlie whimpered from the floor, and Anita glanced at her. She couldn't be ready to wake up already. She'd only been asleep a few minutes.

Anita turned her attention back to Vernon. "Did you find any of the information helpful?"

She'd read every single pamphlet so she would know what each contained. She'd found some of them more useful than others, but if nothing else, they all included a list of additional resources the reader could engage with.

He rubbed his chin. "It's complicated."

When it came to family farms and estate planning, that was an understatement. She nodded. "Do you think—"

A piercing cry interrupted her train of thought. She looked at Charlie in surprise. "My goodness, sweetheart, what's the matter?"

Charlie's face was screwed up in distress. Her fists were clenched. She continued to cry, so Anita picked her up. "Shh, shh. It's okay."

Vernon tapped his empty cup of coffee against the desk before tossing it in the trash can. "Guess I'll leave you to it."

"No, wait." Anita rocked the baby in her arms as the crying continued. "She'll be fine in a moment."

"I gotta get back. We're hoping to wrap up planting before the storm hits."

Anita switched from rocking to bouncing, but Charlie's agitation only grew. She must be feeling miserable.

Anita tried to catch Vernon's eye, not wanting their conversation to end, but he was already halfway to the door. "Maybe I'll see you at Coffee Break?"

If he could hear her over the ruckus, he gave no indication. She blew out a breath and peered at Charlie. "It's okay, sweetheart. Shh, shh."

As the door closed behind the old man, a strange feeling of loss lodged itself in Anita's heart. Something had compelled him to come in today. Something was on his mind. But now . . .

It was surely not the last time she'd ever talk to Vernon, but she might never have an opportunity like that again.

◆ ◣ ◗

Dan's eyes were closed before Anita even finished changing into her pajamas. She tiptoed to the bed and clicked off the lamp, then slid under the covers. Her mind was swirling with thoughts about Charlie and Tad and Vernon and Sam, so when Dan cleared his throat, she yelped.

She pressed a hand to her chest. "I thought you were asleep."

"Sorry." He turned toward her. "I was just thinking."

"With your eyes closed?"

"I was thinking about what you said about Vernon."

She sank into her pillow. At supper, she'd relayed the short version of what happened at the Coalition this morning when Dan asked how her day had been. She'd been upset when she told him, having spent all day stewing about it.

"I'm sorry Charlie ruined your shift," he said.

She stiffened. "She didn't ruin anything. It wasn't her fault, she's only a baby."

Dan held up a hand. "I didn't mean it like that. I just meant things didn't go the way you wanted because Charlie wasn't feeling good, and I'm sorry."

Anita took a deep breath. "I can't help feeling like I blew it. It's not every day someone like Vernon DeVries comes to the Coalition ready to talk, you know? I might never get another chance like that." She covered her face with her hands. "And I don't even know what he was going to say. What if it was important?"

Dan squeezed her shoulder. "Maybe he left because he *wasn't* ready. Or maybe he'll talk about it with someone else. There are lots of other volunteers, aren't there?"

"No, not really. Most people are too busy to help, but you're right. Maybe I'm overreacting."

They lay in silence for a few minutes. In her head, Anita replayed her conversation with Vernon over and over. She examined it every which way and couldn't get past the idea that if Charlie hadn't been there, it might've turned out differently.

"Maybe I should pull back at the Coalition for now." A small lump formed in her throat at the thought, but she swallowed it. "Until Charlie gets a little older."

Several long moments passed before Dan responded. "Is that what you want?"

It wasn't. Not really. The more time she spent at the Coalition, the more she realized the work they were doing there was essential to the community. Even though progress was painfully slow, the handful of people involved with the Coalition were committed to sticking it out for the long haul. Who would help Diana with Coffee Break if she wasn't there?

"I don't know. It would only be for a little while."

She was grateful when Dan didn't point out the obvious: that they actually had no idea how long it might be before Charlie didn't need so much attention. Or how long Charlie was even going to be around.

"I'd hate to see you give up your work at the Coalition. I know it's important to you."

"Yes, but I'm not going to give up Charlie."

"That doesn't mean you have to watch her all the time. It can't be easy carrying that car seat around. I know your fingers have been bothering you."

"I promised Tad I would help."

Again, silence fell. Dan yawned. Anita knew they were both exhausted and needed to sleep. She knew Dan was only trying to help. But the thought of not watching Charlie hurt her heart even more than lugging Charlie's car seat around hurt her hands. If she took it too far, though—if her hands got to the point where they failed to work properly—she could put Charlie in danger.

Dan found her in the dark and kissed her forehead. "If Tad's going to be a parent, he's going to have to take responsibility. Figure it out like the rest of us did."

Her voice was low. "He's got no one else, Dan. No one on his side."

Dan sighed and turned onto his back. "I guess we'll have to pray about it, then, and see what happens."

A variety of responses churned through her mind. Before she could choose one, the familiar sound of deep snoring filled the room.

She sighed. "Good night, dear."

Staring into the darkness, her clenched hands resting on her stomach, she whispered. "God, I don't want to stop volunteering at the Coalition. But I don't want to stop watching Charlie either. Is it wrong to want to do both?"

She was aware of her limitations. For the past few years, her body hadn't let her forget them. But God's power was made perfect in human weakness, right? That's what the Bible said.

"Please show me what You want me to do. If Tad wants to do the right thing and parent his daughter, shouldn't we support him in that? We have so much—family, stability, resources— and he's got practically nothing. Which reminds me, give Bud a kick in the pants, would You? Even this moment, as we speak, put a desire in his heart to be there for Tad and care about his granddaughter. Remind him of the kind of man he used to be."

Her heart twinged as she remembered that man and everything they'd been through together. How had their lives gone in such different directions? Why had she ended up with so many blessings and he'd ended up broken and alone?

They'd each made their choices. But it could've gone very differently.

She yawned a huge yawn and closed her eyes. She didn't want to dwell on the past. It was a burdensome and lonely place.

Before she drifted off, she murmured, "And please help Vernon DeVries."

twenty

I like summer. Even though summer doesn't start until June it feels like summer now because it's warm on most days and there are lots of people coming to the cabins. That means there's more work to do and I like to work. I like to meet all the new people even though sometimes they're not nice and I like helping people saddle the horses but I wish Dad would let me be the trail boss just once but he said no. Mom and Dad are always saying no.

My new favorite thing about summer is Tad. I hope he works at the ranch every summer forever and I love Charlie. She's not my sister but I pretend she is and this morning Tad said I could go with him and Charlie to Sloppy Joe's tomorrow if I ask Mom and Dad if it's okay but I'm afraid they'll say no so I haven't asked. I really want to go with Tad and Charlie.

It's kind of hot and windy out here. My hair is sticking up. I told Curly to stay at the junipers because he was so tired and seemed kind of grumpy and I walked really fast to the hill across from the cabins because if I sit real still between these two big rocks at the top no one can see me but I can see a lot.

I can see Tad when he comes out of the barn and stands in the driveway staring at the house. He stands there and stares sometimes and I think he's thinking about Charlie. I can see every car that comes up to the ranch and every car that drives down Whitetail Road and most of them go way too fast. Dad would be mad if he saw. I can see the guests when they sit on the porches of their cabins but usually only the old people do that. I can see almost to the fence line and sometimes it looks like there's something back there moving around but it's probably just cows.

One day I'm going to go up there and find out if it's cows but it's harder to go that way without being seen so I haven't gone yet. If I go that way and Mom sees me she will say no Sam, stay away from the fence line, that's not our property anymore and there's nothing up there anyway. She thinks there has to be something up there for anyone to want to go but I want to go because it's there. Because it's something to see and I want to see everything.

twenty-one

Saturday morning was bright and clear and beautiful, the kind of morning that reminded Anita why she never wanted to leave Montana. The hills were green, and the mountains were blue and white. Birds were singing, and the air smelled like dirt and grass. As she walked toward the round pen to help Dan prepare for today's trail ride, she could feel summer coming.

Steve and Sarah, the two guests who had signed up for a ride, were already at the pen. Dan was patiently walking them through the steps necessary to get their horses ready to ride. Sam was leaning against the fence, watching, with Curly beside him. Anita couldn't help but notice how thin the old dog was. Like a southwest wind might blow him right over.

As she approached, Dan glanced over and gave her a wink. She loved seeing him like this, in his element.

He turned back to the guests. "When it's time to brush the other side, always walk around the front of the horse, so they can see you." Dan demonstrated on TJ. "You don't ever want to walk around the back."

Steve frowned. "Why not?"

"Horses have a blind spot directly behind them. If they lose sight of you, and then you appear back in their field of vision, they tend to startle. And startled horses tend to kick."

Sarah's eyes grew wide. "You mean we might get kicked?"

Dan's even tone never changed. "If you stay away from your horse's rear end, you should be fine."

"How do they get their tails brushed if you can't go behind them?" she asked. "I saw a horse with a braided tail once. In a parade."

Dan nodded. "It can be done. If a horse knows you well and you keep your hand on him as you go. You have to talk to him to help him keep track of where you are. Then he probably won't kick, but you can never know for sure."

Sarah had been matched with Sandy, and she eyed the mare suspiciously. "I didn't know horses were so unpredictable."

Anita noticed the crinkles next to Dan's eyes that gave away his amusement. "I would say humans are much less predictable than horses."

"I predict Sandy will be good today," Sam called out.

Anita smiled. Dan encouraged Steve and Sarah to continue brushing their horses, and Anita walked over to Sam. "Aren't you going?"

She didn't think he'd miss the chance to join his father on a trail ride. He always begged to tag along.

Sam shrugged. "I don't know."

Her brow wrinkled in confusion. "Did more guests decide to ride?"

It wouldn't make sense. Dan had only gotten gear out for three horses, and if other guests had decided to join them, she would've heard about it. But if Sam didn't want to go riding, that was fine. That meant they could spend some time together. She'd been preoccupied with Charlie lately and hadn't been around Sam as much as usual, and this would be the perfect chance to check in with him. Maybe he would help her in the garden. He'd always loved getting his hands dirty.

The sound of a car winding up the driveway caught her attention. She turned and frowned. That was strange. Tad wasn't scheduled to work today. He was always welcome at the ranch, of course, but she was surprised he'd want to drive over on his day off.

She made her way to the parking area so she could say hi to Charlie and see if Tad needed anything. In a blur, Sam rushed ahead of her to Tad's car.

Tad hopped out but left it running, standing with one arm draped over the open driver's side door. "You ready?"

Sam grinned, and Anita's eyes narrowed as she looked back and forth between the two boys. "Ready for what?"

Tad drummed his fingers on the door and gave Sam a mildly stern look. "You told me you were going to ask."

Sam hung his head. "I forgot."

Anita wasn't sure she liked where this was going. "Ask about what?"

"I invited Sam to go to breakfast with Charlie and me. I'm sorry, I thought he talked to you about it."

"No, he did not." She looked at her son. So this was why he hadn't been begging to go on the trail ride. "He already had breakfast."

It was almost ten o'clock. She and Dan and Sam had eaten hours ago. Sam dug the toe of his boot into the gravel.

Tad tilted his head. "I bet you could still eat, right, Sam?"

Instead of responding, he looked at Anita with a hopeful expression. She knew what that meant. Whenever Sam wanted something really, *really* bad, he stopped begging and turned quiet, almost like he was afraid that if he brought it up, he would jinx it. That explained why he'd never asked if he could go. There was no way he "forgot." It had probably been all he could think about since Tad first brought up the idea.

"I don't know what your father has planned for you today, Sam. He might need you." She was grasping at straws, and she knew it. Dan would be thrilled to see Sam go out to breakfast with a friend. By himself. "I wish you would've asked."

Tad peered into the car to check on Charlie, then straightened. "We won't be gone long. We're just going to Sloppy Joe's, and I'll need to get Charlie back home before her next bottle."

Still Sam said nothing, but the pleading in his eyes was impossible to miss. Anita scolded herself for her hesitation. It shouldn't be a big deal for her twenty-year-old son to go to the diner without her. Yet she had spent years remaining constantly vigilant to his needs and trying to foresee and prevent any possible difficult situations. Had those years conditioned her to resist the unknown and unplanned? Conditioned her to believe that her most important role in life was as a buffer between Sam and the rest of the world?

Like Dan had said, humans were much harder to predict than horses, and the diner would be full of them. Yet Dan had also said, many times, that Sam had his own life to live.

"I suppose it would be fine." She pushed her doubts to the side and forced a smile. She had no good reason to say no. And Tad had proven the other day how protective he was of Sam. "Do you have your wallet?"

Sam nodded eagerly and patted the back pocket of his jeans. Since he turned fourteen, she and Dan had been paying him modest wages that almost all went directly into a savings account for his future care. They allowed him to keep some cash on hand, however, and counseled him frequently on how to use it wisely. Counsel he did not often take to heart.

Sam beamed as he flung himself into the passenger side of the car. "Bye, Mom."

Tad slid into his seat. "We'll be back in about an hour."

As he shut his door and they drove away, all she could think was, what if Sam forgot to wear his seat belt? She heard a huff at her feet and looked down to see Curly had finally caught up to them, just in time to be left behind with her.

"Sorry, old man." She rested a hand on top of his head. "He's gone."

She walked slowly back to the round pen so Curly could keep up. TJ was tied to the outside of the fence with a quick-release knot while Dan led Prince and Sandy, carrying Steve and Sarah, out of the gate. Sarah looked terrified. Anita took hold of the halters from Dan so he could mount TJ.

He was in the saddle in one fluid motion. "Was that Tad? Where's Sam?"

She tried to sound like it was the most natural thing in the world. "He went with Tad to Sloppy Joe's for breakfast."

Dan's eyebrows rose, but she could tell he was pleased. "Oh. Okay, then. Will you be all right here while we're on the trail?"

It was a silly question on one hand. Why wouldn't she be all right? She was a grown woman. On the other hand, she knew what Dan was really asking.

She released the horses' halters and stepped back, wondering how much Dan could see in her face. "I'll be fine."

◆ ◇ ◗

The horses were dark dots against the hill before Anita moved away from the gate and walked back to the house. Curly trudged along half-heartedly beside her, perhaps feeling a similar sense of abandonment.

"We need to buck up, old man." Anita paused at the front steps before deciding to circle around the house to the garden. "It's far too beautiful a day to be feeling sorry for ourselves."

She retrieved her work gloves from the shed. There were a couple of areas that had already been planted that needed water—seeds that could withstand cooler weather. There were weeds to be pulled. There were starters in small plastic trays to be moved from the window in the mudroom to the open air for the day. And was it too early to plant the peas and carrots?

She shook her head. She wouldn't let a nice day like today trick her into believing May didn't still have a hard frost or two up its sleeve. The last freeze was on June third last year. The growing season in Montana was only a hundred days long in some places.

"What do you think, Curly? Should I wait another week for the peas and carrots?" The dog didn't even twitch an ear in response. Anita watched him for a second to make sure he was still breathing, her heart in her throat until she saw his stomach rise and fall. She didn't want to think about the day he would pass over the rainbow bridge, but there was no denying that day was drawing near.

A pleasant quiet settled in as she rolled up her sleeves and pulled on her gloves. There was plenty of noise—the breeze in the grass, the distant rumble of a tractor, the droning of insects—but they were peaceful sounds. She filled the watering can from the spigot at the back of the house, her mind darting in a dozen different directions.

How was Sam doing at the diner? Had he remembered his

manners? Did Charlie miss her when she went home with Tad? What was she going to do about volunteering at the Coalition? When would she see Vernon DeVries again?

It was funny what constituted a big deal in her life these days. When she was in her twenties, none of those things would have mattered to her. Now, they tied her stomach up in knots. If she thought being a teenager had been emotional, it was nothing compared to being forty-eight.

"Hello? Anybody home?"

Anita stopped sprinkling the dirt and looked around. The guests who had not signed up for the trail ride had all left this morning to spend the day in various places, but maybe one of them had returned and needed something. "Hello? I'm in the garden."

When no one answered, she thought for a minute she had imagined the voice. It would be just like her to fantasize that someone needed her. Then Maddie appeared.

"Mrs. Wilson, hi. Sorry to intrude, no one answered the door."

"You're not intruding." Anita smiled and set down the watering can. "I'm always happy to see you. What brings you out to the ranch today? Here to see Princess?"

Maddie hesitated. "Yeah."

"Sam's not here, I'm sorry to say. He'll be disappointed when he finds out he missed you."

"Oh." She looked around. "Where's everyone else? It feels kind of deserted."

Anita chuckled. She'd been thinking the same thing. "Four of the guests are out and about sightseeing, and two of them are with Dan on a trail ride. Sam's with Tad in town. So it's just Curly and me."

Curly wagged his tail twice at the sound of his name but didn't lift his head.

Maddie gestured toward the hills. "They go that way on their trail rides, right?"

"Yes." Anita pointed. "You can sort of see the trail they follow. They go west past the cabins and then turn north and work their way through those trees. Sometimes that's as far as they go, if the guests are struggling."

"What if they're not struggling? Then what do they do?"

Anita was surprised at Maddie's interest but happy to have something entirely unemotional to talk about. "Then they go all the way to the land the Richardsons bought from us. You know the big field where their cattle are?"

Maddie nodded, and her long hair glinted in the sun. "The cattle don't mind?"

"No, they usually stay closer to the barn, anyway."

"What if a storm comes up or something? Is there somewhere they can go for shelter?"

"On the trail ride, you mean? I suppose there are probably a couple old lean-tos out there, but Dan can usually see a storm coming from miles away and would turn around. And the horses always know if one's coming too. They would hightail it back home in a hurry."

"Oh. I see."

Anita tilted her head. "Are you interested in going on a trail ride sometime?" Maddie didn't seem like the outdoorsy type, but Anita had been wrong before.

Maddie's face seemed to flush, but it was hard to tell with how bright it was outside. "Um . . . I don't know. Maybe."

"Anytime you want to, let me know." Anita gave her an encouraging smile. "We'd be happy to take you out."

Maddie looked away. "Uh, thanks." She folded her arms over her stomach. "How's it been going with the baby?"

Anita had been impressed with how much Maddie knew about babies when she'd visited her and Charlie a week and a half ago. "It's going well. She's so much fun. I could stare at her face all day."

Well, it wasn't *always* fun. She thought of the fit Charlie had thrown at the Coalition the other day and how not fun it was carrying her car seat. No need to mention that to Maddie, however. Unless . . .

"Do you like babies?"

Maddie's face brightened. "Yes. They're sweet and innocent, you know? They never . . ."

Anita leaned toward her. "Never what?"

"Oh, nothing." Maddie shook her head and looked embarrassed. "I was going to say they never lie."

Anita studied the young woman. Had she been lied to a lot in her life? Her father was a powerful man in Jefferson County and sometimes there were rumors about his business dealings, but the Pine family always seemed happy when she saw them at church. Of course, appearances could be deceiving.

"You're right." Anita dipped her chin. "There's nothing more honest than a crying baby. And Charlie does her fair share of that."

Maddie laughed. "I love all babies, even crying ones."

The wheels were turning in Anita's mind. Could Maddie be the answer to her prayers? If Maddie could come out to the ranch to watch Charlie during Anita's shifts at the Coalition, Anita wouldn't have to give up either of the things she loved to do.

"Do you have a job these days?" she asked.

Maddie looked a little taken aback. "Well . . ."

"Sorry." Anita waved a hand. "That came out of nowhere. I was wondering how busy you are, that's all."

"I do some work for my dad." Maddie lifted one shoulder. "But I don't have much else going on. Most of my friends are away at college. I'm thinking of going too."

"That's wonderful. In the fall?"

She hesitated. "Maybe."

"No big plans for the summer, though?"

"No." She gave a small smile. "Except playing with Princess."

Anita thought quickly. It seemed like Maddie had time on her hands, but how would she feel about helping out? Neither Anita nor Tad could afford to pay her much. Yet this seemed like such a perfect solution.

She forged ahead. "How would you feel about coming to babysit Charlie for a couple hours on Tuesdays and Thursdays when I volunteer at the Coalition? I've been bringing her with me, and it's been . . . well, a bit of a struggle, to be honest."

Maddie's expression was hard to read. "You volunteer every week?"

"Yes, but you wouldn't have to help every week. Even if you just—"

"I can do it."

"Really?"

Maddie tucked her hair behind her ears. "Totally. If Tad doesn't mind."

Anita blinked. She'd gotten ahead of herself. She should've checked with Tad first. He was the parent, not her. But why would he mind? If anything, he'd probably be happy that Charlie would be able to stay at the ranch when Anita went to town. Right?

"I'll talk to him. I'm sure it'll be fine." She pushed away the feeling that perhaps she had overstepped and embraced the idea that this must be an answer to her prayers. "I really appreciate this."

twenty-two

Tad's hands were sweaty as he downed his second cup of coffee and set it on the end of the table for a refill. His caffeine consumption had gone up since he'd cut back on cigarettes, but that wasn't the reason for his sweaty hands. It was all the staring. It felt like every pair of eyes in Sloppy Joe's was on him and Sam. The residents of this small Montana town were a curious bunch.

Sam poked at the ice cubes in his water glass with a straw. "I don't like coffee. It's gross."

"Ha." Tad shifted in his seat. "You're probably right."

Tad didn't trust his own taste buds anymore. The gallons of Mountain Dew he'd consumed in the past ten years, not to mention the hundreds of cigarettes he'd smoked, had deadened his sense of taste and smell. When it came to food, anyway. He could still smell Charlie's diapers from a mile away.

His daughter remained asleep in her car seat next to him in the booth as the waitress appeared with his and Sam's food. Despite what Anita had said about Sam already having breakfast, he'd ordered the Farmer's Special: two pancakes, two eggs, two strips of bacon, hash browns, and toast. Tad had no doubt Sam would eat the whole thing.

He nodded his thanks to the waitress and poured syrup over his short stack.

Sam made a face. "Aren't you going to put butter on it?"

"Nope."

"Pancakes are supposed to have butter."

"You can put butter on yours."

"Okay."

Sam smeared the butter from the two packets that came with his plate onto his pancakes. When Tad nudged the packets of butter from his own plate toward him, Sam smeared those on too.

Tad snorted. "You ever heard of cholesterol, Sam?"

"Yes." Sam bobbed his head. "My dad has some. Mom always tells him to keep an eye on it."

As they ate in silence for a few minutes, Tad continued to catch people looking their way. He didn't blame people for being curious about them. They were quite the trio. And people probably didn't see Sam very often, especially not without one of his parents.

That's one reason Tad had invited Sam to breakfast today—to get him off the ranch and out on his own for a little while. Anita sometimes acted like Sam was a little kid, but he wasn't. Well, he kind of was. But he wasn't.

The other reason was that Tad liked being around Sam. He was uncomplicated, and he accepted Tad as he was. He made no demands. All Tad's other friends had stopped calling since Charlie came along. Babies and Friday night adventures didn't mix. At least not the kind of misadventures he and his friends usually ended up in.

"Do you ever go out with your friends?" Tad asked. "Like to a bonfire or something?"

Sam spread jam on his toast. "Sometimes they have bonfires at church."

"You only hang out with your friends if it's at church?"

"Sometimes people come to the ranch. Like Maddie. And you."

Ugh. Maddie. At least she wouldn't be coming around much longer.

"Maddie's going to be taking her kitten home soon, remember? Then she won't come anymore." Tad gripped his fork. He wouldn't always be around either. The Wilsons had only hired him through September. He'd have to make a point to keep visiting Sam after that.

Sam frowned. "But she's nice."

Not this again. Tad scrambled for an answer that wouldn't make him look like a jerk. Then Charlie made some baby noises beside him and squirmed in her car seat, saving him from having to respond.

Sam sat up straighter. "She's awake. I want to hold her."

Tad eyed Sam's plate and imagined globs of egg yolk falling on Charlie's head. "When you're done."

Tad unbuckled Charlie's straps and pulled her onto his lap as Sam tore into the rest of his food. Charlie was warm and felt a little damp, but when he checked her diaper, it was fine. She was probably sweaty from being too bundled in her car seat. He was constantly worried about whether she was too hot or too cold. How was a guy supposed to know?

She grabbed hold of his finger and peered around the diner with wide eyes. The whole place was filled with cheerful colors, but suddenly all Tad could see was danger. Hot things that could burn her, sharp things that could cut. People who might not be trustworthy. If he couldn't even figure out how warm to dress her, how would he keep her safe from everything else?

A hulking figure in uniform appeared next to their table, and Tad cringed.

"Howdy, boys." Chief Stubbs grinned down at them from nearly six and a half feet. "And who is this pretty little thing?"

Tad fidgeted. If everyone hadn't been looking at them before, they were now. "This is Charlie."

The chief pulled a chair from a nearby table and sat himself down as if he'd been invited. He appeared carefree and relaxed, but Tad had a feeling he could jump into action at a moment's notice.

"I got seven grandkids now, can you believe that? The youngest one turned three last month. You won't believe how fast they grow up."

Sam swallowed his last bite and set his fork down. "Charlie is only four months. She won't be three for a looong time."

The chief studied her carefully. "Four months, huh? You seen her mom lately?"

Tad didn't like the way he looked at Charlie as if she was a puzzle to solve. "No."

The last thing he wanted to talk about was Jenna. And the last person he wanted digging into his life was the chief.

"Can I hold her now?" Sam asked.

Tad lifted her by her armpits and passed her across the table. He was a lot more comfortable with Sam holding Charlie when Sam was sitting down. The waitress bustled over and set an empty mug in front of the chief.

He turned his oversized shoulders toward her. "Did I hear you asking Sid about his car when I walked in?"

She nodded. "Won't start again. He thinks it's the spark plug this time."

"All right, I'll catch him before I leave." The chief slid his mug closer to the edge of the table. "I've got some spark plugs in my truck."

She filled the chief's mug with coffee, then topped off Tad's cup.

Chief Stubbs saluted. "Thanks, Kathy."

Sam tucked Charlie into the crook of his arm, and she blinked up at him. "She likes me."

Tad fiddled with his cup. "Of course she does."

The chief leaned his elbows on the table and fixed his eyes on Tad. "You guys looking for a place closer to town?"

Tad frowned. He hadn't told anybody about how he wanted to find his own place. Not even Sam. "What do you mean?"

Chief Stubbs shrugged. "Saw your dad coming out of Matthew Pine's office the other day. Figured you might be thinking of moving."

Sam's face fell. "You can't move away, Tad."

Tad's mind raced. Bud had never tried to hide his disregard for Matthew Pine, especially ever since Matthew announced development plans for farmland he'd somehow acquired for a fraction of what it was worth. What on earth had Bud been doing at Matthew's office? It would be just like him to sell the house without telling Tad.

"No one's going anywhere," he mumbled in a less-than-convincing way. "Don't worry."

The chief took a swig of coffee. "It's a tough market these days, son."

Tad grunted. "Yeah."

The chief and Sam began to talk about something else, but

Tad tuned them out as he thought about the house. It was a pile of junk, sure, but why would his dad sell it? Tad needed to get serious about finding a new place to live, but it was going to be a lot harder now that Charlie factored in. He'd need to be pickier about the location. There would have to be two bedrooms. And what about a yard for her to play in when she got bigger?

Maybe it was stupid of him to think about a future with Charlie in it. He'd be unemployed come fall. How was he supposed to support her then? And Jenna could come back any day.

Wasn't that what he wanted? He hadn't planned to be tied down by a child for the next eighteen years. Hadn't planned on becoming a dad.

Hadn't chosen this.

He looked over at Charlie, and his heart twisted. Would he undo it if he had the chance?

◆ ▸ ▸

The drive back to Come Around Ranch had been quiet. Tad had been lost in thought, and he had no idea what kinds of things occupied Sam's mind. Maybe nothing. Maybe he was able to look out at the passing landscape and simply enjoy it without worrying about anything else. Tad hoped that was true.

A red Mazda RX-7 passed them going the other way as they reached the turnoff for the C-A-R, and Tad tensed. It had to have been Maddie. No one else had a car like that. He'd lucked out for once that he missed her. Thankfully, Sam had been looking the other way.

He pulled up to the house and put the Ford in park. "Thanks for coming with me, Sam. It was fun."

Sam opened the passenger door and looked back. "Can we go again next Saturday?"

"We'll see."

"Okay." He shut the door and walked away.

Tad shook his head. He loved that kid. And he swore he was going to stop calling him that.

"Tad." Anita appeared on the driver's side and waved an arm. "Hold on, you got a minute?"

He rolled down his window. "Hey."

"Did you guys have fun?"

He nodded.

"I was hoping to talk to you about Charlie."

His heart constricted as if suddenly clutched in the vengeful fist of God. This was it. This was the moment he had been dreading. When someone would finally bite the bullet and tell him he couldn't keep pretending he could take care of Charlie on his own. He opened his mouth, but nothing came out.

Maybe it was for the best. He'd been a fool to think—

"You know how I go to the Coalition on Tuesdays and Thursdays?" Anita didn't seem to notice his distress. He nodded again, unsure what the Coalition had to do with his failure as a dad.

"Well, I don't think I can keep taking her with me. It's hard to carry her, and she's a bit of a distraction, as I'm sure you can imagine."

Oh. This wasn't about him. What was he going to do with Charlie if Anita couldn't watch her on Tuesdays and Thursdays? Take her to the barn with him? He was no expert, but he was pretty sure a baby couldn't ride a horse. "Uh . . ."

Anita held up her hands. "Not to worry, though. I have the perfect solution."

He swallowed. "You do?"

Anita peered into the back seat at Charlie and smiled. "Maddie said she would come out to the ranch to watch Charlie while I'm gone. Isn't that wonderful?"

The fist holding Tad's heart gripped tighter. No. It was not wonderful. Maddie? Watching Charlie? Twice a week? "Uh . . ."

"I'm sorry to spring it on you like this, but I was talking to her and she was telling me how much she loves babies and I asked her about helping out. I hope you don't mind."

He did. He did very much. But what could he say? Anita was caring for Charlie out of the kindness of her heart, and she volunteered at the Coalition for the same reason. How could he ask her to give that up? But why would Maddie help him? He thought he was about to be rid of her, and now this. Yet he had no choice. It seemed everywhere he turned he was at the mercy of one woman or another.

He took a deep breath. "I can pay."

Anita flicked her wrist. "I mentioned that to her, but she said not to worry about it."

"She'll have to drive all the way out here. I should at least pay for her gas."

"You can take it up with her, if you'd like. She'll be here Tuesday."

Tad didn't know what to think. For years, he'd known Maddie as a selfish, spoiled brat. She'd looked down on him in class. She'd toyed with the hearts of whatever boys she could sink her nails into. She'd lured him out to the bleachers that day and left him high and dry. *Just one more turn.* Hmph.

Unlike Tad, trouble never seemed to stick to Maddie. If it ever tried to, her dad was always there to pull strings and make sure it didn't. Now all of a sudden she was acting nice to

Sam and playing with kittens and offering to help Tad without getting anything in return?

Tad didn't buy it. Maddie only cared about Maddie. His options were severely limited, however. He had no one else to help with Charlie, and he couldn't afford daycare. Even if he could, the thought of sending her off to someone she'd never met, to some place where he couldn't stop in to check on her during the day, made him want to cut off his own arm.

"All right." He nodded at Anita and hoped she couldn't see through him to his inner turmoil. "Thanks. See you Tuesday."

He rolled up his window and turned his old bucket of rust around. As he wound back down the driveway, the feeling he had no idea what he was doing almost overwhelmed him. Even stronger, though, was the sense that how he felt or what he wanted didn't matter anymore. Only one thing did.

Charlie.

twenty-three

"I want to see a moose."

Tad blinked at the short, middle-aged man who had cornered him in the barn. "Uh . . ."

Tad had only arrived at the ranch about twenty minutes ago. He didn't even know the names of this week's guests yet.

"Before we leave on Friday." The man leaned in and lowered his voice. "But don't tell my wife. She thinks moose are dangerous."

Tad shifted on his feet. "They are."

The man waved his hand. "I don't want to pet it or anything. I'm not one of those crazy people who try to ride the bison in Yellowstone Park. I just want to see one."

Tad wasn't sure why the man was telling him this. It wasn't like he could pull a moose out of his hat. "We don't get many moose around here. It's too wide open."

"Your website said there would be wildlife sightings."

Tad scooped some Nutrena SafeChoice into Prince's special black bucket. Prince was already standing at the gate that connected the corral to the round pen, waiting to be let in for his daily helping of senior feed.

"There's a lot of wildlife to see around here." He scooped a smaller amount into Tinkerbell's blue bucket and stood with one bucket in each hand. "But moose are elusive. They stay in the trees and by the river. I don't think—"

"Can we go to the river?"

The man followed Tad as he carried the buckets to the round pen and set them six feet apart on the ground inside the fence. Tad wasn't sure what to say. Part of his job was to ensure the guests had a good experience at the ranch. He was supposed to help them with whatever they needed. But he had too much work to do to go on a wild-moose chase.

"I'll have to see what I can do, Mr. . . . ?"

"Paul is fine."

"Okay, Paul. I'll see what I can do."

Maybe he could ask Dan how he should handle this. Dan was good with people.

He hopped the fence and strode over to where Prince and Tinkerbell stood, eager for their breakfast. He let them into the round pen, and they plodded straight to their buckets.

Paul watched them curiously. "How come the other horses don't get any?"

"These two are the oldest. They need a special kind of grain."

"Why is that one so short?"

"Tink is a Shetland pony. Ponies are smaller than horses."

"How do they know which bucket is theirs? Can they see color?"

"Yeah."

"And they knew where the gate was? That's pretty smart."

Tad started to roll his eyes behind Paul's back but caught himself when he saw Sam and Curly had snuck up on them. Anita wouldn't appreciate him setting a bad example.

"Horses are super smart," Sam said. "They can get you home if you get lost. Even in a blizzard."

"Well, I'll be darned." Paul inched toward the round pen. "Can I touch one?"

Tad nodded. "These two are very friendly. Go ahead."

As Paul stuck his hand through the fence to tentatively pat the top of Tinkerbell's head, Tad listened for the sound of Maddie's car. She should be arriving soon. Would it be weird if he met her at the house to tell her about Charlie's schedule and everything? Anita could do it—she probably knew more about Charlie's needs than he did—but wasn't it his job?

"What's she doing?" Paul asked.

Sam laughed. "Oh, Tink."

Tinkerbell had picked up the bucket with her mouth and was banging it against the fence.

"She's hoping for more grain." Tad reached through the fence to grab the bucket, but Tink wasn't giving up that easily. She dodged his hand and scooted farther down the fence. *Bang, bang.* Tad tried to follow, but she kept herself out of reach.

"She's a feisty one." Paul watched in amusement. "I thought you said she was old."

"In human years, she's in her seventies."

"Reminds me of my aunt. She was pulling pranks on the staff at the nursing home till the very end. They didn't even believe it when she died. Thought she was faking it."

Sam shook his head. "Sometimes Tink pretends to be asleep. I thought she was dead once, and I got sad."

Tad worried that talking too much about dead animals in front of Sam might not end well. He glanced at Curly, who looked pretty lifeless himself. Time to change the subject.

"Were you thinking of signing up for a trail ride, Paul?"

Paul perked up. "Does the trail go by the river?"

"Well, no. But—"

"I'm not too sure about getting up on one of those things." Paul eyed the horses skeptically. "Especially that feisty one."

Sam nodded. "One lady fell off Sandy and got hurt."

Paul's eyes widened, and Tad gave Sam a look meant to remind him of the instructions Dan had given not to mention that particular incident to the guests.

Sam hung his head. "Oh, huckleberries."

Tad patted Sam's shoulder, then inched backward toward Tink as he spoke to Paul. "These are good horses. If you respect them, they'll respect you."

Paul made a face. "I don't know . . ."

"Think about it." Tad got within reach of the fence and quickly poked his hand through the opening to take Tink by surprise and grab her bucket. "We're supposed to have good weather all week."

Paul grumbled something about whether moose would come out in good weather, but Tad's ears caught the sound of gravel under tires, and he stiffened. Maddie was here.

He shoved Tink's bucket at Sam. "Grab the other one and put these away, okay?"

He didn't hang around for a response. All his uncertainty about whether to talk to Maddie and what to say faded to the back of his mind as his feet took him to her car like they'd been given marching orders. He wished he had a cigarette.

She got out of the Mazda in that breezy way of hers and faced him. "Hey, Tad."

He cleared his throat. "Uh, hey."

She waited, tilting her head like he was something strange

to study. She had done something different with her hair, he was pretty sure. He didn't know what. She looked good.

She always did.

He finally managed to spit out some words. "Thanks for coming."

She lifted one shoulder. "I don't mind. Charlie's a sweetie."

She was. She was sweet, frustrating, beautiful, fascinating, wonderful, confusing. "Yeah."

"Can I have your number?"

His brow furrowed. "What?"

"In case anything comes up. Or I have a question about Charlie."

"Oh. Right." He could feel his face flushing. "Anita uses the walkie-talkie if she needs me. There's one in the house."

"Oh. Okay, I'll have her show me where it is."

"But maybe I should give you my number too." He fumbled in his pocket for his phone. "Just in case."

The corner of her lips twitched. "You're cute when you're nervous."

For a second, his insides warmed and wriggled around, then a cold dose of reality washed over him as the bleachers behind the school popped into his mind. This was how Maddie operated. This was how she got guys to do whatever she wanted. He wasn't going to fall for it this time.

Still, she was doing something nice for him. And she had called him Tad.

"Here." He handed her his phone. "Put in your number, and I'll text you so you have mine."

She gave him a half smile. "Just in case."

"Yeah."

She punched in her number and gave the phone back. He

sent a text that said *Hey*, then shoved the phone back in his pocket.

"Maddie." Sam came running over, grinning from ear to ear. "My mom said you're babysitting Charlie today. I know how to hold her, and she likes me."

Maddie smiled. "Then I guess if I have any trouble, I know who to call."

Sam held up his walkie-talkie. "Me!"

Maddie laughed, and Tad couldn't keep from chuckling too. Sam made even hard situations a little bit better.

Maddie gestured toward the house. "I should get in there."

"Will you bring Charlie out to see Princess?" Sam asked.

"Maybe." Maddie caught Tad's eye. "See you later."

He nodded once. She spun around and walked up the front porch steps like she belonged there, and Tad's heart squirmed. He hadn't even said anything about Charlie's needs or schedule. What could he say? Maddie probably knew more about taking care of a baby than he did. If it weren't for Anita, he wouldn't have a clue what to do. And now he was questioning whether Maddie was good enough to watch his daughter?

A lonely feeling pressed on him as he watched Anita open the door and wave Maddie in with a smile. Like he was on the outside looking in.

✦ ✧ ✦

Tad could see the cabin roofs in the distance from where he had been checking the fence that marked the edge of the Wilsons' property. Dan had told him the Richardsons had agreed to let the Wilsons keep using the land for trail rides on the condition that the C-A-R maintain the fence. They didn't want any of their cattle wandering over to the ranch.

Tracks in the dirt appeared to be from a coyote, and Tad snorted. The fence wouldn't keep predators away from the cattle. The whole thing seemed like a waste of time to him, but he would keep doing what he was told so he could keep earning money and putting as much aside for the future as possible. He hadn't asked his dad about the house or his visit to Matthew Pine's office, but he had checked the paper for any rental listings and found nothing he could afford.

He looked at the tracks again a little closer and paused. Hold on a minute. Those were too big to be from a coyote. Curly had pretty big paws, but there was no way he would've roamed this far from the house. He could barely make the trek between the house and the barn these days. That meant . . .

Wolf.

He narrowed his eyes and looked around. Had a lone wolf passed through here, or was there a small pack living nearby? He saw only one set of prints. He thought of Charlie and shuddered. If someone were to lay her down somewhere outside, she would be completely defenseless.

He shook his head and scolded himself. He was being ridiculous. A wolf would never get that close to the house. Dan would want to know about this, though. And they should warn the Richardsons as well.

He climbed on the four-wheeler and checked the time, disappointed to see it was past noon. Anita would've already returned, which meant he wouldn't get the chance to accidentally on purpose catch Maddie on her way out to ask how it went with Charlie today. Not that he wanted her to think he was checking up on her, even though he was.

The walkie-talkie he'd left on the rack crackled, and Anita's voice came through. "Sam, I haven't seen you since this morning. Why don't you come in for lunch?"

Tad listened, but there was no response. Sam had wandered off after Anita left and could be anywhere. The offer of food would draw him back, Tad was sure.

Anita's voice came again. "Tad, are you with Sam?"

He picked up the walkie-talkie. "No. I haven't seen him."

"Okay. Sam, it's time to come in for lunch."

Still nothing. Tad chuckled, picturing Anita's frustration, although Tad suspected Sam probably *had* answered. He just hadn't remembered to push the talk button before he did. Tad would bet a family-size package of pepperoni sticks that Sam was already on his way to the house.

He spoke into the device. "I'll keep an eye out."

"Thanks, Tad. Over."

He tossed the walkie-talkie back on the rack. Then, mindful of the uneven terrain, he slowly turned the four-wheeler around to head back. As he made a wide loop, something caught his eye in a scraggly patch of foxtail barley. Something even more disturbing than the wolf tracks. A cigarette butt. He stopped and hopped off the ATV.

It wasn't his. He was sure of it. He hadn't smoked at the ranch since the day he promised Sam, and even before that he wouldn't have been stupid enough to leave evidence sitting out in the open like this. Not after Dan's warning about smoking.

Who could've been out here? It was possible a guest had wandered this far. He should say something to Dan about this too. Fires that consumed thousands of acres had started from less than a carelessly tossed cigarette. The fields weren't dried out yet, but by July they would be, and an errant butt could lead to disaster. Dan would want to remind future guests of that, just to be on the safe side.

But what if he thought Tad was trying to cover his own tracks? Tad knew Dan didn't trust him. It would seem like Tad was making up excuses to deflect blame from himself in case Dan found a butt somewhere. If Dan already held Tad in low esteem, Tad didn't want to risk sending it any lower.

He would remind the guests himself. And keep an eye out for wanderers.

As he crested the hill and the house came into view, he saw Maddie getting into her car. He frowned. Had Anita gotten home late? No, she and Maddie had probably been talking. It never ceased to amaze him the amount of talking some women could do when they were together.

Maddie was long gone by the time Tad parked the ATV inside the barn. He headed for his car to grab his Mountain Dew.

"Tad."

He turned to see Anita standing on the front porch, holding Charlie. He waved.

"Did you see Sam?"

He shook his head.

She threw up a hand and sighed. "Ugh, that boy. Well, why don't you come in for some lunch? I've got it all laid out."

It didn't feel right. He was already taking advantage of Anita's kindness. But all he had in his car was Mountain Dew and a box of stale powdered donuts, and he wanted to spend time with Charlie. He veered toward the house.

As he reached the porch, loud, running footsteps sounded behind him. It was as he'd suspected. Sam.

"I'm starving, Mom." Sam whooshed past Tad and into the house. "Can I hold Charlie?"

She shook her head. "Go wash up."

Tad approached timidly, and Anita held Charlie out to him without hesitation. When he scooped her up, she waved her arms in the air, and he felt lighter. Why did everything seem a little easier when he was holding Charlie?

"Hello, Charlie-horse."

"Ba-ba-ba-ba."

"Did you already eat your lunch?"

"Ba-ba-ba."

Anita tickled Charlie's neck. "You never have any trouble eating, do you, sweetheart? That's why you have so many chins."

Charlie cooed, her eyes shining bright.

He glanced at Anita. "Did it go okay with Maddie this morning?"

"Yes. That girl is a godsend. She even did the breakfast dishes while I was gone, can you believe it?"

He couldn't. Maddie Pine, the princess of Grady, had done Anita's dirty dishes? On purpose? Maybe he did need to give her a chance. People could change, couldn't they?

By the time they were all settled at the table, with Charlie on his lap, Tad's stomach was turning inside out from hunger. The thick ham sandwich on his plate dripped with some kind of sauce, and he was about to grab it and stuff it in his mouth like some kind of wild animal when Anita spoke.

"Would either of you like to say grace?"

Tad froze, as if his lack of movement would make him invisible. Sam looked down at his plate.

Anita gave them a patient smile. "How about I do it?"

Tad let out his breath, and Sam folded his hands in front of him.

"Lord, we are grateful for this food and this beautiful day. I ask that you keep Tad and Sam and Charlie safe and give them the wisdom to make good decisions. Keep them protected. And help us always remember how blessed we are. Amen."

Tad mumbled "amen" and picked up his sandwich. He didn't feel very blessed. His life was in shambles. He still lived with his dad, he only had a job for a few more months, and his personal life was a joke. Still, here he was with this homemade lunch and a beautiful little girl on his lap. It was more than he deserved.

From the living room, he heard "Take the Low Road" play on his phone from where he'd left it by the door, but he pulled his daughter closer and ignored it.

twenty-four

Tad clicked the car seat into place in the back of the Taurus and hurried to get behind the wheel, his nerves frayed like used baling twine. The call earlier during lunch had come from Jenna. She hadn't left a message, but he'd spent the rest of the day freaking out about what she might have to say. Whether she would answer when he called back. How he was going to handle hearing her voice after what she'd done.

He quickly flipped the car around and pressed the callback button on his phone. The five hours since lunch had already felt like a hundred years. He couldn't wait a second longer.

Three rings, and then a clicking noise. Tad frowned. Had she hung up on him? He pulled the phone away from his ear to check the screen. It said, *Connected.*

"Hello? Jenna?" He strained to listen over the sound of the Ford's engine rumbling. "Are you there?"

"Yeah."

Emotions flooded his body—panic, shock, relief, anger—but he pushed all that aside and took a deep breath. He couldn't go off half-cocked here. He had to think of Charlie. Yet none of the words or questions he'd brainstormed and practiced in his head all afternoon would come to mind.

"You called me."

"Yeah."

He bit back a growl and the temptation to throw his phone out the window. "Where are you?"

"How's Charlie?"

He was sure flames were shooting out of his ears. "Seriously, Jenna? What the heck?"

Silence. The heart-pounding, dreadful kind. He scolded himself for lashing out. He couldn't afford to have her cut the call short before he got some answers.

She sniffled. "I'm sorry, okay?"

He realized he was holding the wheel so tight his fingers were going numb and forced himself to loosen his grip. Jenna's apology was unsatisfactory, but it was a start. "She's fine. She started rolling over. When—"

He started to ask, "When are you coming back?" but stopped himself. He wasn't sure why. He wanted to know, didn't he? But maybe he didn't want to sound overeager for her return because her return would mean . . .

"I want to see her." Jenna's voice was strained like she was holding back tears. "I miss her so much."

"Then why did you leave?" The words came out loud and harsh, but he didn't care. His concern was for his daughter, not Jenna's feelings.

"I had to."

"You *had* to? No one was holding a gun to your head."

"I was . . ."

Unstable is what she was. He couldn't remember how he'd ever gotten involved with her in the first place. "You were what?"

"I had to deal with some things, okay?"

"What things?"

No answer. He huffed. Did he really want to know? He pulled up to his dad's house and turned off the car. Charlie made grunting noises behind him. She was going to need her diaper changed.

"I should probably go. Charlie's going to want a bottle soon, and—"

"Wait. Will you send me a picture?"

He frowned. She was the one who decided to drop Charlie off and disappear. Why should he send her a picture?

For some reason, he thought of Anita and sighed. She would send a picture. She would send a hundred pictures.

"Fine."

Another sniffle. "Thank you."

His "bye" came out like a growl, and he jabbed the end call button with unnecessary force. He hadn't realized how mad he was at Jenna until now. And he was mad at himself too. Why hadn't he demanded answers? Demanded she come back to get Charlie right this minute?

He jerked open the car door. He knew the reason why. And it terrified him.

◆ ◇ ◆

Tad was hungry, the ham sandwich Anita had made for him a distant memory. He had changed Charlie's diaper and fed her a bottle. Then she had spit up everywhere and he had changed her clothes and his own. Then she had pooped again. He was on edge and ready to eat cold chili straight from the can.

He set Charlie on a blanket on the floor. "Time for Daddy to have dinner now, Charlie-horse."

She kicked her feet and cried.

"You're okay." He tucked her favorite stuffie next to her. "Mister Panda will keep you company while Daddy eats."

Her face grew red as her crying continued. From the other room, his dad called out, "What're you doing in there? Pinching her?"

Tad scowled. Bud hadn't said a word to him since he'd been home—hadn't lifted a finger to help—and now he wanted to complain? Tad scooped Charlie up off the floor. The crying stopped.

"Let's go see Grandpa," he whispered. He had yet to call Bud that to his face.

Bud had his customary can of Rainier in one hand and the TV remote in the other. Tad stepped between Bud and the screen.

"Hey, I'm watching that."

"Can you hold her for a few minutes?"

Bud stared at Tad.

"Please? I need to eat real quick."

Now Bud stared at Charlie, and something changed in his face. "All right."

Tad hoped his surprise didn't register on his face. Bud set the beer on the coffee table, and Tad carefully laid Charlie in the crook of Bud's arm. She looked up at Bud and squinted but didn't cry.

Bud waved the remote in the air. "Now, move, would you?"

Tad stepped aside and glanced at the TV. "I don't want her watching *that*."

He wasn't an expert on kids or anything, but he knew *Hacksaw Ridge* wasn't appropriate for a child.

"Fine." Bud grumbled and pointed the remote at the TV, clicking until he found a news channel. "Happy?"

Tad looked at Charlie. She seemed content. "Thanks."

He hurried to the kitchen and grabbed a Mountain Dew from the fridge. Deciding against chili, he pulled two corn dogs from the freezer and tossed them in the microwave. While they cooked, he dug a bag of chips out of the cupboard. It was half-eaten, and the chips were stale.

It would do.

Once everything was ready, he went back to the living room so he could keep an eye on Charlie while he ate. She happily swatted at her feet, and every once in a while, Bud would reach over and rub her head. Tad pretended not to notice.

"I wonder where she got all this black hair," Bud said.

Tad scarfed down his first corn dog, then gulped half the bottle of soda. When he picked up his second corn dog, he decided to slow down a little. Charlie was fine, and Bud didn't seem to be in any hurry to pass her off. Tad turned his attention to the news. They were talking about a Family Day promotion coming up at the Grizzly & Wolf Discovery Center in West Yellowstone.

"People can also adopt a wolf pack for three hundred dollars," the woman being interviewed said. "It's a great way to support these Yellowstone wildlife ambassadors."

Bud snorted.

"I saw some wolf tracks today at the ranch." Tad's hand paused as he reached into the bag of chips. Shoot. He'd totally forgotten to mention the tracks to Anita. He'd been too distracted.

Bud's eyes didn't leave the screen, but he seemed to perk up a little. "Oh yeah?"

"Thought they were coyote at first, but there's no way. Too big."

"Where about?"

Tad shrugged. "Along the fence line. Headed south."

"The Richardson fence line?"

Tad nodded. This was the first normal conversation he'd had with his dad in a long time. He wanted to ask him about his visit to Matthew Pine's town office but didn't want to ruin the moment.

"Only one set?" Bud asked.

"I didn't look too close, but yeah. I think there was only one. Probably passing through."

"Or scouting for calves. Those grays are a nuisance."

Tad stuffed his mouth with chips and didn't answer. Everybody had an opinion about the gray wolf population in Montana. Some people wanted to shoot them all. Some thought there should be strict hunting limits. Some advocated for coexistence. All he knew was that no one he'd ever met could afford to lose any livestock to a predator, whether it was a coyote, wolf, mountain lion, or whatever.

He finished off his Mountain Dew and crumpled up the chip bag to throw in the trash. Once again, he considered asking his dad about Matthew Pine, and once again he decided against it.

He jerked his chin at Charlie. "Let me throw this stuff away, then I can take her."

"Hmph." Bud turned up the volume on the TV and settled deeper into the couch. "She's happy where she is."

twenty-five

Saturday morning, Tad jerked awake with a grunt, pulled from a crazy dream about a horse that could talk. Why was it so light out? He checked the time. Nine o'clock? How had he slept in until nine o'clock?

He threw off the covers in a panic and leaped over to Charlie's bassinet. She should've woken up at seven for a bottle. His heart hammered as he stood over her. Something must be wrong.

Her chest rose and fell peacefully. Her mouth was half open as she breathed. His blood pressure lowered a tiny bit. She seemed fine, but she'd never slept this long before. Should he wake her so she could eat? Was it okay for her to miss a bottle? Maybe he should call Anita.

He picked up his phone and hesitated. No. He couldn't call her for every little thing. Charlie just wasn't hungry. Or was extra tired. She was *fine*.

He, on the other hand, was a tangled-up mess. He gave his daughter one more good look and snuck out of the room. He was trying to quit—he really was—but now would be the perfect time for a cigarette.

Outside, the sun was shining. He checked his phone for new

messages and saw only the picture he'd sent Jenna yesterday. He'd sent her one Tuesday night after she'd asked, then yesterday Anita had given Charlie a new headband with bright red flowers and Tad had taken a dozen pictures because she'd looked so darn cute. He'd sent one of those to Jenna as well, for some reason. He couldn't help it. Maybe he wanted her to see Charlie was doing fine without her.

After a couple deep drags, he flicked the cigarette to the ground and stomped on it. Why was he out here? He didn't want to smell like smoke when Charlie got up. He thought back to a couple days ago when Maddie had stopped to talk to him before she'd left. *"I respect you for taking Charlie in,"* she'd said. *"A lot of guys would've said no."*

He didn't feel respectable. He was Charlie's dad, what was he supposed to do? Leave her in the driveway?

Maddie was confusing. She would drive him nuts for days and then she'd go and say something like that.

He slipped back into the house and heard his dad bumbling around in the kitchen. Bud always moved pretty slow after a night out at Webb's. Tad hadn't gone with him since Charlie moved in. He didn't exactly miss it—Webb's wasn't that great—but he did miss having the freedom to go out if he wanted to. Everything was harder with a baby, and everyone treated him differently now. Had it been like that for Jenna? Had she felt stuck? Had she had someone like Anita to help her?

Probably not.

A squeak came from his room, and he hurried down the hall. Charlie was stretching, her little knees pulled up to her chest, her face scrunched. He peered down at her, his heart also stretching.

"Hi, sleepyhead." He smiled. "You finally decided to wake up, huh?"

She blinked at him. "Ba-ba-ba."

He picked her up and laid her on his bed to get her changed. It hadn't taken him long to figure out he needed to keep a basket nearby filled with diapers, wipes, and onesies. What was taking him a little longer to learn was how to keep up with the laundry. Sometimes Charlie had to wear clothes that weren't exactly clean.

Tad scanned the room. Was there a clean pile somewhere? No, it had been a busy week. If her onesie and sleeper were still dry, though, she could keep wearing them until he ran a load of laundry. Saturdays were for pajamas, anyway.

He stayed intent on his task while he changed her diaper and was proud of himself that he only needed four wipes. When he was finished, he zipped the sleeper back up to Charlie's chin and frowned. What was that on her neck?

He looked closer, his chest tightening. Some kind of bumpy, red rash marred her neck. He gently lifted her chin to find the rash spread across every little fold of her skin. His stomach lurched as his earlier fears resurfaced. Something *was* wrong with her. That's why she'd slept in. She was sick. She had a disease. She had . . . something.

How could he have let this happen?

This time when he picked up the phone to call Anita, he didn't hesitate.

She answered right away. "Good morning, Tad."

"Something's wrong with Charlie."

Anita had suspected for many years now that she would never be a grandma, and she had thought she'd made peace with that. She had many other blessings to be thankful for. Many people to love. But as she drove over the speed limit toward Tad's house, praying desperately for Charlie's well-being, she realized her grandmotherly instincts were not so easily left behind.

"God, please let her be okay." She pulled up to the house. "Please, God, please, God, please."

She hadn't gotten many details out of Tad. He'd only said Charlie had slept through her feeding time and was covered in a rash. Anita slung her tote bag over her shoulder and hurried up the front steps to knock.

Tad opened the door with Charlie in one arm and relief evident on his face. Anita didn't see any rash, but she followed Tad into the house, fighting the urge to snatch Charlie right out of Tad's hands for an examination.

Bud looked up from where he was sitting at the kitchen table. "What are *you* doing here?"

Somehow, Anita had driven the whole way here without once considering that she might run into Bud. A memory of the last time she was in this house flashed through her mind. It stung her heart to think about it, but that wasn't important now.

"I called her," Tad said. "Charlie's sick."

Bud stood abruptly, knocking over his chair. "What's the matter with her?"

Tad sat on the couch and laid Charlie on his knees. "She's got a rash."

Bud and Anita crowded in, all other concerns forgotten as Tad gently pulled Charlie's chin up to reveal a smattering of red bumps on her neck.

"Is that it?" Anita asked. "Where else?"

"That's it. And she wouldn't wake up this morning for her bottle."

Charlie smiled and babbled, happy to be the center of attention. She was not acting like a sick child. And she was not "covered in a rash."

Anita scrunched her lips to the side. "She *wouldn't* wake up, or she *didn't*? Did you try to wake her?"

Tad hung his head. "No."

"It's okay." She put a hand on his shoulder. "There was no need to do that unless something seemed wrong."

Bud jabbed a finger toward Charlie's neck. "Doesn't that seem wrong?"

Anita ignored him. "Have you tried feeding her since she's been up?"

"Yeah. She finished her bottle right before you got here."

Anita felt Charlie's forehead, then unzipped her sleeper and felt her armpit. "She doesn't have a fever. And if her appetite is normal, that's a good sign."

Tad was visibly distraught. "But look at her neck."

Anita looked. And looked again. "I'm pretty sure I know what it is."

Bud's dark eyes bored into her. "What?"

"A yeast infection." She'd seen it before. It was a fairly common affliction for a baby, especially a chubby one.

Tad's face reddened. "I thought yeast infections—uh, I didn't know—"

"I know it sounds weird, but it's pretty normal. If her neck hasn't been getting cleaned and dried as much as it should, this was bound to happen."

Bud smacked the back of Tad's head. "You don't keep her clean?"

"Ow." Tad gave his dad a dirty look. "I do."

"Then how did this happen?"

"Well . . ." Tad studied Charlie and mumbled. "Maybe I don't do it as much as I should."

Anita's heart went out to him. "It could happen to anyone, Tad. Don't worry. You've got to wipe her neck after every bottle and dry it really well. You can't let any milk or spit-up get stuck inside those rolls of hers. You could even put some Vaseline on her neck to keep any moisture from reaching the skin. It'll clear up in a few days."

Tad brushed a finger over Charlie's cheek, and she smiled. "Ba-ba-ba."

"Are you sure?" he asked. "What about the sleeping thing?"

Anita leaned closer to Charlie and spoke in a baby voice. "Someone's learning to sleep better, aren't you, sweetheart?" She straightened and turned to Tad. "She'll be sleeping through the night in no time."

His eyes widened in wonder. "They can do that?"

"Yes, and let me tell you." She leaned against the couch and held up her hands. "It's a game changer."

There'd been many mornings Tad had arrived at the ranch looking like he hadn't slept a wink. It was a rite of passage for parents to be up all night with their children sometimes, but she was happy the end was in sight for him.

"I guess we'll be going to the store for Vaseline today." Tad moved Charlie to his shoulder and stood. "I should go find a washcloth to clean her neck."

He headed down the hall, all his attention on Charlie.

Anita took a deep breath as he disappeared. "He really loves her, doesn't he?"

She'd had her doubts, the first time she saw Charlie in Tad's arms, whether he could do what needed to be done. Despite being patient and gentle with Sam, she'd been afraid the demands of fatherhood might be too much for him. If any of those fears had remained, however, they were gone now. He would do anything for Charlie. She could see it.

Bud grumbled something unintelligible, and she glanced at him, feeling suddenly self-conscious. "How are *you*, by the way?"

It had been a long time since they'd talked. She could remember his last words to her, clear as a mountain stream: *"Keep your big, fat nose out of our business."* He'd been upset that she'd stopped by to check on him and the boys. Again. She hadn't meant to make him feel like he couldn't be trusted to care for his kids, though in hindsight she could see that's what she'd done. The final straw that day had been when she told Bud she'd heard Tad hadn't been doing well in school.

She rubbed a hand over her nose and shifted on her feet.

Bud looked even more uncomfortable than she felt. "We're fine."

"That's good."

An awkward moment passed. She could hear Tad talking to Charlie, and then he must have tickled her because she squealed.

Anita shook her head. "I can't believe you're a grandpa."

When they'd been close, that summer years ago when Anita couldn't imagine life without him, the thought of being grandparents never crossed their minds. They'd cared only about late-night drives and stolen kisses. She blushed, thinking of it now. She'd been such a child then.

"I should get going." She reached into her tote bag and

pulled out a bag of homemade English muffins. "I brought these for—"

"You've gotta be kidding me." Bud's eyes flashed. "We don't need your stupid biscuits."

She winced. "I-I'm sorry. I know you don't *need* them. I was just worried about Charlie and wanted to bring something."

She stood there frozen, the bag in her hands, as he stared at her. Then his expression softened, and he gave an almost imperceptible nod toward the coffee table. She set the bag there and stepped back.

"Say good-bye to Tad and Charlie for me."

He nodded again, and she saw herself to the door. She blinked in the sunlight as she climbed into her Tahoe, her stomach in knots.

"God, I don't know why everything has to be so hard. I don't want him to hate me forever. I don't hate him."

She drove home slowly, the windows down. It was a beautiful day. A small voice deep in her spirit whispered to her. *But do you love him?*

She pressed her lips together. "He pushed me away. He broke my heart." She smacked the steering wheel. "He said I have a big nose."

Dust rose behind her as she drove up the driveway to Come Around Ranch. The wispy clouds shaped like flames reminded her of the time she and Dan saw the Northern Lights. Sitting next to him under a blanket as they watched the lights flicker across the sky had been a magical moment. He was the best decision she'd ever made. She had no regrets.

"Then why do I keep thinking about Bud, Lord?" A bird flew past her window. A horse whinnied in the distance. "Why can't I let it go?"

twenty-six

Tad leaned against TJ to encourage him to shift his weight and asked again, "TJ. Foot."

With a huff, the horse reluctantly lifted his left front foot. Tad carefully examined it, checking for any tenderness or swelling around the hoof before putting the hoof pick to use cleaning around the frog. A guest had heard him talking about frogs the other day and had said, *"I hate those jumpy things. You don't have any around here, do you?"* Tad had been unable to convince the man he'd been referring to part of a horse's foot.

"Some people don't listen." He continued to work, in no hurry. "Do you know what that's like?"

TJ snorted.

"Yeah, I suppose you do. You've probably tried to tell us stupid humans all kinds of things, and we never get it."

Tad set TJ's foot down and straightened. From the corral fence, Bob nickered, and TJ held his head a little higher.

Tad raised his eyebrows. "You two have a thing going on?"

A fly buzzed around TJ's ears, and he tossed his head.

"She's nice." Tad had been around a lot of horses, and Bob

was one of the sweetest. Much nicer than most humans of the female variety. "I won't tell anyone."

He moved around to TJ's right side. The whole herd stood at the corral fence now, curious about the attention TJ was receiving. Or maybe they were curious about Tad. He always got the feeling after he'd been off for two or three days that they wondered where he had been and what he'd been doing. Maybe the time passed slowly for them without a change of scenery or routine.

Time had been racing for him, on the other hand. He couldn't believe it was Tuesday again already. Everything had seemed to speed up since Charlie arrived. Every minute was filled, even though he never seemed to get anywhere.

He put a hand on TJ's shoulder and was about to ask for his right foot when he heard the telltale sound of gravel crunching. He didn't have to look to know Maddie had arrived for babysitting duty. Right on time.

What kinds of things did she do over the weekend while he was doing laundry and wiping up drool? His weekends used to be wild and free without a diaper in sight. Would he ever have that life back? What had his friends been up to without him? He wouldn't mind a night out once in a while. Wouldn't mind blowing off some steam.

He shook his head. That was out of the question right now. Charlie needed him. At least her rash was almost gone.

He thought about Jenna. She'd never texted him back after the last picture he sent. He couldn't help but wonder if she meant it when she said she missed Charlie. Why wouldn't she give him a straight answer about anything? What if she was in some kind of trouble?

What if she never came back?

"Hey, Tad."

He jumped, so far lost in his thoughts he hadn't heard Maddie come up. He fiddled with the hoof pick in his hands. "Oh. Hey."

She was wearing a flowery yellow sundress. He didn't know much about clothes, but he knew she didn't get it at Big R. He wished he didn't notice her long, tan legs.

"I wanted to ask you something." She leaned against the fence. "It's about Sam."

A pit opened in Tad's stomach as he walked toward her. His voice was wary. "What about Sam?"

"It's his birthday on Friday, right?"

Tad nodded slowly, the pit only growing.

Maddie tucked her hair behind her ear. "I was thinking it would be fun to throw him a party. You know, like a real one. At the Oasis or something."

Tad stopped at the fence and blinked. The Oasis was a hole-in-the-wall bar and grill a couple miles out of town. It was famous for its steaks and rumored to have the occasional celebrity stop in, though Tad had never seen one. He'd only been there once. Prices at the Oasis were far outside his comfort zone.

Maddie wanted to take Sam there for his birthday?

"I think Anita's planning a special dinner."

He'd heard her ask Sam if he wanted hamburgers or fettuccini alfredo. He'd chosen the burgers.

"Oh, come on, Tad." Maddie pouted. "It's his twenty-first birthday. Don't you think he deserves to have a celebration?"

Tad crossed his arms over his chest, then uncrossed them. He'd never thought about it before. "Who would even come? I don't know any of his friends."

"I can invite some people from church. I'll take care of everything."

"I don't know. What if no one showed up?" A sick feeling filled the pit in his stomach as he pictured Sam sitting at one of the big, oak tables at the Oasis, waiting and waiting for people who never came. He wasn't going to do that to Sam.

"They'll show up. People love birthday parties."

"A birthday party?" Suddenly Sam was there, standing on his toes in excitement. His voice rose to a high pitch. "For me?"

Tad cringed inside. Great. Now he would have to disappoint the poor kid. "I don't think so, Sam. I think your mom already has plans."

Maddie smiled at Sam. "A party at the Oasis would be more fun, though, wouldn't it?"

Sam rocked back on his heels, nodding wildly. "I love birthday parties."

Maddie raised her eyebrows at Tad. "See?"

"My mom always makes cupcakes for my birthday."

Maddie smirked. "They have chocolate lava cake at the Oasis."

"Ooh." Sam turned to Tad, practically shouting now. "Chocolate lava cake!"

Maddie's smile grew. She raised one shoulder and turned her sparkly blue eyes on Tad. "Like I said, I'll take care of everything. I only need your help convincing Dan and Anita."

He hesitated. It would be a nice thing to do for Sam, wouldn't it? But he wasn't sure he wanted to get in the middle of this. So many things could go wrong at a bar and grill in the middle of nowhere on a Friday night. "I don't know . . ."

Sam tugged on Tad's sleeve. "Please, Tad?"

He sighed. Then again, he would be there the whole time, on the lookout for trouble. He wouldn't leave Sam's side. And it would be the biggest thrill the kid had had in a long time.

If Tad knew Maddie at all, she wouldn't go halfway with the party. She would pull out all the stops. It would be a birthday to remember.

"Okay, fine. I'll help."

Maddie clapped her hands. "Yay!"

Sam spun around and kicked a rock with all his might. "One, two, three, four, five, six, seven, eight. Let's go talk to Mom right now."

"I'll talk to her later when I go to leave." He needed time to think about the best way to bring it up. The right words to say.

Sam's face scrunched. "Why?"

"Tad's working right now." Maddie playfully punched Sam's shoulder. "Don't say anything to your mom until Tad picks up Charlie, okay?"

Maddie gave Tad a look that told him she understood why he wanted to wait, and he was relieved.

Sam whined. "I want to do it now."

"I know." Tad tried to sound sympathetic but firm. "But it will be better if we keep it between us until later."

Sam studied Tad. "Between us? Is this another pinkie promise?"

Tad swallowed. "Sure."

It wasn't like he was asking Sam to keep anything from his parents this time. He was only asking him to wait. He held out his hand over the fence, and they hooked pinkies. From the corner of his eye, Tad could see Maddie watching closely, probably wondering what other promise he and Sam had made.

When the deal had been sealed, Sam grinned and lumbered off to where Curly was laying in the shade and started belting out "Happy Birthday." Curly gave him an irritated look before easing his head back onto the ground. Sam finished the song with his arms raised over his head.

"Happy Birthday to meee."

It did Tad's heart good to see the joy on Sam's face, but he glanced at Maddie and felt uneasiness creeping in. Was the kind and thoughtful Maddie behind this, or the manipulative one with the claws?

Anita flinched as Sam raced through the house, practically shrieking.

"Dad's home!"

He must've been watching the driveway from his bedroom window upstairs, waiting for this moment. After Tad brought up Sam's birthday earlier and asked if Sam could attend a party at the Oasis—a conversation for which she had been wholly unprepared—she'd told Sam she didn't want to hear another word about it until his father got home. She knew he would bug her relentlessly otherwise, begging for an answer.

She didn't have an answer.

The mudroom door creaked open and banged shut. A moment later, it opened again, and she could hear Sam telling Dan all about the birthday party Tad and Maddie wanted to throw for him as Dan took off his boots and hung up his coat. As they entered the kitchen, Sam was saying something about a chocolate lava cake.

"Wow, buddy, that sounds pretty cool." Dan caught Anita's eye, and some unspoken communication passed between them. He rubbed his chin and turned back to Sam. "Why don't you go check on the horses so I can talk to your mom, okay? Make sure they have enough water. It's supposed to be hot tomorrow."

Sam held up his hands. "I want to talk about the party."

"I know, but right now I need to talk to your mom."

"You're going to talk about the party without me?"

Dan's tone was firm. "Yes."

Though Anita had been tempted to hold back the truth from Sam sometimes over the years, Dan never did. He said the truth wasn't something people needed to be protected from.

Sam gave an exaggerated sigh as his shoulders slumped. "Okay." He stopped briefly in the mudroom to tell Curly to stay, then let the door bang shut behind him.

"Hi." Dan kissed her temple. "How was your day?"

She leaned against him. "It was fine until Tad came to pick up Charlie."

"That's when he mentioned the party?"

"Yes."

Dan shook his head. "I wish he would've talked to us about it before mentioning it to Sam. The poor guy won't be able to sleep tonight, no matter what we say."

Anita crossed to the fridge to get out the milk. Supper still needed to be served. "I think Sam overheard them."

"Ah. So it was Maddie's idea?"

Anita nodded.

"That was nice of her to think of him."

Anita pulled the lasagna from the oven and set it on the table. "Yes, but I'm not sure she understands Sam's needs. It seems risky to let him face something like this without one of us there."

"I could tag along."

Anita gave him a grim smile. "Sam made it pretty clear we were not invited."

"I see." Dan took out three forks and three knives from the drawer. "Tad will be there. He understands Sam pretty well."

"But they serve alcohol there."

"Sam knows better than to mess with alcohol."

Anita shook croutons from a bag onto the green salad she had made, her head down. What would Dan see on her face right now? Fear, she guessed. She was afraid of all the things that could go wrong. Yes, they'd taught Sam about the dangers of alcohol, and yes, he was a good kid, but he didn't always make the best choices when left to his own devices. She wouldn't send an eight-year-old to a party without any adults, so why should she send Sam?

She sighed. "I guess Tad and Maddie *are* adults."

Dan filled a glass with water from the sink. "True, though twenty-four seems younger the older we get."

Anita nodded. Not only that, but just because someone was an adult, didn't mean they always acted like it. This morning at Coffee Break, Vernon DeVries had told her his middle-aged sons were acting like "kids who need a spanking."

Dan leaned against the counter and folded his arms across his chest. "You've been spending a lot of time with Maddie. Do you think she's trustworthy?"

Anita pondered this. It was a good question. She had enjoyed getting to know Maddie better the past few weeks. She enjoyed talking with her. Maddie was hard to read, however. Whenever Anita asked about her family or her plans for the future, she was evasive. Still, she seemed kind and responsible. Anita didn't want Maddie to think she didn't trust her. She needed someone in her life who believed in her.

"Yes, I think so."

"Then I think we should say yes. It would be good for Sam."

She looked at the floor, tears inexplicably welling in her eyes. "I was going to make hamburgers and cupcakes."

"You can make them a different day. It's not a big deal."

"I don't know, Dan." She couldn't shake her emotions. What was wrong with her? She shouldn't be crying over a birthday party. "It feels like a big deal."

Dan's voice was gentle. "We've got to let him have his own life. We're not always going to be here to watch over him."

Ha, that's what *he* thought. She planned to be here watching over him for at least another forty years. She sniffled.

"Tell you what," Dan said. "We don't have to decide right this minute. Let's pray about it for a couple days, and then talk again, okay?"

Ugh, he was so reasonable and calm and looked so handsome with the silver in his sideburns and his face starting to darken from the sun. She wanted him to hold her close and somehow feel what she was feeling. How could he understand that letting Sam go felt like losing a piece of herself?

But he was right. About the praying part, anyway.

The mudroom door creaked, and Sam shouted into the kitchen, "Can I come in now, guys?"

Anita laughed and wiped her eyes with her sleeve. "Okay. Let's pray about it."

Dan pushed off the counter and gave her a quick hug. "Okay. I love you." Then he raised his voice. "Come on in, buddy."

Sam burst into the kitchen, his wide eyes darting back and forth between her and Dan. "Can I go to the party?"

Dan raised one shoulder. "We haven't decided yet. There's a lot to think about."

Sam's face fell. He gave Anita an angry look. "You're not being fair."

"Whoa, there." Dan fixed Sam with a fatherly glare. "You don't speak to your mother like that."

Anita's heart squeezed. How had Sam known she was the one who wanted to say no? Was it that obvious? She cringed inside. Of course it was. She was always the one saying no. Always the one keeping him close and saying, *"I don't think you should do that"* and *"That's probably not a good idea."*

She took a deep breath. "Sam, honey, we want to make sure we've thought about everything and—"

"You *don't* know everything, Mom." He stomped a foot. "You don't even know what I want most for my birthday."

He stormed out of the kitchen, leaving her speechless. He loved lasagna, but she had a feeling he wasn't coming back to eat dinner anytime soon. The tears returned to her eyes as Dan drew close and pulled her into his arms.

"It's okay. He'll get over it."

She buried her face in Dan's shirt and didn't answer.

It wasn't okay. Because Sam was right. She had no idea what he wanted for his birthday. She had no idea if she even knew him at all.

twenty-seven

I'm pretty sure I'm not supposed to leave the house by myself at night but I've never done it because I've never wanted to so I don't know a hundred percent sure. I'm being really quiet even though my insides feel really loud because I'm mad.

I want Curly to come with me because it's dark outside but when I go in the mudroom and shake his shoulder to wake him up and he tries to stand his body shakes and I feel bad so I tell him to lay back down. Poor Curly. He has gray hair on his face like Dad but Dad doesn't shake like that. There's not a lot of room but I sit down next to Curly and rub his back until pretty soon he's snoring and then I put on my boots.

I am so quiet when I go outside. I close the door so quiet. I hurry away from the house and I almost kick a big rock but then remember how I am being so quiet. I want to go to the fence line but I'll have to go past the cabins so I can't take the four-wheeler because it would be too noisy so I walk and walk.

There are a lot of stars in the sky. I wish Dad was here. It was warm all day but now it's cold and I wish I had a sweat-shirt but I'm past the cabins now and I keep going. The hill looks like water because the moon is shining on it but it's not water. I get to the fence line and I can see the light from the Richardsons' barn but it's really far away and I can hear cows telling each other stories and I know their voices carry across the field because Dad told me about that.

Mom was right. There isn't much here. I used to go everywhere on the ranch with Dad so I've been up here before but not in a long time because I do more stuff on my own now and try to stay on the other side of the barn where no one can see me. It's dark so I can't see a lot but I know there are no cows by the fence. I wonder if it was cows I saw up here the other day or something else but mostly I wonder if Mom's going to let me go to the Oasis on Friday for my birthday. It would be so much fun but I think Mom only cares about if something's safe not if it's fun.

I spread out my arms and sing the song Mitch sings in *City Slickers* when he's driving cattle and the cows sing too. My insides are a lot quieter now that I walked all the way here and I feel sorry that I yelled at Mom because the Bible says to honor your parents and Mr. Bill says that means you should talk to them with respect. *Respect* is a hard word, like *soon*, and maybe because it seems like it means different things at different times. I still feel sorry I yelled but I'm not sorry for coming out here at night because I like how everything is quiet and no one can tell me what to do because no one knows where I am. I like the way it feels to have so much space all around me. I know I'm going to come up here again.

Now that the rest of my insides are quiet I can hear my stomach telling me how hungry I am so I guess next time I'll have to bring a snack. I can also hear a car somewhere and it sounds kind of close but the rumble must carry over the field like the cow voices so it must not really be close but now I see headlights and they seem close too. I don't want to be up here anymore and I really want a granola bar or a bowl of cereal so I hurry back down the hill and I don't look back because if someone's there I don't want to see them and I don't want them to see me.

twenty-eight

"Them custard-filled ones are my favorite." Vernon pointed at the box and wagged his eyebrows at Anita.

She laughed. "I like those ones too."

She'd taken to picking up a dozen donuts on her way to the Coalition on Thursday mornings so there would be something to offer anyone who stopped by. Just in case. Visitors were still few and far between, but you never knew when someone might come in some other time besides during Coffee Break. Like today.

She used a napkin to pick up the custard-filled donut and handed it to Vernon. Her hands had been feeling a little better now that she wasn't dealing with Charlie's car seat anymore, though her knuckles still looked like they belonged to a much older woman.

"What brings you to town today?"

"Oh, I got some things to pick up at the hardware store." He waved the donut around. "You know how it is. It's always something. I suppose your lesser half is over there?"

She nodded. "I always stop in to see him when I leave. I'll save him a maple bar."

Vernon took a big bite and talked with his mouth full. "What about your grandbaby? Why isn't she here?"

She thought about correcting him but decided against it. "Someone else is watching her while I'm here. She's a bit of a distraction. Makes it hard to talk. Speaking of which, I wanted to ask you about that pamphlet I gave you. You said you read it?"

She'd wanted to ask him about it at Coffee Break on Tuesday, but there were always other people around, laughing and swapping stories.

He chewed another bite of donut thoughtfully and looked around the room. "Yeah, I read it."

"Did you find it helpful?"

He furrowed his eyebrows so hard they were almost touching each other. "I reckon it's all good information and everything, but I don't see how it'll help me any."

"Why not?"

He shrugged. "My boys are going to fight about the farm no matter what my last will and testament says. They already do. I don't see any way around it at this point."

His shoulders slumped, and Anita wanted to reach out and give his gnarled and wrinkled hand a squeeze, but she didn't. She and Dan had been lucky. Dan only had one sibling, a younger sister, and she'd been more than happy to have Dan buy her out of her share of the ranch years ago when Dan took over from his dad.

"Have you tried talking to them about your wishes?"

He barked a laugh. "That's just it. I don't even know what my wishes are anymore. If I split everything fifty-fifty, Jake'll think it's unfair because he's oldest and he worked the farm instead of going to college. If I give Jake more, Ed'll think it's unfair because Jake could've gone to college if he wanted. He chose not to."

Anita poured a cup of coffee and set it beside Vernon's elbow. "That was years ago, though. They're still talking about college?"

"The farm paid for Ed's college. But it's not just that. They've both loaned the farm money. Ed loaned more, but Jake says the money he loaned years ago would be the same amount as what Ed did if it was today because of inflation." Vernon shook his head. "Bah."

"Oh dear. It really is complicated, isn't it?" Anita thought of Sam and the trust she and Dan had planned for him. So far, they'd been unable to decide on a trustee they could, well, *trust*, but at least their main concern was how to give Sam the best life possible after they were gone. Poor Vernon had to be concerned about whether his estate would even survive the probate process.

Thinking about Sam caused a twinge of guilt in her gut. She still hadn't given him an answer about the birthday party. She'd prayed about it as promised, but her conflicted feelings hadn't gone away. If she didn't protect her son, who would?

Vernon finished his donut and wiped his fingers on the napkin. "My wife used to say it's not complicated at all. She said family's more important than land and Ed and Jake's relationship is more important than money. For years she was after me to start transferring ownership and responsibilities to the boys, to not wait until I was gone, but I was too stubborn. I thought I knew what was best."

"She was a lovely woman." Anita remembered Shirley DeVries for her loud laugh and the coleslaw salad she brought to every church potluck. Anita had always liked her.

"I should've listened to her back when Jake'n Ed were still getting along okay. When they might've had a chance to work it out between 'em. I should've let go and let them make the decisions. Now I'm afraid it's too late."

Anita shifted on her feet, Vernon's words hitting awfully close to home. "Maybe you could still sit down with the two of them and talk it out. Maybe there are certain things they both want more than other things and you can find a compromise."

"Maybe." He tapped a finger against the coffee cup, his voice tinged with sadness. "But it's hard to let go."

"I'm not so great at letting go either." For the hundredth time, she thought of Sam's birthday party. "Sometimes even little things start to feel like big things, and the bigger they feel, the tighter we hold on to them."

"You got that right. Shirley always said I was holding on with both hands." He looked away. "I don't know why I'm telling you all this."

Anita knew why. God was answering her prayers for guidance, and this was exactly what she needed to hear. She knew what she needed to do.

◆ ▾ ◢

"Sorry I'm late." Anita bustled into the house and waved at Charlie, who was sitting in Maddie's lap on the couch. "I stopped to see Dan at the hardware store on the way home and got carried away."

Maddie stood and moved Charlie to her hip. "It's no problem. We were having some girl talk. This little munchkin cracks me up."

Charlie had been doing a lot of jibber-jabbering lately, as if she already had a lifetime of stories to tell. Sometimes Anita thought about Charlie's mother and the milestones the young woman was missing, and it made her sad. The sweet child had already changed so much since her arrival a month ago. What might Jenna have missed in another month from now?

Anita turned her attention back to the present. "I'm thankful for you, Maddie, and I need to apologize. I shouldn't have waited this long to decide about the party. Now it's only a day away and I've put you in the difficult position of having to plan everything last minute. I'm so sorry."

Maddie's face brightened. "Does that mean Sam can go?"

Part of Anita's heart still resisted, but she scolded it and nodded, remembering Vernon's words about letting go. This birthday party was a small matter in the grand scheme of things. Not something to grasp with both hands. Dan had been right.

"It was a lovely idea and so thoughtful of you. Sam's lucky to have you for a friend."

Maddie's face flushed, and she looked away, as if unaccustomed to being praised. Anita reached to take Charlie so Maddie could get ready to go.

"Thanks again." Anita kissed Charlie on the forehead and smiled at Maddie. "You can give Sam the good news on your way out if you want. I'm sure he'd love hearing it from you instead of me."

Sam wasn't her biggest fan at the moment. He'd been avoiding her since Tuesday night and moping around like he had a broken heart. Maybe he did. How could he possibly understand why she and Dan couldn't always let him do what he wanted? He didn't know what it meant that he had the mind of a child.

Maddie scooped up her purse and keys from the coffee table

and touched Charlie's cheek on her way to the door. "I'll tell him. It's going to be fun."

Anita smiled, sure the little niggle of doubt in her heart was only a byproduct of two decades of worrying over her son. As Maddie closed the door behind her, Anita carried Charlie over to the window.

"There she goes." Anita bounced Charlie. "Did you have fun with Miss Maddie today?"

Charlie waved her arms around. "Ba-ba-ba."

As Maddie walked toward the barn, Sam came racing out, practically tripping over himself to get to her. Anita couldn't hear Maddie's words, but she saw the moment Sam realized he was going to get his wish. His grin could light up all of Grady. He wrapped his arms around Maddie's waist, lifted her in the air, and spun her around.

Anita blinked. She'd never seen him do that to anyone but her before. Then Maddie, laughing, got into her car, and Sam, beaming, went back to the barn.

Anita kept watching until long after Maddie was gone. Until Charlie began to fuss in her arms. She turned away from the window slowly, her thoughts and emotions tangled up. She felt a measure of joy at Sam's happiness—how could she not?— but it was tempered by two very little but very big things.

One, her son had always wanted to share every bit of excitement with her, even something as ordinary as finding a bird's nest. Yet he hadn't even looked her way.

And two, she still had no idea what it was he wanted most for his birthday.

twenty-nine

Tad rushed home after work on Friday. Though his dad's land adjoined part of Come Around Ranch property, it was out of the way to drive to Bud's house and then back to the ranch to pick up Sam. Tad was in desperate need of a shower and fresh set of clothes, however. He smelled like a horse.

Maddie had made a reservation at the Oasis for eight o'clock. He'd been surprised she could get one on such short notice, but she confessed she made the reservation days ago. *"I had my fingers crossed,"* she'd said.

It seemed like everything had fallen into place. Sam had been over the moon all day. Yet Tad felt a little anxious. Maddie said her dad was paying for everything, but why would he do that? And who was going to be at this party? He didn't want Sam to be disappointed if the party didn't live up to his expectations.

Tad parked the Ford and hurried to get Charlie out of the back seat. Here was another problem. He'd somehow not considered, until he was driving home, what he was going to do with his daughter during this party. Bringing her along didn't seem like a great idea. He didn't know how late the party would go, and it would be hard to watch over both Sam and

Charlie at the same time. But bringing her back to the ranch and asking Anita to watch her was out of the question.

He lugged the car seat into the house and unbuckled Charlie. "Your daddy's not very good at planning."

"Ba-ba-ba."

He was still getting used to being solely responsible for another human being's schedule, safety, and wellbeing. All. The. Time.

There *was* a long-shot third option, but . . . no. He couldn't do that. Could he?

Bud was in the kitchen, rummaging around. Tad was starving but he would wait to eat at the party. He planned to order the most expensive thing he could find if Matthew Pine was paying the tab. That guy made plenty of money off the people of Grady, so Tad figured this was one way Matthew Pine could give back.

He carried Charlie into the kitchen. "Hey."

Bud pulled his head out of the freezer. "Hey." Then his face and his voice both softened as he looked at Charlie. He leaned close to her sweet, chubby face. "How's my little Charlie-horse today?"

Charlie batted Bud's nose as Tad cringed inside. That was *his* nickname for her. No one else was supposed to call her that. "She's fine."

Bud straightened and waved an arm toward the fridge. "Well, she's lucky she doesn't eat food yet. There's nothing in here to get excited about."

"The food at the Oasis is pretty good, though. She might get jealous." He would have to bring her along and hope for the best.

Bud scowled. "You're going to the Oasis?"

"Yeah, for Sam's birthday." He and Bud were not in the habit of sharing their plans with each other, but maybe he should've mentioned the party since he'd been doing nothing but staying home on Friday nights since Charlie arrived. Bud probably wondered if Tad was ever going to go out on a Friday night again.

Bud narrowed his eyes at Charlie. "And you're bringing her?"

Tad shrugged. "I guess. I mean, what else am I supposed to—"

"That's ridiculous, give her to me." Bud held out his hands. "I'll watch her."

Tad didn't move. Yes, he had considered it. Briefly. The long-shot third option. But there was no way he could actually leave his daughter in Bud's care for more than a few minutes.

"It's no big deal." He held Charlie tighter. "She'll be fine with me."

Bud crossed his arms and scoffed. "It's going to be crowded and loud in there. She won't like it. And what're you going to do if you gotta change her diaper? Set her on one of those big oak tables?"

It was Tad's turn to scoff. "What would *you* do if she needs changed?"

"I raised you and your brother, remember? I've changed plenty of diapers. Now, hand her over." He reached out again, and this time Tad stared at his outstretched hands, considering. It *would* be a lot easier to keep tabs on Sam without Charlie along. And hadn't he been wishing he could go out on his own once in a while?

"She would need a bottle around—"

"Three scoops at nine o'clock, I know. And then to bed. I'm not stupid."

Tad let Bud take Charlie from him and stepped back, dumbfounded. He had no idea Bud had been paying attention to anything he or Charlie did. He wasn't sure sometimes if Bud even knew they were home. He wasn't sure what to think.

Bud waved him away. "Go on. I'll take it from here." He rubbed noses with Charlie and spoke in a baby voice. "You're going to have lots of fun with Grandpa, aren't you, Charlie-horse?"

Tad wanted to remind him to check the heat of the water when he made the formula and to make sure she could reach her elephant blanket if he laid her on the floor, but he didn't. He just slumped out of the kitchen and jumped into the shower with the unsettling feeling his heart was now in Bud's hands.

◆ ◆ ◆

Tad took the driveway to Come Around Ranch slowly so he wouldn't stir up a bunch of dust. Twice on his way back here, he almost turned around. What was he thinking, leaving his daughter with Bud, of all people? What if something happened? What if Bud reneged on his promise not to drink while Tad was gone? *"I wouldn't do that,"* Bud had said, but Tad drummed the steering wheel nervously and glanced up at the sky.

Should he try to pray or something?

No. That was Anita's thing, not his.

He parked and walked toward the Wilsons' house. Curly was sprawled out on the porch, which meant Sam was inside, and as Tad studied the poor, old mutt, he found he had a new appreciation for Anita's protectiveness of Sam. There were so many ways for a kid to get hurt in this world. Even giving a kid a dog could cause them pain.

Had Anita been dealing with the kind of anxiety Tad was

feeling right now every day for the past twenty-one years? Was she constantly wondering about all the things that could go wrong? No wonder she hadn't jumped for joy at the idea of a birthday party for Sam.

Sam threw open the door before Tad could knock and raced down the front steps. "I'm ready!"

Tad smiled. "I can see that."

Sam practically danced on the balls of his feet. "Let's go."

"Hold on, I have to make sure your parents know I'm here."

"They know. Come on."

Dan and Anita appeared in the doorway.

"Have fun," Dan said.

Sam waved wildly.

Anita fixed Tad with a serious look. "Promise you'll keep an eye on him."

"I promise." He loved Sam too. He didn't want to see anything bad happen to him, but there was nothing to worry about. The biggest risk was that Sam would eat too much dessert and get a stomachache.

"Promise you won't let him have any alcohol," Anita pressed.

Tad nodded. He would not be drinking tonight either. "I promise."

Dan put his arm around Anita's shoulders and spoke gently. "Okay, dear, that's enough. They're going to be fine."

"Yes. Sorry." She made a brave attempt at a smile. "What time will you be back?"

Dan chuckled. "Anita."

She raised her hands. "Okay, okay. Just get him home before midnight, would you?"

Sam called from where he stood beside the Ford. "Tad, come onnn."

Tad looked back at Anita. "I will."

As soon as he turned to head back to his car, Sam scrambled to get into his seat. When Tad slid into the driver's side, Sam was already buckled.

He tilted his head at Tad. "Where's Charlie?"

Tad fought against a frown. "She stayed home with her grandpa."

"Oh. Okay, let's go." Sam strained against the seat belt as if he could propel the car himself, and as Tad drove away from the house, he saw Anita watching them in the rearview mirror.

thirty

Tad had been right. Maddie had pulled out all the stops. There were over a dozen people waiting in the west room she had rented when he arrived with Sam, and they'd greeted Sam warmly and had even brought gifts, which was more than Tad could say for himself. The room was decorated with a million blue and silver balloons, and Maddie had given Sam a cardboard crown to wear. Tad had never seen Sam so happy.

"Save some room for your cake, Sam." Tad shook his head. The kid had ordered a giant steak and finished the whole thing. Now he was halfway through a heaping pile of mashed potatoes and gravy, which he kept washing down with lemonade the waitress had already topped off twice.

Sam chewed and swallowed. "But this is really good."

Tad worried his fear over a stomachache was about to become reality. "I know, but maybe you can take a break. There's no hurry."

Sam considered this and set his fork down. "Okay."

"Maybe you should go say hi to your friends for a few minutes."

Sam eyed his plate. His cheeks were flushed, but Tad was sure a break was all the kid needed.

Tad shooed him with his hands. "I won't let them take your plate. Go talk to some people. They all came here to see you."

There was another room on the east side of the Oasis with one giant table that could seat thirty people, but this room was arranged with five smaller tables that seated four people each. It was open to the rest of the dining area but still provided some privacy. As Sam left the table to visit his friends, glass of lemonade in hand, Maddie took his place.

"Hey."

Tad struggled to look directly at her. She was hotter than a tin roof in August with her hair curled and her short black shorts and a sparkly top. "Hey."

"Is Sam having fun?"

As hot as she was, Tad had to admit maybe there was more to her than her looks. "Yeah. He's practically buzzing. And, uh . . ."

She raised her eyebrows slightly, waiting.

He swallowed. "Thanks. For all this. It was nice of you."

She brushed back her hair and shrugged. "It was nothing."

"It's not nothing. Sam will remember this party forever."

"Maybe." Maddie grinned. "Or maybe next year we'll throw him an even bigger party that will make him forget all about this one."

Tad shifted in his chair. Next year? Would he work for the Wilsons again next summer? Would Maddie still be hanging around Grady? He never understood why she hadn't gone away to college like most of her friends had. She wasn't dumb. She got good grades.

His tongue was too tripped up to respond, but Maddie nudged him with her elbow. "Did you leave Charlie with Anita?"

His chest tightened. By next summer, Charlie would be one and a half. She'd be walking. Talking. "No, she's with my dad."

Something flashed across Maddie's face. "Oh?"

He couldn't blame her for being surprised. He was surprised about it himself. She must think he was a loser, still living with his dad. He hoped the embarrassment he felt wasn't all over his face.

"He said he wanted to watch her." Tad checked the time on his phone. Almost ten o'clock. "She should be in bed by now."

It took every ounce of self-control he had to keep from texting Bud to ask how it was going. Almost as much to keep from bailing out on the party early to go home and stand in his bedroom and watch Charlie sleep. How had he gone from tipping cows and drag racing to counting formula scoops and obsessing over his daughter's bedtime? He hardly recognized himself. His friends would think he was out of his mind.

Maddie rested her elbow on the table, her chin in her hand. "You're a good dad."

A loud voice from the main dining area cut through the moment, and he and Maddie both turned around at the same time to check out the disturbance. Tad stiffened. Oh great.

Scooter MacDonald.

"I got a right to be here same as everybody else." Scooter bent over the front counter toward the hostess and glared. "Give me a table."

Maddie leaned close to Tad's ear and whispered, "Someone's looking for trouble."

He cringed. The hostess couldn't be more than seventeen, and he didn't like the way Scooter was berating her, but he didn't want to get involved. He would be happy to avoid any kind of interaction with that guy.

As Tad and Maddie watched, a man who looked like he was in charge came to the hostess's rescue. "Mr. MacDonald, we've discussed this before. You are no longer welcome here. Don't make me call the cops."

Maddie turned back around with wide eyes. "Yikes."

Tad quickly turned back to the table as well, scanning for Sam as he did so. The kid was at a table in the corner with two other guys Tad didn't know. Sam's back was to Tad, but he could hear Sam laughing as the waitress filled his glass once again.

Suddenly, Maddie gasped and tilted her head toward the main dining room. "Listen! It's my favorite song. Let's go dance."

She stood in a swish of expensive fabric and looked at him expectantly. Tad blinked. He knew there was a dance floor along the back of the restaurant. He knew people danced on that dance floor. But the thought of him and Maddie on that dance floor at the same time—near each other, in fact—did not compute. He did not dance. He especially did not dance with rich, beautiful women whose long fingernails were painted silver.

She tugged at his arm. "Hurry up, before the song's over."

He'd spent so many years viewing Maddie as the enemy that it was surreal to stand and take her outstretched hand. It was like she was holding a magnet and he was powerless against its tug. As they passed into the main room, he looked back.

"Wait. I should check on Sam."

"Oh, come on." Maddie pouted. "You sound like Anita. He's fine."

Tad allowed her to drag him to the dance floor, thankful Scooter seemed to have taken the hint and hightailed it out of the Oasis. That guy was a real piece of work.

Three strings of white lights hung over the dance floor as

the music played, and Maddie began to dance, her lips silently moving along with the words. Tad hoped no one was watching him. He was mesmerized by her hips moving, her arms swaying above her head, her hair glinting under the lights. He clumsily stepped side to side and bobbed his head, glad her eyes were closed. He must look like a total fool.

When the song ended, he let out a heavy sigh of relief, but before he could even make a move to get away, Maddie's hands were on his shoulders.

"One more song." She was close enough he could see the diamond horseshoe studs in her ears through her wavy locks. "Please?"

He'd never felt sorry for the ocean before tonight. What chance did it have to resist the pull of the moon? He gave in and rested his hands lightly on Maddie's waist as an old and slow country ballad about the keeper of the stars played.

Maddie moved a little closer so they were almost cheek to cheek. She smelled like wildflowers and raspberries.

"I still live with my parents too," she said.

He winced. She *had* noticed his embarrassment earlier. "It's just for now. I'm looking for a place for me and Charlie."

"In town?"

He nodded.

"I could help you."

He was glad she couldn't see his face. Did he want her help? Did he want to spend more time with her than he already did? A couple weeks ago he would've said no way, but now . . .

"I've got the inside scoop because of my dad," she continued. "There aren't many rentals available, but I bet I could find you something decent. My dad's always the first to hear about vacancies, even before they hit the market."

The final notes of the song faded away. Tad dropped his hands and took a step back, a spark of hope igniting in his chest. He'd almost given up on finding a place he could afford. But why would she help him with this, especially after what she was already doing for him? He almost asked but faltered. Maybe it wasn't fair to be so suspicious of her.

"Tad!"

Tad jumped at the sound of his name and spun around looking for its source. It sounded like Sam.

"Tad." Sam staggered out of the dimly lit depths of the dining room. "You were looking for me." He scratched his forehead. "I mean, I was looking for you."

Tad's heart dropped a beat. He shouldn't have left him alone. "Are you okay?"

The crown on his head tilted to the side as the kid stumbled closer. His cheeks were still flushed, and now his pupils seemed dilated. Panic jolted through Tad's body.

"Sam, what have you been drinking?"

"Just lemonade." The unmistakable smell of alcohol wafted from Sam's mouth as he slapped Tad's shoulder. "And it was goood."

thirty-one

"Careful." Tad hovered as Sam attempted to fold himself into the Taurus. "Watch your head."

"I don't wanna go home." Sam got his rear end on the seat but kept his legs sticking out of the car as he sulked.

Tad tried to keep his voice calm, though he was raging with fear and fury on the inside. "I know, but it's getting late. The party's over."

It was sort of true. Maddie had rented the west room until midnight, which was still an hour away, but Tad had stormed in there and shouted at the guys Sam had been sitting with, which had effectively killed the party vibe and sent the other guests slinking out the door. He didn't know if those guys were actually to blame or how long Sam had unknowingly been drinking hard lemonade, but the specifics didn't matter at this point.

How could this have happened right under his nose?

Tad had wanted to leave immediately, but when Sam had begged to eat his mashed potatoes, Tad had relented. He figured getting some carbs into the kid's stomach wouldn't hurt. Now, however, it was time to face the music.

"Sam, put your feet in the car."

Sam crossed his arms and stuck out his lower lip. "No."

Tad shook his head as a tight pain formed deep in his chest. How was he ever going to explain this to Dan and Anita?

Maddie's voice came from behind them. "Tad, wait."

He ignored her.

"At least let me load his presents into the car." She came up beside Tad and touched his arm. "Please."

Sam gazed up at her with a lovesick expression. "Hi, Maddie."

Tad jerked his arm away. "I think you've done enough."

He couldn't believe he'd fallen for it. The dancing. The soft words. The "just one more song." It was senior year all over again.

She tugged on his shoulder, trying to get him to turn and look at her. "I didn't do anything. You have to believe me. I had no idea—"

"You had no idea this would happen at the party that was *your* idea, that *you* planned, with people *you* invited?" His voice was harsh and low. "Real nice church friends you got there. The Wilsons trusted you."

Her face hardened. "They trusted you too. You were supposed to be watching him."

"Guys. Hey, guys." Sam struggled to speak, his words slurring. "I'm always watching him."

Tad waved an arm at him and glared at Maddie. "I hope you're happy. Sam, get in the car."

Sam's brow furrowed. "Why're you mad?"

Tad lowered his face to Sam's level and softened his voice. "I'm not mad at you, okay? I'm sorry I yelled. Would you please get in the car? It's time to go home."

Finally, Sam pulled in his legs and shut the passenger door with a bang. Tad stomped around the front of the car, but Maddie slipped around the back and blocked him from reaching his door.

"Please, Tad, I didn't mean for this to happen. I'm sorry."

Tad's thoughts raced in a hundred directions. Maybe she was telling the truth. Maybe it was his own fault for not checking Sam's drink. For leaving Sam in that room without supervision. But it all seemed rather convenient that she had distracted him and lured him away. And it had all been her idea from the beginning.

At least she hadn't said he'd bungled it up. He didn't know if he could take that.

He forced himself to look her in the eye. She looked sad. Stricken. Was that real? The crocodile tears she'd given the principal their senior year had seemed real.

His shoulders drooped. "I don't know what to believe, okay? I need to get him out of here before any more people see him like this."

"Okay." She moved out of Tad's way, and he quickly got into the Ford before she could say anything else. The smell inside the car caused his heart to sink. There would be no hiding the state Sam was in. Dan would be angry and probably fire Tad and feel justified in his earlier doubts about hiring him in the first place. That part was going to suck, big time, but Tad could handle it. It was the thought of facing Anita that made him want to cry.

      ❖❖❖

Tad took his time driving back to the ranch. He was in no hurry to lose his job. How was he going to buy formula for Charlie? Who would watch her if he had to find a different job? How would he even *find* a different job after his long and depressing string of employment fails?

He briefly considered taking Sam to Bud's house and coming

up with some excuse to give the Wilsons about why their son was going to spend the night on Tad's couch, but he quickly dismissed the thought. It was a dumb idea. Even if he could think of a decent excuse, which was unlikely, it was only a matter of time before they found out the truth. There'd been too many witnesses to keep the incident a secret.

"Are we driving slow or fast?" Sam asked.

Despite the grim circumstances, Tad had to chuckle. "Slow."

"Can we go fast?"

"No."

"Huckleberries. I want my birthday presents."

Tad chided himself. He should've let Maddie load them in the car. Sam hadn't even opened them. "We'll get them later. I promise."

"I want my cake."

"I know."

"Were you dancing with Maddie?"

Tad sighed. "Yes."

"She's nice."

Tad didn't respond.

The road that led to the C-A-R turnoff was dark and winding. The Ford's right headlight had burned out two weeks ago, but Tad hadn't replaced it yet, so he gripped the wheel tightly and strained to see ahead of him. The last thing he needed was to hit a deer or a skunk, although the stench might cover up the telltale smell of alcohol coming from Sam.

"Happy birthday to me," Sam sang. "Happy birthday to me. Happy birthday, dear Maddie, happy birthday to me."

Tad shook his head, thankful Sam would probably never understand what had happened to him tonight. Then, a flashing light caught his eye in the rearview mirror, and he groaned.

"Really?"

He pulled over to the side of the road, and Sam turned to look behind them. "I like the police. They're nice."

Tad pressed his lips together. One day Sam was going to learn that not everyone was nice, and maybe it would be good for him, but he didn't feel like tackling that issue right now. He rolled down his window and waited for the officer to make his way to the Ford, his blood pumping hard as he wondered how bad this night was planning to get.

A large man shone a flashlight into the car. "Good evening, gentlemen."

Chief Stubbs. Tad let out the breath he was holding. At least it wasn't Officer Beaumont the Bonehead.

He forced himself to respond. "Hey."

"You got a headlight out, son."

"Yes, sir. I've been meaning to fix it."

"And you were driving pretty slow." The chief bent closer. "You haven't been drinking, have you?"

Tad stifled a growl. "No, sir."

"I was drinking, sirrr," Sam shouted. "Happy birthday to meee!"

Chief Stubbs frowned at Tad and lowered his voice. "Is that true? What's going on here?"

Tad hung his head. There was no point in attempting a cover-up. "It was an accident. Maddie Pine threw him a birthday party at the Oasis, and somebody must've spiked his lemonade with alcohol. Sam didn't know what he was doing, and I—"

He cut himself off. He could hear how ridiculous it sounded. Like one more excuse in a long line of excuses Tad had made to try to keep himself out of trouble over the years. He was unreliable and immature. Everyone knew it. Why would anyone believe him?

The chief leaned his forearm against the top of Tad's door with a sigh. "You've been a good friend to Sam. I'm sure you didn't mean for this to happen."

"I didn't." Tad shook his head, his throat tightening in response to the chief's unexpected compassion. "I promised his parents everything would be fine."

Sam began to fiddle with his seat belt. "Everything's not fine. I don't feel good."

Tad's whole body tensed. Oh no. He pushed the button Sam couldn't quite manage to find to release the latch, and Sam untangled himself from the belt and opened the passenger door just in time. Most of the vomit landed on the side of the road with a sickening splash, but some splattered the inside of the door and Sam's pants.

Sam slumped. "I wanna go home."

"Hold on." Chief Stubbs pushed off the car. "I've got disinfectant wipes in the truck."

Was there anything the chief didn't have in his truck? Tad got out and met the chief on the passenger side. Together they cleaned up Sam and the car the best they could while Sam groaned in misery. Tad helped him get buckled back in and shut the door. The poor kid was going to smell even worse now.

He turned to the chief but was glad it was too dark for him to see his face. "Thanks."

"Ah." The chief waved Tad's words away. "To serve and protect and all that. Always happy to help. Just make sure you get that headlight fixed."

"I will."

"Say, you seen any strange activity around here lately? I got a report about 'suspicious lights' from a concerned citizen." He cupped a hand over his mouth and whispered, "Mrs. Duncan."

"No. I'm not usually over here after dark." Tad wondered how often the police had to drive all the way out here because of Mrs. Duncan.

The chief peered at him intently. "You'll let me know if you notice anything?"

Tad hesitated. "Yeah."

"All right, well, you better get Sam home."

Tad glanced at Sam through the window and cringed. He looked awful.

The older man put a hand on Tad's shoulder. "He's going to be fine, and hopefully he'll forget all about this. But"—He put his hands on his hips and looked north, where they could see the old barn light flickering at Come Around Ranch. "I don't envy you facing the wrath of Anita."

thirty-two

Anita thought she heard a noise and scrambled over to the window, almost stepping on Sabina. The cat protested and stalked off. Outside, the barn light illuminated the parking area and round pen. There was no sign of movement.

"I'm sure they'll be here soon." Dan yawned from the couch and patted the cushion next to him. "Come sit down."

Anita didn't want to sit down. She wanted Sam to come home. About an hour ago, she'd texted a message to Tad that said, "Hope you guys are having fun!" despite Dan's strong suggestion to the contrary. Tad hadn't responded. Hadn't gotten the hint that she was fishing for some kind of status report. Maybe she should've added a couple smiley faces or something.

"Ugh." She plopped down beside her husband. "I can't even remember the last time we stayed up this late."

She was usually in bed by nine thirty. Ten, at the latest. Dan sometimes had to stay up later due to ranch responsibilities, particularly in the summer, but for the most part, he was an early-to-bed-early-to-riser along with her.

Dan looped his arm around her and pulled her closer to him. "Remember how late we used to stay out back in the day?"

It felt like a different life, but she remembered. She and Dan and Bud and some of their other friends would be out until well past midnight the summer after high school. They were never troublemakers. They never did anything too stupid. They just had fun together—roasting marshmallows, throwing rocks in the river, going to the drive-in. Whatever they could find to entertain themselves. Whatever excuse she could think of to be around Bud a little longer.

The nineteen-year-olds they'd been had no idea what life was really like.

"Sometimes it feels so unfair that Sam will never have what we had, you know?" Dan's voice was wistful. "He'll never have a summer like that."

It was hard to think about all the things Sam would never have. Never do.

"Maybe that means he'll never be hurt like we have either."

Dan rubbed her shoulder. "Everyone gets hurt."

Anita heard another noise, and this time she was sure it was the sound of wheels crunching over gravel. When she sprang up from the couch, she could see Tad's car.

"They're back."

Dan pushed off the couch with a grunt and joined her at the front door. She opened it with a smile, but her smile froze somewhere in the vicinity of a grimace. Sam was stumbling as the boys approached the house, and Tad was holding one arm out behind Sam as if he might fall.

"Hey, guys," Dan called.

Sam looked up and wiped his face with his shirt. "I threw up."

Anita exchanged a glance with Dan. This wouldn't be the first time Sam had overdone it with food. He didn't always know when to stop.

Tad kept his eyes focused on his feet as he helped Sam climb the steps. "I'm sorry."

"There's no way you could've known how much food he could handle," Dan said. "No need to be sorry."

Anita took in Sam's bloodshot eyes and the despondent look on Tad's face and felt her heart wobble as intuition kicked in. Was Sam . . . drunk? She put her hand on Dan's arm. "I don't think that's what he meant, dear."

Sam swayed a little, and Dan's eyes widened. "Tad?"

Anger began to bubble up in Anita's chest, and she tried to tamp it down. How could this have happened?

"Tad danced with Maddie," Sam said. "And I drank a lot of lemonade."

Tad looked like he'd stepped on a rusty nail. "I shouldn't have left him. I'm sorry. There was more than lemonade in his glass. I think some of Maddie's friends—"

"Are you saying this is Maddie's fault?" All sorts of unidentifiable emotions surged through Anita's body. "You're going to blame her when she's not here to defend herself?"

"No, I . . . yeah, maybe. I don't know."

"You don't know." She turned to Dan, her voice icy. "I knew this was a bad idea."

Dan scowled at Tad. "Have *you* been drinking?"

"No. Nothing but Mountain Dew, I swear."

"You assured us you would keep your eye on him."

Tad nodded, misery evident on his face. "I know. I'm sorry. I thought—"

"I'm tired, Mom." Sam leaned down to hug Anita, almost knocking her over. "I wanna go to bed."

She patted his back. The poor thing must be feeling horrible. "Just a minute, honey. We're talking to Tad."

Dan rubbed a hand over his face. "It's too late to talk about this right now. I think we all need to go to bed."

Anita bit her tongue. She didn't want to go to bed. She wanted to wring somebody's neck. But Dan was probably right. It was late and everyone was tired. Tad looked like he'd been dragged behind a horse.

She studied him and caught a glimpse of his father in his broody eyes. She hadn't realized how much Tad was starting to resemble Bud as he aged. Her voice softened. "Are you all right to drive home?"

"Yeah." He frowned at Sam. "I'm sorry you got sick."

Sam groaned. "Bye, Tad."

Dan sighed. "Why don't you come by on Monday. We'll talk more then."

Tad dipped his head in response and trudged back to his car, his shoulders slumped. Anita's chest tightened. She couldn't believe he'd let this happen, but she knew he did care about her son. She knew better than anyone that being responsible for Sam could be a heavy burden. She never should've agreed to this party in the first place.

Remorse over her harsh words a minute ago flooded her heart.

"Send me a text when you get home," she called as Tad opened the driver's side door. "So I know you made it."

❧

The house was quiet, and Sam was sound asleep in his bed, but Anita tossed and turned in hers. It wasn't only tonight's events that troubled her too much to allow rest. It was the thought of hundreds, even thousands more nights when she would have to wonder if she was doing everything in her power to keep her son safe. When she would pray with all her might but have no guarantee that Sam would be protected. She'd read the Bible cover-to-cover multiple times and nowhere did it promise sons would always come home. Would always make good choices. Would always be happy.

"Are you all right?" Dan's sleepy voice interrupted the thoughts that threatened to pull her into a downward spiral.

She turned toward him, kicking at the sheets tangling her legs. "Sorry if I'm keeping you awake."

He heaved a sigh. "It's okay. I can't sleep either. I keep think-ing about what might've happened if Tad hadn't been there to bring Sam home."

Anita's eyes widened in the dark. "Nothing would've hap-pened because Sam wouldn't have been out at a party to begin with if it weren't for Tad."

"I don't know about that. Sam's not going to live the rest of his life without ever going to a party. He was lucky he had someone around looking out for him."

"That's what you call what Tad did?"

"Come on. Just because Tad got a little distracted—"

"He promised."

"It sounded like Maddie had a part to play in all this too. We don't know the whole story."

Anita huffed. Maddie was a nice girl trying to do something nice for Sam. She'd heard plenty of tales around town about poor choices Tad had made and the poor company he kept, but never once had she heard a word spoken against Maddie Pine.

Her gut twinged with guilt. Maybe she wasn't being fair to Tad.

"I think Sam got lucky this time, is all," Dan continued. "I think it's important we make sure he has lots of good friends in his life to help keep an eye on him. We can't watch him every minute."

"Why not?" Anita clenched the corner of her pillow. She would happily keep Sam on the ranch within hearing distance of her voice forever.

"Anita." Dan's voice was one part chiding and two parts compassion. "You know that's not possible."

She slid her head over and buried it in his shoulder. "I know. We need to decide on a trustee for Sam's trust. We've been talking about it for ages."

Dan blew out a breath. "Easier said than done."

Anita laid her arm over Dan's chest. They'd talked about this before. Both their parents were in their seventies, which pretty much counted them out. Dan's sister was a lovely woman, but she lived in New Hampshire and could not be expected to uproot her life and move to Montana to supervise Sam and the ranch if something should happen to Dan and Anita. And Anita was an only child.

That left . . . who? She loved and trusted her friend Diana, but Diana already had three grandkids and would likely end up with more in the future. She would have her hands full.

"What about Bill from church?" Dan asked. "He's known Sam his whole life."

Bill was the volunteer youth leader, a single man in his thirties who had grown up in Grady.

"Yes, that could be an option, if he was willing. We should pray about it."

"I have been."

She pulled her head back. "You have?"

"Of course."

She'd been praying about the trustee problem too, especially since talking with Vernon DeVries about the situation with his sons. "Okay, then let's both pray about Bill specifically and see what happens."

"Okay."

"Now what are we going to do about Tad?" She was ashamed to still feel a flash of anger when she said his name. It felt like he had betrayed them.

"I think the only thing there is to do is extend grace."

She wrestled with Dan's words, remembering the way Sam had staggered into the house earlier.

"Mistakes were made," Dan said. "But Tad was repentant, and Sam is going to be fine once he sleeps it off."

The corners of Anita's mouth twitched. "You didn't even want to hire Tad, remember? Now you're sticking up for him?"

"He's growing on me, I guess. Plus"—Dan leaned over and kissed the top of her head—"it's too late to hire someone else for the summer. Every ranch hand in a hundred-mile radius has been snapped up already."

"Oh, you." She playfully smacked his arm. "You're turning into a softie."

He yawned. "Maybe. Or maybe the older I get, the more I see the value of second chances."

"And third and fourth and fifth chances?"

"Well, yes, that's grace, isn't it?"

It was her turn to yawn. They were going to be exhausted tomorrow. "I love you."

"I love you too. And just think." He turned onto his side. "Some parents have their kids coming home drunk *every* Friday night."

No. She squeezed her eyes shut. She didn't want to think about that.

thirty-three

It had been a long and wretched weekend. Tad had refused to leave the house, choosing instead to wallow, imagining what everyone in Grady was probably saying about him and Sam and obsessing over what would happen when he had to "talk more" with Dan. Bud had left him alone for the most part, which suited Tad fine, but Jenna had not.

What r u doing hanging around Maddie Pine?

Small town news traveled fast and loose, far and wide. He'd wanted to respond that it was none of her business, but instead he'd said nothing. Later, Jenna texted again.

I heard u two were pretty cozy at the Oasis

Having people think there was something going on between him and Maddie was the last thing he needed, but at least if people were worked up about that imaginary relationship, they might forget about Sam. People in town, anyway. The Wilsons wouldn't forget. And now it was Monday.

"I guess we better get over there, huh, Charlie-horse?" He scooped up his daughter and blew a raspberry in her neck, which had cleared up since he'd taken Anita's advice. Charlie squealed, her eyes bright, and Tad's heart expanded. He would do anything to keep his job at the ranch. He would beg on his knees in a pile of horse manure. But he had a feeling even that wasn't going to be enough.

The morning was sunny and warm, and the lilacs were beginning to bloom. It would've been easy to feel cheerful, but Tad only felt weighed down and depressed as he parked near the barn at Come Around Ranch and got Charlie out of the car.

Sam must've been watching for him because he came running up before Tad had even closed the passenger door.

"Hi, Tad."

"Hey, how are you feeling?"

"Good. I want to hold Charlie."

"Maybe later. Right now I need to find your dad."

"He's checking the fence between the pasture and the round pen. Tink keeps finding a way through and he thinks she's being sneaky, but I said maybe she's magic."

Tad chuckled. "A magic twenty-four-year-old pony. Sounds about right."

He started walking around the barn to find Dan, and Sam followed. Tad turned around.

"I need to talk to your dad alone this time, okay?"

Sam frowned. "Why?"

"Because."

"I want to come with you."

"I'll find you when I'm done, and you can hold Charlie, okay?"

Sam grumbled. "Okay."

The kid hung back as Tad continued around the barn, but

Tad knew he wouldn't go far. Tad would need to keep his voice down when talking to Dan.

Dan was standing inside the round pen, scratching his head. When he saw Tad, he walked over and leaned his elbows on the fence. "I can't figure it out. There aren't any loose boards or holes or anything, but that darn pony has been waiting in here for me the past three mornings."

Tad set Charlie's carrier on the ground, facing her away from the sun. "Sam told me she's magic."

Dan threw up his hands. "I'm starting to believe it."

An awkward silence fell between them, and Tad shifted on his feet. After a minute, he cleared his throat.

"Look, I'm sorry about what happened Friday night. I would never do anything to hurt Sam."

He wanted desperately to add that he'd thought he could trust Maddie's friends from church, but he knew it would sound like an excuse. He'd never actually talked to those guys at the party, anyway, and had no idea who they were. He was the only one here to take the fall.

Dan climbed over the fence and stood in front of Tad. "We know you wouldn't. We were very disappointed about what happened, but—"

"Please give me another chance." Tad could hear the desperation in his voice. "You can't fire me. I have to take care of Charlie. I promise I'll work extra hard and—"

Dan held up a hand. "You didn't let me finish. We were very disappointed, but we know sometimes things happen. People make mistakes. Life is hard. I'm not going to fire you."

Tad blinked at the ground, repeating Dan's words in his head to make sure he'd heard them correctly. *"I'm not going to fire you."* Could this be real? He'd messed up as trail boss and a guest got injured. He'd chased another paying guest off the property. He was more trouble than he was worth now that Charlie had come along and he needed childcare, and Sam had gotten drunk on his watch. Yet Dan wasn't going to fire him?

"Have you ever heard of grace, Tad?"

Tad raised one shoulder, an uncomfortable lump in his throat. "You mean like in the song? 'Amazing Grace'?"

He'd never been to church, but everyone knew that song. People were always singing it in movies and at funerals and stuff.

"Yes. It's about God's grace that He shows to us. We're also supposed to show that same kind of grace to others. Do you understand what that means?"

"No."

Dan leaned back against the fence and folded his arms. "It means we give people chances and love them even when maybe they don't deserve it."

Tad shifted on his feet. This was getting weird, fast. He wasn't used to hearing people talk about these kinds of things. But Dan's words caused relief to fill his chest, along with the air he felt like he'd been missing all weekend. He took a deep breath.

"I'll work extra hard. I'll put in extra hours."

Dan straightened and clapped Tad's shoulder. "You just keep doing what you've been doing. You're a good worker. We're glad to have you around."

He walked away, but Tad didn't move. No one had ever said that to him before. Not even his own father was glad to have him around. And he wasn't the kind of guy who got second chances. He wasn't smart enough, rich enough, popular enough. He wasn't good-looking or charming or talented. He was nothing but a dumb, scrawny guy with bad teeth and an addiction to Mountain Dew.

Suddenly, he noticed how blue the sky was and how loud the birds were singing.

◆ ◆ ◆

If he would've left ten minutes ago like he'd planned, Tad wouldn't have to face her. But he'd let Sam talk him into a rock kicking competition with Charlie as the judge and now Maddie was here, climbing out of her RX-7 with a white box in her hands.

She held it up. "I brought you a chocolate lava cake from the Oasis, Sam."

He yelped with excitement and stampeded to her car. "What about my presents? Did you bring my presents?"

When she nodded, he threw open the passenger door with a shout and began rooting around.

Maddie turned to Tad. "Hey."

He wasn't ready to talk to her yet, but there was no avoiding it. "Uh, hey. Thanks for bringing everything."

"I didn't think you usually worked on Mondays."

"I don't. I came to talk to Dan."

"Oh." She knelt beside Charlie's carrier. "Hello there, little miss."

Charlie fussed in response.

"She's tired," Tad said. "I should get her home."

He knew she'd probably fall asleep in the car as soon as he started driving. Sam had held her and played with her for almost an hour. Tad grabbed the handle of the carrier and heaved it off the ground. His chubby little Charlie-horse was getting heavier every day.

"See you, Sam," he called.

Sam pulled his head out of the car, and his hair was sticking out all over. "Don't you want to see my presents?"

"You can show me tomorrow."

"Okay." He dove back into the Mazda.

Tad gave a half smile and nodded once at Maddie. "See you."

"I didn't mean for any of this to happen, you know." She took a step toward him. "That wasn't how the party was supposed to go. Those jerks made some kind of arrangement with the waitress. They thought they were being funny."

Tad set the carrier back down. "I thought they were your friends."

She took another step closer and lowered her voice. "I had to take whoever I could get, okay? People weren't too excited about coming to the party until I told them there would be an open bar tab."

Tad winced. "You said people love birthday parties. You said you would take care of everything."

"I already feel bad enough." She pouted. "You don't have to make it worse."

"I almost lost my job, Maddie."

She wrinkled her nose. "I said I was sorry."

He grumbled to himself and thought about Dan and his words about grace. "Fine. I'm sorry too. For freaking out at you that night. Can we make a deal to have Sam's birthday party here next time?"

Her eyes sparked, and she gave him a teasing nudge. "I don't know if I can agree to that. The whole point was for him to have a new experience."

Tad gave her a look. "That wasn't the kind of new experience any of us were hoping for."

She opened her mouth to respond, but Sam appeared beside them, breathless. He held up a small, plastic cat carrier. "Maddie, are you taking Princess home today?"

She nodded. "If that's all right with you. Last week you said she was ready."

"Yes, yes, yes. But first I will show *both* of you my birthday presents." He tilted his head toward Tad. "Please?"

Tad glanced at Charlie and saw she was now sound asleep. She wouldn't need a bottle for about two hours, and she would probably sleep until then.

"All right." He made a grand sweeping gesture toward the Mazda. "Let's see what you got."

thirty-four

The next day was a scorcher. Though it was only early June, the sun beat down on Tad and sweat dripped from his face as he completed jobs around the ranch in record time. He was determined that Dan would not regret keeping him around, and when he'd dropped Charlie off at the house this morning, Anita had given him a banana nut muffin she'd saved for him. She'd set it aside just for him, she said.

He wanted to be worthy of their kindness.

The Mountain Dew in his car was warm, but he washed down an Oberto stick with it anyway. It was going to be a hot trail ride later this afternoon. He should've tried to schedule it for eight or nine this morning when the temperature was more comfortable, but most guests didn't like to get up early. And this week's guests were particularly . . . particular. So much for "an authentic Montana ranch experience."

Ha. He could only imagine how much the guests were going to complain out in this heat. The couple from Las Vegas had already complained that their cabin smelled like grass and the path to the cabin door was too rocky.

Sam and Curly had disappeared somewhere, so Tad decided it was a good time to scout around for more wolf tracks without having to worry about the kid tagging along. He made sure he had his walkie-talkie and headed up past the cabins and toward the fence line. He never did tell Dan about the tracks. It seemed kind of silly now to make a big deal about it. Lots of different creatures passed through here, and they rarely caused problems. They'd all been here first, anyway. If Tad found any new tracks today, however, he should probably mention it, just to be on the safe side.

From the top of the hill, he could see dark clouds forming to the southwest. It was thunderstorm season, and those clouds looked like they could bring hail. He might not have to worry about the trail ride after all. As he approached the fence line, he scanned around for wolf tracks or anything else unusual. A granola bar wrapper was stuck in a tumbleweed, and his brow furrowed. Why did the guests keep coming up here? It wasn't that the area was off limits. It just seemed odd because there was nothing to do. Nothing to see.

Well, out-of-towners were unpredictable. Maybe they liked the cows. He pulled the wrapper loose and shoved it in his pocket to throw away and that's when he saw them. Fresh tracks. Definitely wolf. Dan had shown him where he kept a .22 locked up on the top shelf of the mudroom, and Tad wondered if he should've brought it with him. Not that he would try to kill a wolf with a .22, but the gun would scare a predator off if needed.

After a moment's hesitation, he followed the tracks. The chances of encountering the wolf were slim to none, as they avoided humans whenever possible. He trekked over the uneven ground for about half a mile and stopped when he noticed a run-down outbuilding. He'd never been to this corner of the property before. The structure looked like an old shed.

Tad hurried toward it. The shed had clearly been abandoned for a while, and he could clean it out and take it apart. Maybe this was something he could do for Dan. A guy could make good money selling weathered wood to builders and people who made custom rustic furniture. Or maybe Dan would want to use the wood to build something himself.

When he reached the shed, though, his senses kicked into high alert. There was a cigarette butt on the ground and a shiny padlock on the door that appeared much newer than the rest of the building. Maybe Dan *did* use this shed. Was he hiding something out here?

No, that wouldn't make sense. Dan hated cigarettes. He didn't allow smoking on the ranch, and he didn't seem like the kind of guy to have a secret shed. Who else would have access to this place? The Richardsons could reach it through the fence, but it was a long way from their house. The only other house within walking distance was . . . his father's.

Tad shook his head to keep his imagination from running wild. There was probably a logical explanation for all this. Yet he remembered how Mrs. Duncan had reported "suspicious lights" to Chief Stubbs and felt a fist of dread form in his stomach.

He looked around and listened but noticed no other clues. The wind began to kick up as the storm clouds lumbered closer and dust swirled around his boots. What was in the shed? There were no windows, but some of the boards had wide-enough gaps between them that he could peer inside. He pressed his face to one of them and squinted.

The interior was dark. Thunder rumbled in the distance. Though some sunlight shone through the cracks in shafts, most of the inside was too shadowy to tell if anything was in there. But something must be. Something valuable, by the look of that hefty padlock. He moved to a different spot and peeked again, and his mouth went dry. There appeared to be a stack of bags or boxes or something in there, but what caught his attention and made the blood freeze in his veins was the light glinting off a can of Rainier beer.

❦

Tad had wrestled with himself all the way home. After his discovery, he should've gone straight to the Wilsons' house and told Anita what he'd seen. Really, he should have. But some sort of twisted sense of loyalty kept him from doing that. He figured he should at least give his dad a chance to explain himself, right? Maybe Bud wasn't even involved in whatever this was. Maybe Tad was totally off base.

Then there was Tad's own situation to consider. The Wilsons had no reason to trust him at this point. What would they think? Would they even believe his reason for being out in the far corner of the property, anyway? He wouldn't, if he were in their shoes.

He pulled up to Bud's house and sat with the car running for a minute. Bud wasn't home yet. Tad had left work a little earlier than usual because the trail ride had been cancelled, as he'd anticipated. Lightning and equines did not mix.

"What should we do, Charlie-horse?"

She didn't answer, but he could hear her kicking her feet. She loved to move. With a heavy sigh, Tad turned off the Ford. A few fat drops of rain spattered the windshield.

"We better get inside."

He covered Charlie's carrier with a blanket so she wouldn't get wet and scrambled into the house as the skies opened up.

A strong gust of wind slammed the screen door shut, and rain fell in sheets.

"Whew. Just in time."

Inside was hot and stuffy, so he left the main door open and pushed the front windows open as well, allowing the smell of rain into the house. Through the roar of the rainfall, he heard Bud's truck pull up, and Tad growled to himself. He wasn't ready. He didn't know what to say. He didn't want to start a fight.

"What should we do?" he asked again. Charlie kept kicking her legs. He pulled her out of the car seat in the middle of the living room and tucked her against his side, facing the door. That's how Bud found him when he plowed into the house, wiping water from his face.

He gave Tad a suspicious look. "What're you doing?"

Tad shifted on his feet. Was it any of his business what his dad was up to or what was happening on C-A-R property or who was involved in what? He had more than enough of his own problems to worry about. He had never been in the habit of poking his nose where it didn't belong. Whenever his friends had been up to no good, he always looked the other way and expected them to do the same for him. An unspoken agreement.

But this didn't feel the same. He'd already let Dan and Anita down so many times. After all they'd done for him . . .

A loud clap of thunder shook the house.

Bud tossed his keys on the side table with a scowl. "You get in trouble at work again or something?"

"I, uh . . . I . . ."

Bud snorted and brushed by him, giving Charlie's foot a squeeze as he passed. He was halfway in the kitchen when Tad finally found his voice.

"I found something today."

Bud stopped. His back was to Tad, but Tad's gut told him his words had made Bud nervous.

"What do you mean you found something?"

Emboldened, Tad raised his chin. "Something at the ranch, in the southwest corner."

Bud's back and shoulders tensed. Still, he didn't turn around.

Tad tried to sound confident. "You know anything about that?"

Slowly, Bud turned to face him. The dark glint in his eye was all too familiar to Tad, and Tad fought the urge to take a step back.

"You don't know what you saw," Bud said.

Tad swallowed, any doubt he'd been clinging to gone. "I know you've been out there. I know you know about the shed. I'm not stupid."

Bud laughed derisively. "I don't know about that. But fine. You got me. I know about the shed. So what?"

"What's in there?"

Bud's eyes darkened even more as he came closer, and Tad instinctively shifted to put himself between Bud and Charlie. A bolt of lightning struck nearby, so close he could hear it sizzle.

Bud fixed his gaze on the baby. "You need to think about your daughter. What's in that shed has nothing to do with you. If you know what's good for you, you'll forget about it."

Tad wavered. "But if the Wilsons find out—"

"If you want to keep living in this house, they're not going to find out. You got it?"

Charlie whimpered, and Tad realized he was holding her too tight. He relaxed his grip and gave her a little bounce as his mind raced. If Bud was keeping something bad in that shed, the Wilsons needed to know about it.

"I'm not going to lie to them."

"Don't lie then. Just don't mention it."

"But—"

"What do you think would happen if I told them you knew about it all along, huh?" Bud poked his finger into Tad's chest. "If I told them the only reason you applied for a job at their ranch was so you could have easy access to that shed? That the whole thing was your idea?"

Panic flooded his heart. No. No! They would think Tad had betrayed them. They would think . . .

"You can't do that. Please." He hated the pleading in his voice, but he hated the thought of Anita looking at him with sadness and disappointment in her eyes even more.

Bud glared at him for a long, painful minute. The downpour stopped as suddenly as it had begun, and a heavy silence filled the house.

Charlie waved her arms around. "Ba-ba-ba."

Bud glanced at her and something inscrutable rippled across his face, like the passing of a storm. Then his jaw twitched, and he turned away. His voice sounded different when he spoke. "You have to forget about this. All of it. For Charlie's sake."

He stomped into the kitchen, leaving Tad gaping after him. In a daze, Tad pulled his daughter up to his shoulder and pressed his cheek to hers. Her skin was soft and warm, and she smelled like shampoo and drool and all of Tad's hopes and dreams.

"Don't worry, Charlie-horse." He rocked back and forth as she pressed into him. "Daddy will find a way out of this."

But his heart did not—could not—believe.

thirty-five

Driving home from the Coalition on Thursday, Anita's heart was heavy. Vernon hadn't stopped in, and he hadn't been at Coffee Break on Tuesday either. She hoped he was okay. Hoped his crops had survived the hailstorm the other day. Hoped he'd found a way to get his sons to sit down and talk about the future.

But Vernon wasn't the main thing on her mind. The Coalition had received an email from a woman named Kerry who wrote that she suspected her father-in-law, a dairy farmer in nearby Broadwater County, was severely depressed. She worried about what he might do.

Anita's job as a volunteer was to funnel those types of emails to the appropriate person, in this case one of the licensed counselors who donated their time to the Coalition. The counselor would follow up with Kerry and try to work with her to get her father-in-law the help he needed. Anita was thankful for the counselors, but it was hard not being able to do anything in these situations. It was hard to sit on the sidelines and hope for the best when she wanted to call Kerry right this minute and drag her over to her father-in-law's house to give him hugs and homemade cookies.

The thought that he might do something everyone would regret before anyone could intervene caused tears to sting the back of her eyes.

"Lord, I don't even know this man's name, but I don't want him to hurt himself. And I know he probably needs more than hugs and cookies, but I'm sure hugs and cookies wouldn't hurt, would it? Please send someone to brighten his day. Maybe get him to talk. Right now, if possible, please. Kerry said he never takes a day off and rarely leaves the farm, so they're going to have to go up there and track him down." Anita took a deep breath. "You know all that already, of course. I just feel so helpless."

She turned down the C-A-R driveway and felt a stirring in her spirit. She was wrong to say that. She was never helpless as long as she could pray, so that's what she would do. She would pray for this man every day, and for Kerry too. It had taken courage to send that email.

Anita parked and slowly climbed the front steps, her knees protesting.

"Hi, Mom." Sam's voice made her jump as he appeared around the corner of the house, followed by Curly. "Did you do a good job volunteering?"

She sighed on the inside. He always asked her that, but it felt like an impossible question to answer. Especially today.

"I did my best."

"Can I go with you next time?"

She hesitated. He'd bounced back from the birthday party incident and was no longer avoiding her as he had last week. She didn't want to go back to him acting like she was the bad guy. "You want to volunteer with me?"

She heard a hint of hope in her voice. It seemed like they

hardly spent any quality time together anymore. Maybe this could be a way to do that. She missed the way it used to be between them.

"No." Sam made a face like he smelled something rotten. "I want to go to town while *you* volunteer."

She had to work hard to keep her own face from giving anything away. "What do you mean? What do you need to do in town?"

"I want to hang out. I could walk around and stuff." He grabbed onto the porch railing and swung himself back and forth the way he'd been doing since he was little, only now Anita worried the railing would give way to his weight.

"Stop pulling on that."

"I'm not pulling. I'm hanging."

"Well, then, stop hanging."

He huffed and let go of the rail. "Can I go with you next time?"

Her heart squeezed. How could she let him wander around town for two hours by himself after what just happened? Any number of things could go wrong. "I'll have to talk with your dad about it."

He grumbled. "That's what you say when you want *him* to tell me no."

"Sam." She put a hand to her chest. "That's not fair. I need to—"

"Bye, Mom." He spun around and headed for the barn. "Come on, Curly."

She opened her mouth, then closed it. Held up a hand toward him, then put it down. What had gotten into him? He'd never acted like this before.

He kicked at a rock and shouted at the top of his lungs,

anger in his voice. "One, two, three, four, five, six, seven, eight, niiine."

An uncomfortable feeling swirled around somewhere between her chest and her stomach. It felt like her life was spinning out of control. But she heard Charlie crying inside the house and shook her head. She would have to think about Sam later.

Maddie was walking the floor with Charlie on her hip when Anita opened the door. Charlie's face was tear-streaked and red.

"Oh my. Come here, sweetheart." She reached out her arms. "Tell Miss Anita what's the matter."

Maddie let Anita take the baby with a relieved sigh. "She's been fussy almost the whole time, I don't know what it is. She didn't even want her bottle."

Anita held Charlie close. "Are you having a hard day?"

Charlie whimpered and buried her face in Anita's shirt. Anita gave Maddie a sympathetic smile. "Maybe she's getting a tooth. Sam was always a wreck when he was about to pop a tooth."

Maddie picked up her purse. "Maybe."

"Do you have time for a glass of iced tea before you go?"

On Monday, Maddie had dropped off gifts for Sam but never came in the house. On Tuesday, she'd arrived at the last minute and bolted out the door the moment Anita got home. Anita knew the young woman was probably trying to dodge talking about the birthday party, but it had been almost a week since the incident and Anita didn't want Maddie to spend the rest of the summer trying to avoid her. She got enough of that from Sam.

Maddie glanced at the door, then set down her purse, resigned. "Okay."

Charlie continued to fuss, but when Anita put her in the bouncer and handed her a teether ring to chew on, she calmed down. As Anita poured two glasses of iced tea, she decided to start with an easy question.

"How's Princess adjusting to her new home?"

Maddie groaned as she slid into a chair at the table and accepted a glass from Anita. "That cat. She gets into everything. My mother said Princess will have to live outside with Jasper—that's my puppy—if I can't keep her from scratching the furniture."

Anita slid Charlie's bouncer closer to the table and sat where she could bounce the seat with her foot. "Have you tried a spray bottle?"

"That's what I was going to pick up on my way home today. And a brush for shedding."

Anita chuckled inwardly at the thought of Teresa Pine picking white cat hair off a pair of fancy black slacks. "That should do the trick."

"My mom isn't overly fond of animals."

This didn't surprise Anita. Animals were messy and difficult to control. Not the kind of thing Teresa appreciated. "How's it going living at home?"

Maddie shrugged. "My parents aren't there very much. They're always busy."

"Are you still thinking of going to college in the fall?"

Maddie clinked a fingernail against the glass. Clink, clink, clink. "I haven't decided."

She seemed anxious. Whether it was due to talking about college or because of the elephant in the room called *Sam's Birthday Party*, Anita couldn't tell.

"Which colleges have you looked at?"

Maddie shrugged.

"Is there something in particular you'd like to study?"

Maddie's face brightened a little. "I want to be an attorney." The brightness faded. "I don't know if I could do it, though. I heard law school is really hard."

"Of course you could do it."

"My dad says he's not going to pay for school unless I'm sure I'll 'follow through and be successful.'" Her imitation of her father's voice included a hint of bitterness.

Anita pressed her lips together. No wonder Maddie was hesitant to commit to going to school.

Charlie began to fuss again, and Anita lifted her from the bouncer to hold her on her lap. Clear snot ran from her little nose. "Well, I think you'd make a great attorney. And you could always find a way to pay for it yourself if you don't want to worry about meeting your dad's expectations."

Maddie fidgeted with her glass and studied the table. "Yeah, maybe."

"I can see this is weighing on you. I'm going to pray about it."

Maddie looked up, a flash of panic in her eyes. "Right now?"

Anita chuckled. "I don't have to do it right now. I just wanted you to know I'm going to add it to my list of prayer requests. God cares about you and your future, and so do I."

Maddie shifted, clearly uneasy as silence fell between them. Anita could only imagine what the young woman was thinking. She and her parents had attended the same church as the Wilsons for years, but God and prayer did not seem like a comfortable topic for her. Anita wasn't sure God or prayer were *ever* comfortable topics, or if they were supposed to be.

After a long minute, Anita stood to grab a tissue for Charlie's nose. When she returned to the table, Maddie's expression showed a sense of seriousness and resolve.

"I'm sorry about Friday night." She sounded like a little girl who'd been shoring up the courage to confess to stealing from her mother's purse.

Anita sighed. "Thank you, dear. I know it wasn't your fault."

"Yes, it was." Maddie leaned forward. "I'm the one who invited those guys."

"Tad was the one responsible for watching Sam."

"He did. I mean, he tried. You should blame me, not him."

Anita snuggled Charlie closer and pondered Maddie's words, surprised by the girl's vehemence. "I don't necessarily blame anyone, dear. I'm hoping all of us who care about Sam learned a lesson from the situation. It's easy to forget how much Sam depends on us to help him."

Maddie squirmed, and again Anita found herself wondering what was going through her mind. Was she trying to cover for Tad? Did she realize how devoted Sam was to her?

"I'll be more careful next time," Maddie said.

Anita buried her face in Charlie's wild, dark curls, the words *next time* echoing through her brain. There wouldn't be a next time, if she had anything to say about it.

thirty-six

I like it when I'm the only one awake. This is my third time staying up and going outside real quiet and I left Curly behind again but I took a flashlight and a granola bar like last time. I don't turn the flashlight on until I get past the cabins and over the hill because I don't want to wake anyone up and I don't want anyone to see me and I like to see how good I can walk around in the dark.

When I get to the fence I can hear some cows and I moo back but not loud. I wonder how long it would take to walk to town from here because I want to go but Mom and Dad said no. They think I'm a baby but my new friends from the party said I was cool and should go hang out with them sometime. They were really nice and didn't know that lemonade was going to make me throw up.

I turn on my flashlight and walk south a little ways because I'm pretty sure that's the way to town but after a few minutes I stop because I remember no one would be in town right now because it's night and everything would be closed. Mr. Bill always says nothing good happens after midnight but I'm pretty sure coming out here is good so maybe he's wrong.

I go a little farther because I think I should walk to town

anyway for practice so I can go by myself sometime but then I stop again because I hear a noise. It's not a cow. It's like a door or something. I see a light up ahead and it's moving around and my heart feels funny. I think I want to go home now but then a guy says, "Who's there?"

I don't know if he's talking to me and I breathe hard and drop my flashlight and when I pick it up again the other light is really close.

"Tad, is that you?"

The light shines in my face and I hold a hand up to cover my eyes and I shake my head because I'm not Tad and my heart is beating so fast I think I might be sick.

"Sam?"

There's a man and he holds a flashlight up to his face and says, "What are you doing out here?"

My heart calms down a little bit because I've seen this man before but when I try to talk nothing comes out.

"Sam, it's me, Bud. Tad's dad."

Tad doesn't talk about his dad because he doesn't talk about anything but I've seen Bud lots of times. Suddenly I feel like I can breathe again and I think about how fun it would be if Tad was here too and I ask if he is but Bud says no and shakes his head.

"Are you looking for him?" I ask because I think maybe Tad likes to walk around at night like me and then I get another idea and get excited. "Are you playing a game?"

One time at church when I was still in high school we played a game in the dark with flashlights and it was really fun and at the end we were supposed to find Mr. Bill and it was hard because he was a really good hider.

"Uh, yeah," Bud says.

"Can I play too?"

"No. It's time to go home. But this game is a secret so you can't talk to anyone about it, not even Tad, okay? You gotta keep it between us."

I nod because I know all about "between us" now because of Tad and Maddie. I hold up my pinkie and Bud looks at it and I say, "Pinkie promise, right?" and he nods and holds out his pinkie too. I link it with mine and smile because I can't believe I have *another* pinkie promise and I ask if maybe next time I can play the game and Bud says maybe but only if I keep my promise.

"Tad will tell me if you don't, and then you can't play," Bud says.

Bud is nice if he's going to let me play and I don't want to tell Mom and Dad anyway because they might say no so I say, "Okay."

"You better get on home."

I feel pretty tired now so I say bye and turn off my flashlight and walk all the way home in the dark. In the mudroom I whisper my new secret in Curly's ear and he licks my face because he's happy when I get to do fun things because he loves me even if he can't do it. It seems like he's panting hard and he groans when he puts his head back down so I lay next to him and carefully set my hand on his shoulder and close my eyes.

thirty-seven

As soon as Tad saw Anita return from the Coalition on Tuesday at eleven thirty, he planted himself in the shadow of a tree near Maddie's car. He had to talk to her. It had been a week since he'd discovered Bud was up to something on C-A-R property. A week since his dad had threatened to kick him and Charlie out of the house if he said anything. Moving out seemed like the only way he could even consider taking the risk of telling Dan and Anita what he'd found, but to move out . . . he needed Maddie's help.

He'd wanted to talk to her last Thursday but had chickened out. What if she'd changed her mind about helping him look for a rental after what happened on Sam's birthday? They'd seemed to reach a tentative truce the day she brought Sam's gifts, but that didn't mean she was willing to give him any more of her time. For all he knew, her offer had only been part of a ploy to distract him that night. He still didn't know if he could trust her.

What he did know was that he had to get out from under Bud's roof as soon as possible.

The front door of the house opened, and Maddie stepped out, glancing back over her shoulder to wave at Charlie and Anita. She looked so young in her denim cutoffs and flip-flops. As she made her way to her car, he strolled out of the shade and tried to act nonchalant.

"Hey."

She'd been checking her phone as she walked and startled at his voice. She dropped her phone in her purse and studied him. "Hey."

"How was Charlie today?"

"A lot better now that her tooth popped out. Poor thing."

His daughter had spent all weekend moping until finally on Monday morning a tiny bit of white had poked through her bottom gum. Her first tooth. He'd sent a picture to Jenna, and she'd sent back a video message telling Charlie how she was such a big girl now and Mommy was so proud. Tad had reluctantly shown Charlie the video but had regretted it. Hearing her mother's voice had only confused her.

To be honest, he was pretty confused himself. Two nights ago, he'd dreamed that Jenna was living in the loft of the barn but there was no ladder, so no one could go up and she couldn't come down.

He shook his head. He needed to deal with one problem at a time.

"Uh, thanks again for watching her."

Maddie fiddled with the bottom of her shirt. "You don't have to keep thanking me. I like doing it."

A long moment passed as he tried to talk himself into bringing up the offer Maddie had made at the birthday party. Now was the time, before Sam showed up. Tad didn't want to talk about moving in front of the kid.

"I should go," Maddie said. "I need to make sure Princess isn't tearing the house apart. She goes crazy when I'm gone."

Tad gulped. "Wait. I need to ask you something."

Maddie tilted her head and raised an eyebrow.

Tad adjusted his hat, then shoved his hands in his pockets.

"Uh, remember when we were talking about rentals in town? And you said sometimes your dad finds out about vacancies before they go on the market?"

Maddie laughed. "You're pretty serious about moving, huh?"

"Yeah. We need to get out of Bud's house."

She mulled that over with a frown, her arms wrapped around herself. "I don't like living with my parents either."

It kind of seemed like she was talking to herself, so Tad wasn't sure if he should respond. Then she straightened and flicked her hair.

"Tell you what, I'll talk to my dad tonight. If we're lucky, we might even be able to look at some places this weekend."

Hope swelled in his chest. "Really? You're not too busy?"

He had imagined her spending the weekend gallivanting around, maybe driving to Bozeman to shop or going to the movies with friends. She'd always been the most popular girl in school.

"No." She looked off into the distance, as if studying something. "I'm not busy. I'll text you when I get something lined up."

After she left, he looked up at the sky. It sure seemed more than lucky that Maddie happened to be in a position to help him not only with Charlie but also with house hunting. Were Anita's prayers behind all this? He wasn't about to pray himself, but he was glad if Anita was. She didn't even know he was looking for a new place, though, did she? He looked at the sky again.

Huh. With all her talking to God . . . maybe she did.

He heard loud laughter coming from inside the barn, followed by a thud, and then a surprised, "Holy huckleberries."

He chuckled to himself and hurried off to make sure Sam was okay.

◆ ▾ ◆

Tad heard the words Bud was saying, but he struggled to make sense of them. "You want me to do *what*?"

Bud glowered. "Don't make this a big deal. All you gotta do is keep everyone on the east side of the cabins tomorrow morning during the hunt. Especially the kid. We don't need anyone getting in the way."

Tad clenched his fists, thankful Charlie was already in bed. "Who's 'we'?"

"That doesn't matter. Just do it."

"They're going to notice a helicopter."

"Then tell them it's a sightseeing tour."

Tad's body trembled with barely contained rage. Aerial wolf hunts were a contentious issue in Montana. The state's Department of Fish, Wildlife, and Parks seemed to say it was legal under certain circumstances. The federal law seemed to say it wasn't. Either way, Tad was positive the hunt Bud had planned for tomorrow was against the law and posed a greater danger to the ranch than a lone gray wolf.

"I never should've told you about the tracks."

Bud snorted. "Doesn't matter now. Someone is paying a lot of money for this, and I need you to do your part."

He didn't say the words *or else*, but Tad heard them all the same. Bud had the upper hand, and not only with his ability to kick Tad and Charlie out onto the street if he wanted to. Since Tad never told Dan about the wolf tracks, he knew what it would look like if Bud got caught hunting and told the Wilsons Tad had scouted the wolf for him. He kicked himself for never bringing it up to Dan. He was an idiot.

Tad felt like he was falling deeper and deeper into a hole but didn't know how to get out. He would never do something like this to Charlie. Never put her in this kind of position. Parents were supposed to protect their kids, right? The thought of looking at rentals with Maddie this weekend was the only thing keeping him from losing it. And the fact he and Bud both knew it was unlikely anyone would pay much attention to the sound of a helicopter in the distance. With an international airport and two major hospitals within a hundred-mile radius, the people of Grady were accustomed to seeing all kinds of aircraft.

"Fine." He didn't want Bud to see how upset he was. "I'll try."

"You'll do better than try. This guy's liable to shoot at anything that moves. He wants the wolf bad. Got it?"

Tad's jaw twitched as he gritted his teeth. "Got it."

Was that what his dad had hidden in that shed? Guns and other gear so yuppies from out of state could hunt illegally? And who was Bud's partner in all this?

He stomped outside for a cigarette, hating himself for giving in to the urge and for not daring to ask any of his questions out loud. He had no choice but to bide his time until he could find a place to live and come up with a backup plan in case he lost his job once the Wilsons found out about whatever was going on with Bud. For all Dan's talk about grace, Tad knew this was a whole different level of betrayal. Dan had been right all this time not to trust Tad. And Tad had been wrong to convince himself he would never let Dan down.

He took a drag as he thought of all the food and kindness Anita had given him and felt sick to his stomach. Had it been part of her prayers in recent weeks that Tad would be a good employee, a good friend to Sam, a good dad? If so, it was perfectly clear to him that God was not listening.

thirty-eight

Anita couldn't remember the last time she and Dan and Sam had all stopped at Sloppy Joe's together for lunch. On a Saturday, no less, like normal people. It almost felt like old times, except—

"Mom, please?" Sam begged for the hundredth time. "I can walk home later by myself."

"It's seven miles," Dan said. "And it's almost ninety degrees."

Sam shoved a fistful of French fries in his mouth. "I don't care."

Anita pushed her southwest salad around her plate. She had no idea where Sam's obsession with "hanging out in town" had come from, but it was troubling. Would he know what to do if there was an emergency? They hadn't brought along the walkie-talkies. What if a stranger offered him a ride? She wanted to believe he knew better than that, but she'd also believed he knew enough to be suspicious of strange-tasting lemonade.

The fact was that there was a lot he didn't know and would never understand. The fact was he was always going to be a child. But she didn't like to treat him like a little kid. Dan reached over and squeezed her hand with a knowing look.

She cleared her throat. "Your father has to get back to the ranch, but if there's someplace you want to go, I'd be happy to take you when we're done eating."

Sam slurped at the bottom of his milkshake and shook his head. "No, thanks."

"I could use your help back at home, anyway," Dan said. "I've got to install that new latch system on the round pen gate, remember?"

Anita chuckled. After two weeks of Tinkerbell magically appearing in the round pen every morning, Dan had finally caught her in the act. She'd learned how to open and, more impressively, close the gate. He'd bought a more complex latch this morning at the hardware store with the hope of outsmarting her.

Sam didn't answer but seemed resigned to the plan. He slumped in the bench seat across from her. Were they doing the right thing by imposing so many restrictions on his life? She'd asked God for wisdom about this issue so many times that she wondered if He'd answered already and she missed it. Parents were supposed to protect their children and guide them and provide for them. They were also supposed to prepare them for a life without parents, but what did that look like when a child was never going to be able to live independently?

She and Dan were planning to talk with Bill tomorrow at church about the need for a trustee to be appointed for Sam's trust. Someone who would always look out for Sam's best interest. They had decided not to ask Bill outright to consider the role but instead would ask if he had any suggestions. They were hoping his response would give them an idea of how open he would be to taking on that role himself. They would prefer to find someone who would willingly and voluntarily take on the responsibility so they wouldn't have to worry about anyone feeling obligated or coerced.

A man walking by their table caught Anita's attention. It was Jake DeVries, Vernon's oldest son. His face was pinched and drawn as he joined a half dozen other farmers at a large round table in the corner. They all nodded in greeting and Jake wearily leaned his elbows on the table like a man carrying the weight of the world on his shoulders. Or the weight of a nine-hundred-acre farm.

Again, she felt a sense of helplessness, like after she'd read that email from Kerry about her father-in-law in Broadwater County. All these people were hurting, and there was nothing she could do about it. She couldn't even figure out what was best for her own son, let alone Vernon's, and her prayers were beginning to feel empty and futile. That had never happened before, and she didn't like it.

Dan caught her staring at the farmer's table and gave her a supportive look. She'd told him about all of Vernon's visits to the Coalition, knowing he would never mention it to anyone.

"You ready to go?" he asked.

They paid their bill and walked back to the car, Sam dragging his feet and hanging back. Anita tried hard to keep herself from looking at him every other step.

"Are you worried about him?" Dan asked quietly.

She pushed back hair from her face. "And Vernon, and his sons, and that depressed dairy farmer. Not to mention Tad and Charlie and—" She caught herself before she could say *Bud*. Dan knew about her history with that man, knew she still cared about his wellbeing, but he preferred not to talk about him.

Dan took hold of her hand. "You can't save everyone."

But she wanted to.

Tad gazed down at his daughter in his arms as she finished her bottle. She was beautiful in the bright blue and yellow sundress Anita had bought her. Like a butterfly. He kept telling Anita she didn't need to buy Charlie clothes, but she kept doing it anyway. It seemed to make her happy, so he wasn't going to protest too much. He wouldn't know what to pick out if he did it himself.

Maddie sat beside them on the park bench, the only place they could find in the shade to take a break from their house hunting. "Whew, it's hot today."

Tad sat Charlie up to burp and nodded. "Supposed to be ninety-four tomorrow."

That was hot for Montana in June, and it didn't bode well for fire season later in the summer.

"Did you hear about Scooter MacDonald?" Maddie asked.

Tad stiffened at the name. "No."

"They've got a warrant out for his arrest, but no one knows where he is. Probably skipped town."

"A warrant for what?"

"A bunch of stuff, I heard. He beat up some girl, and they found drug paraphernalia in his house. I think he stole someone's car too."

Tad couldn't say he was surprised. He gently rubbed Charlie's back and hoped Chief Stubbs would find Scooter soon and throw the book at him. Throw it hard. That guy had always given him the creeps. Not that Tad had the right to judge anyone else after everything he'd done. It had made him want to puke the other day when he'd lied and told Sam the helicopter they heard was probably an emergency Life Flight. *"Oh, huck-leberries,"* Sam had said with a frown. *"I'll tell Mom to pray for the person they picked up."*

Tad hadn't asked Bud if they shot the wolf or not. He didn't want to know.

Maddie reached for Charlie. "Here, let me burp her. You're taking too long."

She took the baby from Tad and propped her on her shoulder, then stood and paced while pounding on her back. Tad might've winced at how hard she was smacking her if Charlie wasn't smiling so big.

"She likes you."

Maddie kissed Charlie's cheek. "I like her too."

Charlie giggled and then produced a giant burp, followed by a stream of spit-up that cascaded down the back of Maddie's green, silky-looking shirt.

Maddie gasped. "You little stinker."

Tad laughed. "That's what you get for rushing her."

He pulled some wipes out of Charlie's diaper bag and held them out to Maddie, but she shook her head. "I can't reach. You're going to have to do it."

As he tentatively dabbed at the mess on her back, his mind flashed back to the slow dance they'd shared at the Oasis. It had been nice, holding her like that. He would've never expected a girl like her to be so good at caring for babies. It was beautiful when she smiled at his daughter.

"I'm sorry about your shirt."

Maddie rubbed noses with Charlie and spoke in a baby voice. "It doesn't matter, does it, little miss? No, it doesn't."

"Ba-ba-ba." Charlie's arms flailed around and whacked Maddie's nose.

Maddie pretended to pout. "Ow."

"She's out to get you today." Tad packed up the diaper bag and took Charlie back to get her settled in her car seat. "Where are we going next?"

They'd looked at two apartments already. It had been kind of awkward because the tenants had still been living in them, but Maddie had assured him they were both planning to move out by the end of the month. The apartments had been . . . fine. Small. In his price range. But neither of them had offered much of a place for a kid to play.

"I've only got one more option for you at the moment." Maddie climbed into the passenger seat. "It's not in the greatest shape, so don't get your hopes up."

It was too late for that. His hopes were way up as he followed Maddie's directions to the next place and imagined living on his own, away from his dad and all his demands. Just him and Charlie. He swallowed. Just him and Charlie? What if he couldn't do it? What if something happened to him?

He gripped the wheel. What if something happened to *Charlie*? Being a father had opened up a whole new part of his brain that he'd never tapped into before. The part that ran through nightmare scenarios over and over and laid awake at night worrying about someone other than himself. How long could he give Charlie what she needed? And what about the thing she needed that he might never be able to give her?

A mother.

Maddie pointed. "Turn right there."

He turned and drove down a short gravel lane that ended in front of a run-down single-wide trailer. Weeds grew up around it, and the screen door leaned against the side, having been removed at some point and never put back.

Tad hardly noticed those details. All he could see was the patchy grass stretched out for yards and yards on either side. The huge cottonwood tree with branches shaped perfectly for holding a small fort. The kind he'd always wanted as a kid.

"I know it doesn't look like much," Maddie said. "But I was told it's clean inside and there's a swing set out back."

He opened his door and listened. It was quiet. "I love it."

She came to stand beside him. "It's only six hundred dollars a month. It's been empty for a while because it looks like a dump. And there are a lot of mice out here, I guess. You'd need a cat or two. I couldn't get a key, but do you want to poke around?"

He quickly unbuckled Charlie and gestured for Maddie to lead the way. As they peered through the windows and laughed at the shag carpet in the living room and carefully avoided the rotted-out back steps, deep in his heart Tad couldn't help but imagine a different life for himself. A normal life with a nice, little family and a happy, little home. Why not? Why couldn't he have that?

Well, he could think of plenty of reasons. He understood that he didn't deserve it.

But Charlie did.

thirty-nine

Anita hugged Charlie to her hip with one hand and tried to move wet sheets from the washer to the dryer with the other. This was a Friday job she usually asked Sam to do, but when he'd hurried outside after breakfast this morning without a glance back, she'd let him go. All week she'd felt the strain between them, and she didn't have it in her to ask him to stay at the house and help her when he clearly wanted to be somewhere else.

Anywhere else.

The oven timer beeped, and she wrinkled her nose at Charlie. "The muffins are done. Good thing we set that timer, or we would've forgot all about it."

She abandoned the laundry and plodded to the kitchen, the pain in her knees keeping her pace slow and steady. She peeked into the oven and set the timer for three more minutes, then heard her phone ding.

She looked around. "Oh dear, where'd I leave it this time?"

After a minute of searching, she located the phone in Charlie's diaper bag. There was another message from the incoming Cabin B guests. This was the third time they'd texted her so far today to "double-check" on something. First it had been to ask if they could check in an hour early, then to ask what specific plants were in bloom in the area this time of year.

She puffed out a breath. "Let's see what they need this time." She read the message and snorted.

Are your cabins stocked with spatulas? And if so, are they made from plastic, metal, or silicone?

"I don't know if anyone's ever used the spatulas in the cabins, Charlie." Anita shook her head. "I can't remember what kind they are."

Charlie squirmed. "Ba-ba-ba."

"Do you want down?" Anita groaned as she bent to set the baby on a play mat she'd picked up the other day. "Was Miss Anita squeezing you too much?"

Anita loved holding Charlie, but sometimes she worried her arms would give out. Charlie was getting big and wasn't always content to calmly hang out on Anita's hip. She wanted to move. She was going to be an early crawler for sure. Anita had already seen her try to get up on her hands and knees.

Anita smoothed a hand over Charlie's dark hair. "You're ahead of the curve, aren't you, sweetheart?"

Drool covered the baby's chin as she gazed up at Anita with the kind of expression that made you wonder if babies knew a lot more about the world than they let on. Anita's heart grew in her chest. Oh, how she loved this child. She didn't want to think about Jenna coming back or summer ending and Tad finding a different job. She didn't want to imagine a life without Charlie.

The timer beeped again, and Anita removed the muffins from the oven with a wary glance at the clock. It was well past the time Sam would normally come in for lunch. He wasn't the type to miss a meal, but then again, he'd been acting strange lately. Unpredictable.

She set the muffins on a cooling rack and addressed the baby. "Should I call him?"

Charlie offered no opinion, but watching the baby play deepened Anita's concern. Sam never missed a chance to hold Charlie. She'd had to make a rule that he couldn't go in the house when Maddie was here babysitting, otherwise he'd spend the whole three hours unwilling to be more than a foot away from the two girls. It concerned her that he hadn't at least swept through the house for a snack and a Charlie kiss.

"I told Dan I was going to give Sam more space." She threw up her hands, which were sore and swollen. "What am I supposed to do?"

Charlie was unfazed. She seemed happy to keep waving around the toy in her hand, a fabric book that made a crinkling sound. Anita smiled. Life was simple for babies.

"Lord." She eased into a chair, though there was much work still to do. "I haven't known how to pray lately. I feel like everything's changed and I don't know what part I should play in my own life. My son wants nothing to do with me."

She folded her arms on the table and let her head rest on them. "What if Vernon dies and his sons put up a big fight over the farm? Will they end up losing it? What if that man in Broadwater County kills himself? What if . . . ?"

She took a deep breath, unsure if she wanted to voice her next question, even to God. Her voice was muffled as she spoke into her arms.

"What if Bud spends the rest of his life bitter and broken and there's nothing I can do about it?"

She wouldn't deny she still loved him, in a way. Not like

she loved Dan, of course, but she had given Bud a piece of her heart and never got it back, and you don't just move on from that. You build your own life and pour the rest of your heart into other loves, but sometimes you're still haunted by who your love used to be and the love that could've been.

"You've given me so much, Lord. I have so much to be thankful for, but why won't You show me how to keep Sam safe? Why won't You intervene in Vernon's life? Why won't You help Bud heal?"

Weariness tugged at her, and she forced herself to sit up. She couldn't afford to drift off right here at the table when she needed to watch Charlie and finish the laundry and get the beds made in the cabins. How was she going to get it all done before the weekend guests arrived?

"That's it." She carefully stood and wagged a finger at Charlie. "I'm going to call Sam."

❧

The first time Anita called Sam on the walkie-talkie, there was no answer, but that was expected. Even when he didn't answer, he almost always heard her and showed up a short time later. After thirty minutes had passed, however, then forty-five, Anita called again.

"Sam, come in. Sam, I need your help. Over."

She released the button and listened, but there was only silence. Her mother's intuition did not approve of the situation.

She pressed the button again. "Tad, have you seen Sam?"

The walkie-talkie crackled. "No. Sorry. If I do, I'll send him in. Over."

"Okay, thank you. Over and out."

She set the walkie-talkie on the counter with a frown. Charlie had taken a bottle then fallen asleep in the port-a-crib in the living room, so Anita quietly snuck out the mudroom door. She didn't like leaving Charlie alone in the house, even when she was sleeping, but it would only take two minutes to run to the barn and check for Sam. There was a good chance he and Curly were in there, and she could bribe him with a muffin. Or it might take two or three muffins, but she was willing to part with any number of muffins at this point if it meant finding her son and getting the cabins ready in time.

She blinked in the dim light of the barn. "Sam? Are you in here, honey?"

A mourning dove startled and flew out the back, and two kittens played beside a pallet of mineral blocks, happily wrestling. Otherwise, the barn was lifeless. Hot and stuffy. Sam had probably found a much cooler place to be than this.

She sighed. Maybe she should get back on the walkie-talkie and offer a popsicle. That might be more enticing than a muffin on a day like today. She walked all the way through the barn, planning to circle back to the house around the outside, and found Curly lying in the shady spot he liked to use when he was waiting for Sam to return from somewhere.

"Hey, old man." She knelt beside him, ignoring the pain in her knees. "Where's our boy, huh?"

Curly didn't move. She put a hand on his side and frowned. "Curly?"

The dog did not respond. Dread filled Anita's lungs with thick, heavy air. Her skin prickled as she rubbed Curly's head and called his name again. He was still warm, but the stiffness of his body and the absence of the familiar sound of his labored breathing told her all she needed to know. A lump formed in her throat.

Not Curly. Not now.

"Why, Lord?"

She pressed the back of her hand to her mouth and fought the tears welling up in the back of her eyes. Sam's faithful friend. She'd known this was coming, yet it sent a shock through her. She couldn't guess how Sam would react.

Grief threatened to overtake her, but she didn't have time to break down. She needed to get back to the house, and someone needed to tell Sam about Curly before he came along and found the dog himself. If only Dan was here.

She heard a gate squeak and hurried to her feet. Around the corner, she found Tad entering the round pen with a rope halter in his hand.

"Tad."

He turned. "Hey. I was going to work TJ for a little while. I want him to be ready for Dan this weekend. Is everything okay?"

She looked back over her shoulder to where she could see Curly's front paws. "It's Curly."

Tad's face fell. "Oh no." He laid the halter on the fence and closed the gate before meeting her at Curly's side. He stared at the dog for a moment, shaking his head, then Anita wiped her sweaty forehead on the shoulder of her T-shirt.

"You still haven't seen Sam?"

"No." He squeezed the back of his neck. "I'm sure he's fine, but . . ."

"I don't want him to find Curly like this." Anita couldn't help the strain in her voice. "Do you think you could look for him? Break the news? I think he'll take it better coming from you."

She wanted to be there when Sam found out, to comfort

him as she always had when he was sad or hurt or scared, but she had a feeling he would prefer talking to Tad about it. He would probably blame her for Curly's death somehow.

"Sure." Tad lifted his hat and ran his fingers through his hair. "I can do that."

Anita jerked her thumb in the direction of the house. "Charlie's taking a nap, so I better get back. Will you let me know once you've found him and told him?"

Tad nodded, and she headed back to the house, her thoughts racing. Someone had to stay with Charlie, but she wanted so badly to go out looking for Sam too. She felt like it was her fault he was spending more and more time off on his own somewhere. Was he searching for some semblance of his own life?

The house was quiet. Charlie was sound asleep with her arms and legs splayed out. Anita needed to get those wet sheets into the dryer, but first she should let Dan know what was going on. If only she could remember where she'd left her phone.

forty

The sun beat down on Tad's head, and he thought about the pioneers who'd first come to Montana. As they'd stood in the open like this under the enormous sky during their first summer here, had they wondered what they were getting themselves into? Or those people who were passing through in wagons on their way to the West Coast. Had they seen all those mountains and wondered how they would ever find a way across? The view had always made him feel content, but there must have been times in the history of Montana when that same view had inspired fear and doubt.

He shared a small sense of that fear and doubt now as he looked at the acres and acres he would need to search. The dozens of places where Sam could be. The vastness of this land could be both a friend and an enemy.

Tad checked the overgrown juniper bushes first. He'd seen Sam hiding there once or twice, though he'd pretended not to notice. There was a slight indentation in the dirt where Sam must have sat many times but no sign the kid had been there recently. He eyed the ranch from this vantage point, hoping to see something from this angle—an obscure trail, a slight movement—that he wouldn't see from down at the barn. Anything that might give him a clue.

There. Beyond the cabins, way in the distance, the sunlight reflected off something near the fence line. It was small—maybe nothing more than another one of his dad's Rainier beer cans left behind, wouldn't that figure—but it was something out of place. Something to investigate. He didn't know why Sam would go over there, but he better check it out.

As he scrambled out of the bushes, his stomach turned cold. What if Sam found the shed?

By the time Tad made his way back to the barn and then past the cabins and to the top of the hill, sweat poured from his face. He always wore jeans and boots at the ranch to protect his feet and legs, and for riding purposes, but the sun scorched his bare arms. He regretted cutting the sleeves off this T-shirt, and he longed for a cold Mountain Dew. Or even a lukewarm one.

He scanned slowly from left to right, searching for a glint of light to indicate where the shining mystery object might be. What if it was something left over from the wolf hunt last week? Would his dad be that careless?

He couldn't even guess what Bud might do anymore, and Tad was way past fed up with him. He pictured the single-wide trailer on the edge of town and smiled to himself. If he worked hard, he could make it a nice home for Charlie. He would spray the weeds and mow the grass and fix the broken steps. He'd filled out the rental paperwork but hadn't heard anything yet. He shouldn't get his hopes up, but he couldn't help it.

When he saw nothing from where he stood, he took a few steps and scanned again, convinced now, after thinking of his father, that the object must be something related to the wolf hunt and not something related to Sam. The kid would never come out here. But Tad needed to find whatever it was. Maybe it would be something he could use against Bud.

Another couple of steps, and then he saw it—a metallic object ahead of him and to the left. He strode toward it, his irritation at Bud growing, but his annoyance quickly turned to alarm as the shape of the object became clear.

A walkie-talkie.

"Shoot."

His heart began to pound as he picked it up. Why had Sam come up here? Where had he gone?

"Sam," he shouted. "Sam, can you hear me?"

Nothing. He checked the dirt for sign and spotted a boot print pointed southwest. Someone with bigger feet than him had gone that way, toward the old shed. Someone Sam's size. He held the walkie-talkie to his mouth and pressed the talk button but quickly released it. He couldn't call Anita and tell her what he'd found until he had more answers. He didn't want to scare her. And he didn't want anyone else coming up here right now.

He tucked Sam's walkie-talkie into his belt and faced southwest. If Sam had gone that way, he would too.

● ● ●

Tad's anxiety had grown with every step, his stomach twisting and turning as he tried not to think the worst. What if Sam was lost? He could get sunstroke out here. If he would've answered his walkie-talkie like he was supposed to, Tad could be riding TJ right now. And if Tad did find Sam, how was he going to break the news about Curly?

He hadn't been able to find any other boot prints in the

rocky dirt—his tracking skills were rudimentary at best—but he'd kept going southwest until the old shed came into view. Now that he stood twenty feet from the dilapidated building, his heart coiled tight like a rattlesnake.

"Sam?"

He walked closer. The shed door hung open. What about the padlock Tad had seen last time? Hope sparked in his chest. Maybe Bud had moved his stuff out of here and abandoned it. Maybe once Tad had confronted him, he'd thought it was too risky. Maybe he'd found a different location for whatever dumb scheme he was involved in.

That was a lot of *maybes*.

He approached the doorway and peered inside.

"Sam."

The kid turned toward him, his eyes wide and troubled, his cheeks flushed. "I didn't mean to."

Tad's brow furrowed. "It's okay, Sam. Whatever it is, it's not your fault."

"I was kinda mad and then I got really hot and when I kicked the door, it broke."

Tad glanced at the doorframe and saw the splintered wood where the force of the kick had caused the padlock to break free. "It's okay. Let's get out of here."

"No, I want to go to town."

Tad stifled his irritation. "I'll take you to town later, I promise. But we've got to go back to the house. Your mom needs your help."

"What's all this stuff?" Sam stepped aside and pointed at a darkened shelf that appeared to have several boxes sitting on it. It was too dim to tell what they contained, but whatever it was, Tad was sure it was bad news.

His jaw twitched. So much for Bud clearing his stuff out of here. "It doesn't matter, let's go. We need to get you some water."

He'd been a fool not to bring some. A fool not to go directly to Dan the moment he found this shed the first time. A fool to think this time would be different and he wouldn't bungle everything up and lose his job. He tugged on Sam's arm, but Sam pulled away.

"Is that stuff part of the game?" he asked.

Tad frowned. "What game?"

Sam started fidgeting the way he did when he was agitated. "We're not supposed to talk about it, right?"

Tad was starting to worry Sam did have sunstroke because he wasn't making any sense. He needed to get him back to the house, but Sam was bigger and stronger. There was no way Tad could physically force him out of this shed if he didn't want to go. He'd have to find another way.

"Aren't you hungry, Sam? I'm starving. I bet your mom would make us some ham sandwiches."

Sam hesitated, clearly torn. "And lemonade?"

"Yes. Lots of lemonade. Come on."

"Okay."

Tad practically wilted with relief. Finally. He didn't want to spend another minute in this shed.

"I'm just going to look in this box first."

"Sam, no—"

The kid reached for one of the boxes, and Tad panicked. "Listen, Sam. I have to tell you about Curly."

Sam stilled and withdrew his arm. "Curly was sad he couldn't come with me."

"Yes. And he's . . . uh, not doing well. We need to go check on him."

"He's okay." Sam picked up the box. "He's just sad."

Tad held up his hand, frustration building in his chest. "No, Sam. Put it back. He's not okay. He's dead."

Sam's face was blank for a long moment, then it twisted with shock and confusion. In that moment, Tad hated himself. He shouldn't have blurted it out like that. The kid shouldn't have to find out that way, but what was Tad supposed to do?

"Who's dead?" A voiced boomed from behind them, and they both jumped, startled out of their skin. Sam dropped the box he was holding and the bottom split open, spilling hundreds of white pills onto the dirt.

Tad stared at them. No. No, no, no. He suddenly couldn't breathe. This couldn't be happening. This couldn't be real.

He slowly turned around. It was real.

Officer Beaumont the Bonehead glared at the pills, then glared at them. "I'm gonna need you boys to put your hands up where I can see them. Nice and easy."

Tad complied, silently willing Sam to do the same.

He didn't. "I want to go home and see Curly."

"I mean it." Officer Beaumont moved one hand so it hovered over the gun tucked into his holster. "I'm guessing that's not a stockpile of aspirin. Hands up. Now."

Adrenaline raced through Tad's veins. "Do it, Sam."

Officer Beaumont pointed a finger at Tad. "You shut up."

Sam looked at Tad—his eyes glistening with unshed tears, his chin quivering—then raised his hands.

"Sam's got nothing to do with any of this." Tad couldn't shut up. This was all his fault. "Take me and I'll explain everything. Let him go back to the house."

Officer Beaumont grunted. "Not a chance. Now both of you come on out of there. Slowly."

Tad walked out of the shed and squinted in the sun as Officer Beaumont radioed for backup. Sam followed close behind.

"When I got a tip there was some shady stuff going on at Come Around Ranch, I thought no way those Holy Roller Wilsons would be doing something illegal. They're so squeaky clean. But it looks like I was wrong." The officer gestured toward the side of the shed. "Put your hands on that wall. No funny business now."

Tad's mind raced as he and Sam did as they were told. Dan was going to kill him. Forget Dan, Anita was going to kill him. But the face that filled his mind was Charlie's. His sweet, innocent Charlie-horse who deserved a better father than someone like him. Anger—at Bud, at Officer Bonehead, at himself—churned inside him like a tornado, but he had to stay calm. He didn't want to make this any worse than it already was.

Sweat stung his eyes as the officer patted him down. "We don't have any weapons. And the Wilsons don't have anything to do with this."

"I believe you," the officer sneered. "Really, I do. Now hold still."

Tad obeyed but pleaded, "At least let me call Sam's mom. Please. She's already worried sick about him."

He needed to tell her he'd found Sam. And he needed to tell her he didn't know when he would be picking up his daughter.

"He's a grown man." Officer Beaumont snorted. "He's got to accept the consequences of his actions like everybody else. He'll get a call after he's processed, same as you. I'm taking you boys in for questioning."

Sam sniffled. "I don't want questioning, Tad. I want to go home."

"I know." Tad gritted his teeth as Officer Beaumont pulled

both walkie-talkies from Tad's belt and attached them to his own. "But first we're going to ride in a cop car, okay?"

Sam's eyes widened. "A cop car? Holy huckle—"

"Don't say it." Tad shook his head and stared grimly at the wall. "Don't you dare say it."

forty-one

"I'm really really sorry and I'm really really sad," I say and I feel so sad I can't even lift my head and Tad puts his arm around my shoulders and says I have nothing to be sorry about. We're in the holding tank inside the police station. That's what Officer Beamont calls it but there's no water in here and it's hot and I'm hungry.

"I don't want Curly to be dead."

Tad sighs like he's an old man and says, "Me neither."

We're the only ones in the holding tank but the officer and a lady at a desk are on the other side of the bars and the lady is talking on the phone but I know she's not talking to my mom because the officer said we couldn't have our phone call yet but he said soon and I still don't like *soon*. The lady keeps turning to look at me and Tad and she smiles so I think she's probably nice but she also seems busy.

I wonder if this is all part of the game that Bud plays with Tad but I don't want to ask because I don't want to break my pinkie promise because then Tad might never pinkie promise with me ever again. I don't care if I never get to play the game with them though because I don't like it not one bit. Tad is walking back and forth now and he looks mad and he stops when the lady on the phone says the name Scooter MacDonald.

Tad leans against the bars and listens to the lady and we can hear her tell Officer Beaumont that Scooter finally got picked up all the way over in Sheridan County and I don't know what that means but the officer seems happy and calls Scooter a bunch of mean names and Tad starts walking again and looks like he's really thinking about something.

"Can we have a funeral for Curly?" I ask. "Like in *City Slickers* when they're out on the range and Curly dies and they bury him under a stick cross and Mitch says he'll never forget him?"

"I bet we can do that, if that's what you want," Tad says and I think I know the perfect spot for Curly to be buried where he can feel the sun and see the barn and the house and the hills so he'll always know where I am.

Up by the junipers, that's where.

I hear a noise coming from the lobby and when my mom and dad and Charlie come around the corner I can't believe my eyes. I stand up and shout "Mom" because I've never been so happy to see her and her face is all crumpled up like when her knees hurt and I know I shouldn't because I'm too big but I start to cry.

forty-two

It had never been more fitting that everyone called him Tad, because he'd never felt so small. He stood next to Sam behind the bars and tried to look Dan in the eye but couldn't. Dan had told him that grace meant giving people chances and loving them even when they didn't deserve it, but Tad didn't have to be the brightest crayon in the box to realize even something as nice as grace must have a limit. He had no doubt he'd reached it.

The woman behind the desk gave the Wilsons a sympathetic look. "Hello, Anita."

Anita nodded, her face pinched. "Hi, Suzanne."

Sam wiped his eyes with his sleeve and sniffled. "How did you find me?"

Anita reached her hand through the bars and touched Sam's arm. "Mrs. Duncan called. She saw you and Tad drive by in the back of a police car and was very concerned. What on earth happened? Are you okay?"

"Please step back, ma'am," Officer Beaumont the Bonehead said. "You're not supposed to touch the prisoners."

Anita pulled her hand back but remained close.

Tad stepped forward. "This is all my fault. I . . ."

His words fell away as his eyes fell on his daughter. She was in her car seat, and when she saw him, she began kicking her feet.

"Ba-ba-ba-ba."

His heart constricted. He wanted to hold her more than anything, to bury his face in her hair and kiss her cheeks and pretend everything was fine, but he had failed her. Shame burned in his chest. He was no better at being a dad than Bud.

Dan spoke to Officer Bonehead. "What exactly is the charge against these boys?"

"I found them in possession of what is suspected to be illegal drugs. On *your* property, I might add. We have to wait for the lab results to know for sure."

Dan looked at Tad, dumbfounded. "Drugs?"

Tad shook his head. "I don't know what they were. Sam found them. Some kind of pills."

Officer Bonehead hooked his thumbs in his belt. "I don't suppose you know anything about it, Dan."

"Of course not." Dan crossed his arms over his chest. "Where'd you find these supposed drugs?"

"In an old shed in the southwest corner," Tad said. "You know it?"

Dan turned on the officer. "That shed's in the middle of nowhere. I haven't touched it in years. Anyone could've been using it."

Officer Bonehead huffed. "I caught them red-handed."

Charlie began to fuss, and Tad's muscles tensed as she held her arms out like she was reaching for him. He hated that she had to be here for this, see him like this. At least she was too young to ever remember this day.

The back door flew open and Chief Stubbs came barreling into the station from the alley, his large frame filling up the room. "What in tarnation." He parked himself in front of Officer Bonehead and jerked his thumb at Sam. "Let that boy go."

"But—"

"No buts. Do it. Now." The chief turned to face Dan and Anita. "I'm real sorry about this, folks."

"I want to go home," Sam said.

"We'll get you home in no time." Chief Stubbs gave Sam a reassuring smile, then turned his eyes on Tad with a look of regret. "Not sure I can release you yet, however."

Tad nodded. "I understand."

He did. He couldn't prove he had nothing to do with the drugs, and he had no evidence to implicate his dad aside from his word, which meant next to nothing at the moment. He'd keep himself locked up too, if he was in the chief's shoes, but a hole opened in his heart when he thought about spending the night here, away from Charlie. Would she miss him? Would she be sad?

Officer Bonehead wasn't happy about it, but he unlocked the holding tank and motioned for Sam to come out. The kid fell into Anita's arms, and she rubbed his back as he repeated, "I want to go home, I want to go home," over and over. The officer shut the holding tank door with a clank and relocked it, giving Tad a smirk that said he was glad at least one of his perps was staying behind bars.

Anita kept her arms tight around her son and looked wide-eyed over his shoulder at Dan. "We can't leave Tad here."

Dan threw up his hands. "Not sure there's anything we can do. Bail hasn't even been set yet."

Chief Stubbs was apologetic. "It's almost five on a Friday.

Might not see the judge until Monday, but we'll see what we can figure out."

Monday? The hole in Tad's heart gaped wider, and he could feel his face fall. That was three days away.

Chief Stubbs gave Tad a solemn look. "You claiming you got nothing to do with the drugs?"

Tad nodded.

The chief sighed, looking very old. "Any idea who does?"

Tad hesitated. "My dad."

Anita gasped, and Chief Stubbs narrowed his eyes.

Tad knew no one had any reason to believe him, but he scrambled to explain. "He admitted he was keeping something in the shed but wouldn't tell me what." Tad finally looked Dan in the eye. "I'm sorry I didn't tell you before. Bud said if I did, he'd kick me and Charlie out of the house."

Something flashed in Anita's eyes. "How dare he."

The chief held up his hands. "Let's not get ahead of ourselves. You got any proof, son?"

Tad shook his head.

Chief Stubbs rubbed his chin. "I'll look into it. If you're telling the truth, there's got to be evidence somewhere. And he probably hasn't been working alone. Who does he run with?"

Tad shrugged. "I don't know." He searched his mind for a clue but came up empty. Bud didn't have many friends. Who had he been spending time with lately?

He drew in a sharp breath as a memory struck him. "I don't know if it means anything, but you said . . ."

The chief raised his eyebrows. "Go on."

"You said you saw him coming out of Pine's office, remember? But he's never said anything about selling the house. And he hates that guy. Why would he be at the office?"

Now Chief Stubbs looked not only very old but very tired. "Pine? You think Matthew Pine's got something to do with this?"

Tad shifted on his feet. If he did, would Maddie know about it? "I—I don't know."

"I think we've heard enough." Officer Bonehead waved an arm at the hallway that led to the front door. "The rest of you better get going. Office hours are over, and I'm sure Suzanne here wants to go home."

Anita looped her arm through Sam's, and Dan reached down to pick up Charlie's car seat. She started to cry, and Tad's throat tightened. They were going to take her away from him. He didn't know when he'd see her again.

"Can she stay with you? Until . . ." His voice was rough and broken and he suddenly had an idea of what Jenna must have felt the day she left their daughter at Come Around Ranch.

"Of course." Anita rested a hand on Charlie's foot as Charlie's crying grew in intensity. "She can stay as long as she needs to."

"She goes to bed at nine. And she likes the elephant—"

"The elephant blanket, I know." Anita stuck her hand through the bars to squeeze Tad's arm, and it was hard to read her face. "She'll be fine, don't worry."

Tad nodded once, hardly able to breathe. Officer Bonehead shooed them down the hall, and Sam kept looking back. Tad stood tall and forced himself to hold up a hand in farewell until they were out of sight. Then his shoulders slumped, and he leaned his forehead against the bars.

forty-three

Anita winced as she rubbed her knuckles Saturday afternoon. Her doctor was always telling her to avoid high-stress situations to reduce the risk of flare-ups. Up until a couple of months ago, that hadn't been a challenge. Her life had been pretty consistent and manageable. Ever since they'd hired Tad at Come Around Ranch, however . . .

Charlie cried out from the port-a-crib in the guest bedroom where she'd been napping, and Anita resumed the task of preparing a bottle.

"Hold on, sweetheart," she called. "I'm coming."

She wished the poor baby would've taken a longer nap. She'd woken up three times during the night, needing reassurance. Wanting her daddy. And she'd been out of sorts all day.

Anita couldn't blame her. She was out of sorts herself. In the past month, her sweet, innocent son had gotten drunk, gone to jail, and developed a new and not entirely pleasant personality. She remembered what Dan had said when Tad first started working for the ranch. *"I'm worried it's always going to be something with him."*

It seemed he'd been right. Yet Anita remembered what Tad had said about his dad and felt compassion working on the knots in her heart, kneading at them as if they were lumps of dough. It wouldn't be fair to direct all her anger at Tad.

A text notification sounded, and she scanned the room for her phone. Why was the darn thing so hard to keep track of? Where had she set it down? When it dinged again, she followed the noise to a tote bag on the counter. Yep, it was in there.

She read the text and sighed. The guests in Cabin B—the spatula lovers—had been unhappy when their cabin had not been ready on time yesterday. Now they wanted to know how often the pH level of the well water was tested.

"Oh for heaven's sake."

She would send Dan to talk to them. She had more important things to take care of.

Her eyes were bleary from fatigue as she checked the temperature of the formula and yawned. Was she really only forty-eight years old? Because today she felt a hundred.

In the guest bedroom, she found Charlie whimpering to herself. She had soaked through her clothes.

"Oh my, no wonder you woke up."

She dug through the diaper bag and found there were only two diapers left, and the last set of extra clothes, wadded up in the bottom of the bag, was a size too small. She held up a crumpled onesie. "We'll have to make do with this for now."

As she changed Charlie, she remembered doing the same for Sam. She remembered smiling down at him, her perfect little son, blissfully unaware of the challenges he would face as he got older. The hard road that lay ahead.

It didn't seem possible that was twenty-one years ago. Wasn't it only yesterday? She sang the hymn she used to sing to her son.

"Come home, come home. Ye who are weary come home.

Earnestly, tenderly Jesus is calling, calling 'O sinner, come home.'"

Charlie's mood improved once she was in dry clothes and was drinking her bottle with Anita on the couch. Anita yawned again, big enough her jaw cracked, and thought about Tad, stuck in jail. Dan had given permission for the police to search the shed and surrounding area for evidence, hoping something might be found to exonerate Tad, but they'd heard nothing yet. Could they trust Tad and the story he'd told? She hadn't forgotten what she'd told Dan during Tad's first week on the job. "*I know he's rough around the edges, but he's a good kid.*"

Had she been wrong? She didn't know anymore. And could Matthew Pine be involved in all this? He never came around here.

But Maddie did.

Anita shook her head. It was hard not to—*really* hard—but she didn't want to jump to conclusions before the whole picture had been revealed. She and Dan had tried this morning to get more information about what exactly had happened yesterday out of Sam, but he'd been flustered and evasive. He wanted only to talk about Curly, whose grave he and Dan had dug last night out to the east of the barn, by the junipers.

"*Why'd he have to die?*" Sam kept asking.

"*He lived a long, full life.*" Dan had said. "*His body was very tired, and he was ready to rest.*"

Rest. Anita wished that's what she could do, but she gazed down at Charlie's sweet face and sighed. She knew what needed to be done next. Rest would have to wait.

◆ ﹅ ◗

A stone settled in Anita's stomach as she turned onto Buck Road.

"I'm not ready, Lord." Her hands gripped the wheel. The drive had passed far too quickly. "I don't even know if I should be doing this."

At the last second, she'd decided to tell Dan where she was going, and he had been concerned. She knew he had good reason to be, but she also knew this might be the only way she could help Tad. And Charlie too.

"Lord, please help me. I need Your wisdom and discernment. I don't like any of this."

She parked in front of Bud's house and took a deep breath. His truck was here. He was not going to be happy to see her, but she'd brought a secret weapon.

"Ready, Charlie?"

"Ba-ba-ba."

Anita grabbed the two large tote bags she'd brought, then opted to unbuckle Charlie from the car seat and carry her on her hip rather than lug the carrier in the house. She kissed the top of Charlie's head and knocked on the door.

A long moment passed. Would Bud recognize her car and pretend he wasn't home? She wondered how there could be such a chasm between two people who'd known each other their whole lives. And how someone could change so much.

It was hard to grow up and grow old in the same town. In a lot of ways, it was like living two different lives in one place.

She was about to knock again when the door opened slowly.

Bud wiped a hand over his face and stared at Charlie with bleary eyes. "What're you doing here?"

Anita knew he meant her, not the baby. "I came for Charlie's things."

He scowled, and Anita feared for a second that maybe he didn't know his son was in jail. Maybe he had no idea why Charlie was with her, and she was going to have to explain. But when he stepped aside and jerked his head to indicate she should come in, she got the sense he knew exactly what had happened. It had surely been the main topic of conversation at every restaurant and bar in Grady last night.

"Their room's down there." Bud pointed down the hall. "On the right."

Anita hesitated, then held Charlie out to him. "Will you hold her while I pack?"

He took the child in a way that seemed almost reverent, and Charlie went willingly. Anita limped down the hall. As she filled the tote bags with clothes, diapers, and wipes, she could hear Bud talking to Charlie. She couldn't make out the words, but his voice sounded serious, like he was telling Charlie something important, and she could picture the baby watching his face solemnly, as if she understood.

Did he know how lucky he was to be a grandpa? Did he realize what could happen to Charlie if Tad was convicted of doing something illegal?

When she came out of the bedroom, she found Bud on the couch with Charlie on his lap.

Anita cleared her throat. "Do you know if there's extra formula anywhere?"

"Next to the microwave."

She retrieved the container and tucked the bottle sitting beside it into one of the bags as well. What if Charlie had to stay at the ranch for a long time? She would be ready to start baby food soon. Then she would start to walk. What if . . .

Anita shook her head and carried the bags back to the living room. Charlie was contentedly drooling on a toy while patting Bud's arm with her palm.

Bud glanced away from the muted TV to look at Anita for a brief moment. "What happened to your leg?"

Her cheeks burned. She always hoped she was doing a good job concealing her limitations and discomfort, but sometimes her body gave her away. "It's nothing. Just some arthritis."

He grunted. "You been to the doctor?"

Her brow furrowed. "Yes. There's not a lot they can do."

He grunted again, and silence fell between them. She shifted on her feet, preparing herself. This was it. The moment of truth. The real reason she'd come here.

"Did you know about the drugs in the shed?"

Bud frowned but kept his eyes on the screen. "Like I told the chief, I don't know anything about anything. Tad got himself into this mess, and he can get himself out."

She narrowed her eyes. "Did the chief ask why you were at Matthew Pine's office?"

"Had a property-related question, that's all."

"Come on, Bud." Anita pushed hair back from her face in frustration. "You might be able to fool the chief with that but not me. I can tell when you're lying."

"Oh yeah?" He turned his eyes on her now. "One time, I told you the biggest lie of my life, and you bought it hook, line, and sinker. Believed every word. So don't tell me you know when I'm lying."

Anita's heart wrenched. What was he talking about? "Don't change the subject."

He tucked Charlie against his shoulder and stood, his eyes flashing. "There is no other subject between you and me besides that summer. That's the only subject."

Anita's eyes widened. "That summer? You really want to talk about that?" She'd come here to reckon with Bud about Tad and the drugs, but she couldn't deny a reckoning about their past was long overdue as well. Heat coursed through her veins as unwelcome memories pounded her brain and long-buried anger resurfaced and she was nineteen again. "Was the lie that you cared about me? That I made you happy? Because you're right, I did buy that for a while. I believed you when you said you—"

She cut herself off, unwilling to speak the words out loud. Unwilling to believe a person could tell someone they loved them one day and callously dismiss them the next.

Bud scowled. He opened his mouth, then closed it. He shook his head. When he finally spoke, his voice was quiet. "I meant all that. That part wasn't a lie. I didn't stop coming around be-cause I didn't—uh, because I didn't care about you." He clearly didn't want to say the words either. He took a deep breath. "It was because I realized we were on different paths. You were into church, and you wanted to get married, and I was . . ."

She froze, every muscle in her body taut, as his words spun around and around in her head.

He looked at the floor. "I knew Dan loved you. And he—he deserved you."

Strength seeped from her body, and she leaned against the couch as images flashed through her mind. Pictures of her and Bud laughing together. Holding hands. Watching the sunset from the back of his truck.

Other pictures appeared too. Less pleasant ones. Bud teas-ing her for not drinking alcohol. Bud's hands on her, wanting more as they kissed, and her always saying no. It was true she'd thought they would get married. She wanted to be a wife and a mother. But Bud had been wild and carefree and had told her he didn't want to be tied down. He'd told her she meant nothing to him. Less than nothing. Now he was saying that was a lie?

He got Holly pregnant less than six months later, and Anita had never been able to understand. It had hurt when they seemed so happy. So in love. Six years later, Tad had come along, and things started to change between Bud and Holly. They had never married, and when Holly left one morning and never came back, that's when Bud started drinking in earnest.

Different paths. Yes, it was easy to see now, but how had he seen it then? She hadn't been able to see anything past her love for him. At least, she'd thought it was love. And after his cruel words, she hadn't been able to see anything past the pain of a broken heart. Pain she had never quite been able to let go.

What might have happened if Bud hadn't told that lie? Would they have stayed together? A chill swept through her chest as she tried to imagine a life without Dan, without Sam, without Come Around Ranch.

"I'm sorry about Holly," she said. She'd shown up with food, made herself a nuisance, but she'd never told him she was sorry.

He grumbled. "I guess it wasn't easy living with an ornery cuss like me."

"That's not how I remember you."

He looked up, and they locked eyes for a moment, something passing between them that Anita couldn't name. Acceptance, maybe. Why had she held on to this hurt for so long?

Charlie squealed and began to squirm. Bud turned his gaze on her and gave as much of a smile as Anita had seen from him in years, which still wasn't much, but it transformed his face.

He leaned close to Charlie. "Is my Charlie-horse getting hungry?"

Anita shook her head, the present reality crashing back into the room. "That's what Tad calls her. If the judge sets bail on Monday, will you bail him out? Charlie needs her dad."

Bud's face darkened. "I don't have any money. It's those Pines who have it all."

Anita tensed. "So Matthew *does* have something to do with this?"

"Not just him. The girl."

Her heart skipped and scuttered like a rock Sam had kicked across the drive. "Maddie?"

Bud didn't respond. Wouldn't look at her. What had Maddie done? Whatever it was, was it the reason she'd kept coming around the ranch? The reason she'd been so willing to help out with Charlie?

Anita drew in a sharp breath. The birthday party. Could Maddie have planned for Sam to be taken advantage of? But for what purpose?

Anita steeled herself. The biggest question of all was whether she could trust anything Bud said.

"You need to go to the chief, Bud." She straightened, her voice growing in intensity. "You need to tell him whatever you know."

He growled and held Charlie out to her. "You better go."

Anita took the child and held her close. "Please. He's a good dad, you know."

Bud's shoulders sank. "I know. I've seen it."

"You're a good dad too. Somewhere inside."

His laugh was hollow and tinged with sadness. He reached out and gently squeezed Charlie's foot. "Bye, Charlie-horse."

297

forty-four

Tad paced the holding tank, wishing for a bottle of Mountain Dew and a cigarette but out-of-his-mind desperate for even a glimpse of his daughter. Even though she'd only been with him for a month and a half, he couldn't remember life before Charlie.

Saturday and Sunday had been torture. He'd been a zombie, dead on the inside but somehow still walking around. His head a jumbled mess. His stomach a tangle of knots.

The judge would be around "sometime before lunch," Officer Beaumont had said. The thought of being released was the only thing keeping Tad from banging his head against the bars, but the thought of emptying his meager savings account to make bail made him want to puke. So much for putting down a deposit on that rental Maddie had shown him.

Speaking of Maddie . . .

He couldn't get the thought out of his head that if her dad was involved in the shady stuff happening on the Wilson property, then she might be as well. He didn't want it to be true, but hadn't he had a bad feeling that first time she drove out to the ranch? Hadn't she always been nothing but trouble?

That's what people said about him too. He'd been a fool

to think he could have a different kind of life. A family and a home. A fool to think he could give Charlie what she needed.

Lost in thought, he didn't hear the chief approach until the dead bolt clicked. Tad startled.

"Chin up, son." Chief Stubbs opened the door. "You're free to go."

Tad blinked at him. "The judge is here?"

"He's on his way, but not for you."

That's when Tad noticed his dad standing behind the chief's oversized frame. The chief moved aside, and Tad stepped out of the holding tank. Bud wouldn't look at him. Once Tad was clear, Bud entered the cell, and Chief Stubbs locked the door behind him.

Tad's eyes widened. "Dad."

Bud shook his head, his back to Tad. Even when Tad called to him again, he didn't turn around.

Chief Stubbs nudged Tad toward the lobby and spoke gently. "Come on. Time to go."

In a daze, Tad walked down the hall with the chief close behind. When they'd turned the corner, Chief Stubbs put a hand on Tad's shoulder.

"I'm sorry about all this. Your father assured me you had nothing to do with the drugs."

"He said that?" Tad turned around, but Bud was out of sight. "What about Pine?"

The chief rubbed a hand over his face and raised one shoulder. "He's always been a slippery ol' fish. From talking to your dad, it sounds like Matthew gave all the orders, but always in person. There's nothing written down, no phone calls, no texts. Nothing to tie him to the drugs but Bud's word, and you know that's not enough for a conviction. Unless you got something?"

He gave Tad a hopeful look, and Tad shook his head. "Wish I did."

Chief Stubbs sighed. "Ah, well. I'll keep digging."

A man about Tad's age approached and handed the chief a bag. "Here's the personal items you asked for."

"Thanks, Jeff." The chief handed the bag to Tad. "Here's your stuff. Now I'm sure you're anxious to go get that precious daughter of yours. You better do right by her, y'hear?"

Tad swallowed, the thought of seeing Charlie again overwhelming him. "Yes, sir."

"The Wilsons dropped off your car last night. Keys are in that bag."

They had done that? They had thought of him? Well, of course they couldn't help it with Charlie in their house.

Tad pushed open the door and looked back over his shoulder. "Thanks."

The chief raised one hand, and Tad walked into the fresh air. Despite the distinct odor of cow manure, it smelled like heaven after the sweaty stink of the holding tank. The sun was bright, and the air was warm.

He'd hardly eaten anything over the weekend, and his stomach grumbled for food. As he got into his car, he debated whether to stop at the gas station on his way to Come Around Ranch. He wanted to see Charlie as soon as possible, without delay, but once he had her in his arms, who knew how long it would be before he'd want to put her down to eat.

He better stop. Just for a minute.

He drove to the gas station, his mind on his father. He'd looked small in that holding tank. Different. What had he told the chief? And why? As much as Tad wanted to believe Bud's confession was for his sake, he had strong doubts. Bud hadn't cared about Tad's life, whereabouts, or future for years.

Why would he care now?

◆ ◇ ◆

As Tad walked out of the gas station, he twisted open the big, green bottle of Mountain Dew and took a satisfying swig. Aaah. The good stuff. He tore the wrapper off an Oberto snack stick, shoved the processed meat into his mouth, and pulled his keys from his pocket. When he turned to throw his garbage in the can outside the door, there she was.

Maddie.

"Oh." He spoke with his mouth full. "Hey."

Of the five thousand people in Grady, why'd it have to be her here at the same time as him? He didn't want to talk to her right now. Didn't know what to think. But the look on her face told him there was no avoiding a conversation.

She stared at him. "You're out."

"Yeah. Got released a few minutes ago."

"I'm so sorry." She fidgeted with her purse, her usual confidence and sparkle missing. "I never meant for this . . ."

Her words dropped off and faded to nothing. Tad was chewing on the spicy meat, wondering how to get away, when Maddie's words sank in and everything suddenly became clear.

He drew in a sharp and accusing breath. "You *did* know about the shed, didn't you? That's why you kept showing up."

She held up a hand. "You don't understand."

He gripped the Mountain Dew bottle tightly. "You're right. I don't understand why I ever thought maybe you were actually a pretty cool person. Were you there to spy on us or what?"

She looked at her feet. The sun beat down on them as they

stood on the hot cement walkway in silence. Tad wanted to turn away in a huff, get the heck out of there and go find his daughter, but he also wanted answers.

When Maddie finally spoke, her voice trembled. "Is Sam okay?"

Heat burned in his chest. "First Curly died, then he got arrested. What do you think?"

Her eyes welled with tears. "Oh no, Curly died?"

"What do you care? You're not his friend. Time to stop pretending."

"I do care. I'm sorry. I thought if I went along with my dad's plan, I could protect Sam. He said all I had to do was find out if anyone ever went back in the southwest corner. And keep Sam distracted. Then I got to know you, and Anita, and I realized—"

"Save it, Maddie." Tad spun on his heels and stomped toward his car. He didn't want to hear her excuses. He just wanted Charlie.

"Wait." Maddie ran after him. "There's something else you should know."

He ignored her.

"It's about Scooter."

He stopped. Man, he hated that guy. He'd be fine if he never saw him again. "I already know he got caught."

"It's not that."

Tad turned and narrowed his eyes at her. "Then what?"

Her cheeks flushed as she hesitated. "Everyone's saying that he ... um ..."

She chewed on her lip, and Tad wanted to pull his hair out.

"What?" he shouted.

She flinched. "He's Charlie's real dad. That's what they're saying. That Jenna's friend Lexi heard it from her."

The world tilted. Spun backward. Shook under his feet. What had she said? No. *He* was Charlie's dad. Him. Thaddeus Bungley.

He stumbled to his car and braced himself against it with his arms, his chest and throat constricted.

"I'm so sorry," Maddie said.

He fought for air and pushed off the car. "Why should I believe you?"

She opened her mouth, but nothing came out. With a growl, he threw himself into the Ford and slammed the door. He vaguely heard Maddie trying to tell him something, but he backed out of the parking space and hit the gas.

No. She was a liar. She was a phony. A master manipulator with long, sharp fingernails who wanted to distract him from what she'd done. That was all. She'd only ever cared about herself. But as he sped down the highway to Come Around Ranch, he couldn't stop thinking about Charlie's dark, curly hair.

Dark, curly hair just like Scooter's.

forty-five

Anita's heart was heavy as she watched Sam pick at his dinner. Nothing was worse than seeing your child in pain. Your child struggling. Your child pulling away.

She pushed her own food away, her stomach roiling too violently to eat. "How are your kittens today, Sam?"

He poked at his beans with his fork and shrugged. "They're not my kittens."

Anita gave Dan a desperate look. She'd never seen her son like this. He'd already been acting different—distant and irritable, which was so unlike him—but since Curly's death and being taken to jail, he'd become even more sullen and withdrawn. Charlie had been able to get him to smile a few times over the weekend, but when Tad came this morning to pick her up, Sam had refused to come downstairs to talk to Tad or say good-bye.

Dan cleared his throat. "Do you want to take the four-wheeler out after dinner?"

Sam leaned back in his chair. "No."

Dan's brow furrowed with concern. Anita's chest felt like there was a swarm of bees inside trying to get out as her anxiety grew. "Is something wrong, honey? Are you feeling okay?"

Sam held his hands up, fingers splayed, then slapped them down on either side of his plate. "Can I be excused?"

She exchanged a glance with Dan and nodded. "Sure."

His chair scraped as he slid it back, and she flinched. As he stomped across the kitchen, Dan pointed at the table and said, "You need to clear your place," but Sam was in the mudroom and out the door before he'd even finished speaking.

Dan turned to Anita. "What's gotten into him?"

Anita would've laughed if she didn't feel so sick at heart. Everyone always expected the mom to know everything. To have all the answers. The truth was, moms were as lost and hopeless as everyone else. They were just better at hiding it. "I don't know. He's sad about Curly."

"Maybe we should get him a new dog."

"I don't think that's the only thing bothering him."

Dan sighed. "I know. I wish it was that easy."

Anita hid her hands in her lap so she could rub her aching knuckles without Dan noticing. "I was thinking maybe it's time for him to get a job in town. Something part-time."

Dan raised his eyebrows. "I've been saying that for years and now . . ."

"You were right. He needs to have his own life."

The words tasted raw and unfamiliar. Wasn't his life here with them good enough? Didn't he have everything he needed? Wasn't he safe and, up until recently, happy? But he wanted more, and he'd been trying to tell her. Dan had tried to tell her.

It was all too clear now, looking across the table at Sam's empty chair, that she'd been holding on too tight.

"We need him here, especially in the summer." Dan tapped a finger against his water glass. "You can't take care of the horses and cabins by yourself."

"What about Tad?"

Dan leaned back. "I don't know . . ."

"You talked about grace."

"Yes, but—"

"You gave a whole big speech about it."

Dan raked his hand through his hair and grumbled, "That was before he went to jail."

"He had nothing to do with the drugs."

"He should've told us."

Anita stood and carried her plate to the sink, the word *should've* echoing through her mind. She should've done a lot of things too. "If we bring Tad on year-round, we can give Sam more freedom. And Tad can do things around the ranch that Sam can't."

"Can we afford that?"

"Maybe we raise the rates on the cabins."

Dan frowned.

Anita smiled. "Just a tiny bit. People will pay it."

Dan threw up his hands. "And then you have to watch Charlie every day for the next five years until she starts kindergarten?"

Anita's heart squeezed. Charlie. It had been exhausting keeping the girl over the weekend, yet Anita had loved every minute of it. Could she do it? Could she keep Charlie safe as she grew up?

"We don't even know how long she'll be here." Her voice faltered. "It might only be for the summer."

"It could be forever."

Anita tried not to cling to his words. Tried not to show how much she hoped for that. "If I keep taking my medication and pay attention when my body tells me to rest, I think I can do it.

Tad would always be close by. And Sam would still be around, right? I don't know if he could handle working more than a couple days a week. At least for now."

Dan stood as well and picked up his and Sam's plates. "It's a lot to think over. We're going to need to pray about it."

Anita began clearing the food dishes from the table. "Yes. But right now you're going to go check on Sam, right?"

Dan was already headed toward the mudroom. He flashed a smile over his shoulder at her. "Yes, ma'am."

When he was gone, the house seemed quiet and forlorn. Sabina the cat watched silently as Anita finished cleaning up dinner and walked slowly to the living room. Though it was almost eight o'clock, the sun still shone brightly outside. It didn't become truly dark until well after ten this time of year. She hoped Dan had found Sam and that they were having a good talk, although with Sam, a good talk often meant no talking at all.

She carefully knelt in front of the couch and rested her elbows on the cushion, her eyes squeezed shut and her hands squeezed together. "Oh, Lord . . ."

She took a deep breath and opened her eyes. Blinked at her swollen knuckles, white from the pressure. Slowly, she relaxed her grip and pulled her hands apart. She turned them over so her palms faced up.

Yes. Better.

She bowed her head. "Lord, help me let go. I can't do it all. I can't keep everyone safe and happy all the time, no matter what I do. I don't know why I thought I could."

Sabina rubbed against her side with a purr, and Anita smiled. "You have given me many blessings, Lord. And many trials. Please help us understand what's best for Sam. I guess what You have in mind might not be what I would choose, and there are a lot of things I don't know."

Her hands itched to clasp each other tightly, the force of a long-held habit, but she fought against the pull. "And, Lord, about Tad . . ."

forty-six

It was eight thirty on Tuesday morning, and there was no sign of Maddie. Anita checked her phone one more time. Still nothing.

She looked down at Charlie. "I don't think she's coming."

Anita needed to leave immediately if she was going to arrive at the Coalition in time to prepare for Coffee Break. She set Charlie on her bottom in the port-a-crib and hurried out to the car with the car seat. She'd learned it was much easier to carry Charlie to the car and buckle her into the already latched-in car seat than it was to lug the heavy and awkward carrier with Charlie in it.

The little girl squealed with delight and waved her arms when Anita came back in the house, which caused her to wobble and tip over backward. She was getting pretty good at sitting up by herself, but she was still a little top-heavy. Her face puckered, but Anita scooped her up before she started to cry.

"You're okay, sweetheart." She kissed both of the baby's cheeks. "You're trying to do things you aren't ready for, aren't you?"

Those words replayed in Anita's mind as she drove to town. How many times had she said the same about Sam? That he wasn't ready? But how would anyone know if she never let him try? Charlie had to keep sitting up by herself, over and over, until she could do it without tipping. She would learn. Her body would adjust, her muscles would grow, and she would figure it out.

There would also be times she would get hurt in the process.

Part of Anita's heart couldn't help but believe she'd failed her son. She'd loved him the best she knew how, yet there were so many things she wished she'd done differently. So many mistakes she could see easily now, looking back. And what about Maddie? Anita had wanted to be her friend, her mentor, but it felt like she'd failed at that too.

At the Coalition, with only ten minutes to spare before Coffee Break was supposed to start, Anita left the car seat in the car and carried Charlie inside. Diana was setting out folding chairs around the room, and her face brightened at the sight of the baby.

"I haven't seen you in a while." She walked over and tickled Charlie's cheek. "You've grown."

Anita chuckled and shifted Charlie to her other hip. "That's for sure. I can't hold her for long without my hands going numb."

Diana nodded. "You had quite an exciting weekend, I heard."

Anita groaned. "Does everyone know?"

She hadn't talked to her friend since last Tuesday, and the whole Wilson clan had stayed home from church on Sunday. She'd told herself it was for Charlie's sake—she didn't want to put the baby in the nursery with someone she didn't know—but there was no denying it was also to avoid having to face everyone's questions about Tad and Sam and jail and drugs.

"Not everyone." Diana gave Anita a reassuring pat on the shoulder. "People are also very keen to talk about the police chasing down Scooter MacDonald. At first, there were three police cars on the scene when they finally captured him, and now the story goes that there were a dozen police officers and two snipers." Diana winked. "Sam only required one officer, so his story is not nearly as sensational."

Anita made a face. "I'm not sure if that makes me feel any better."

Diana smiled. "No time to dwell on it now. People will be arriving any minute."

Anita laid Charlie on a blanket by the desk and helped Diana finish setting up. Summer was a busy time for farmers and ranchers, so attendance at Coffee Break had dwindled in recent weeks, but the Coalition had decided to keep the meetings going anyway. Anita was glad. When Vernon DeVries walked in at nine o'clock on the dot, she was especially so.

"Good morning." She glanced at the box of donuts on the table to be sure one of Vernon's favorites was in there. "It's good to see you."

She hadn't talked to him in three weeks, and so much had happened since then that it seemed like even longer.

He shuffled slowly toward the table. "Mornin', ladies. Coffee smells good."

He poured himself a steaming cup, and Anita smiled to herself. Farmers loved their coffee hot, even when it was ninety degrees outside. She placed a custard donut on a napkin and handed it to him.

He thanked her and jerked his chin in the direction of the desk. "I see you got your grandbaby with you today."

Rather than correct him, she picked Charlie up so Vernon could see her. He set his cup down so he could lean close and hold out his finger. When Charlie reached out and grabbed it with her chubby hand, Vernon grinned.

"She's a strong one."

"She sure is."

"Better watch out." His face sobered. "Next thing you know, she'll be all grown up and telling you she don't need your help no more."

Anita held back a sigh as Sam's face flashed through her mind. "It happens fast, doesn't it? They say the days are long, but the years are short."

Vernon nodded. "My Jake turns sixty this year. Can you believe it? I don't know how that happened."

Anita gently tugged on Charlie's hand so Vernon could have his finger back. She was almost afraid to ask, but she wanted to know how things were going on the farm. "How are Jake and Ed doing?"

Vernon shook his head, and Anita braced herself for the worst. He scratched the back of his neck. "You know, we had that big storm a while back."

"Yes, with the hail?"

"It was a disaster for us. One of our lower fields got washed out in a flash flood, and the hail damaged almost thirty percent of the upper fields."

Her heart sank. She hadn't heard. She'd been so preoccupied with her own problems. "I'm so sorry to hear that. What are you going to do?"

His eyes twinkled as he shrugged. "Don't know how this year'll turn out, but darned if it wasn't the best thing that ever happened to the farm."

Anita's brow furrowed, and she hugged Charlie tighter. "What do you mean?"

"Well, it's a real blow when something like that happens. A real blow. And the boys were spittin' mad wonderin' what're we going to do and how're we going to recover, and then . . ."

She held her breath, grimacing inside as she pictured Jake and Ed yelling at each other in the middle of a torn-up potato field, their hopes for a bountiful crop shattered.

Vernon smiled. "Then they started talkin' to each other. Not just talkin' but listening. It was like they had a common enemy, a common goal. They didn't want to hear each other before, but all of a sudden, they were speakin' the same language again."

Charlie wriggled in Anita's arms, so Anita set her down on the blanket. As she straightened, her mind raced. "They're not fighting anymore?"

Vernon took a bite of his donut and chewed for a moment, looking thoughtful. "It's not as simple as that, I guess. They don't see eye to eye on *everything*, but they got all these new ideas and plans, and when they told me about them, I realized I'd heard them all before. They'd each talked about it at different times, in different ways, and it was *me* who wasn't listening." He took a deep breath and got a faraway look in his eyes. "Guess it was my fault all along. I should've . . ."

There was that word again. *Should've*. Anita looked down at Charlie. If the dear child stayed with Tad for a long time and Anita had the chance to help raise her, would she do better guiding a child into adulthood the second time around? Would she see things more clearly? Have a more mature perspective?

"Guess it don't matter much what I should've done," Vernon continued. "What matters is what I'm going to do now."

Anita raised her eyebrows. "And what's that?"

Vernon gave her a lopsided grin, and there was a little bit of chocolate frosting in the silver-specked scruff above his upper lip. "Remember that pamphlet you gave me about estate planning?"

She nodded.

"That's what I'm going to do. With Jake'n Ed's help."

"But what about your crop?"

He popped the last bite of his donut into his mouth and washed it down with a swig of coffee. "The hail damage happened early enough that the plants could recover. Maybe, maybe not. Either way, we'll start making plans for next year because that's what farmers do."

"It's not an easy way of life, is it?"

"There is no easy way of life."

Anita glanced down at Charlie. Wasn't that the truth.

❦ ❦ ❦

Anita opened the door when Tad knocked at the end of the day. He looked tired.

She stepped aside and smiled. "How many times do I have to tell you, you don't have to knock?"

He looked down at his boots and shrugged. "Is Charlie ready?"

"She's playing with her new toy." Anita gestured for him to follow her. "Over here."

He stayed close on her heels. "New toy?"

She waved a dismissive hand. "Something I picked up at the dollar store."

One side of his mouth lifted. "How many times do I have to tell you, you don't have to keep buying her stuff?"

Anita laughed. "Maybe I'll stop buying her things when you stop knocking on the door."

Tad grumbled, but when they entered the kitchen and he saw Charlie, the tension in his face eased a little. Anita could see it had been hard on him to be separated from his daughter over the weekend.

"Any word on what's going to happen to your dad?"

Tad's back was to her as he picked Charlie up. "No."

He had stiffened at the mention of his father. Bud had turned himself in for Tad's sake, but clearly all was not forgiven. "Are you and Charlie okay at the house by yourselves?"

Tad held Charlie close. "Yeah."

Anita shifted on her feet. Tad didn't seem like himself. Was it because of what he'd been through or something else? "Let me pack up some leftovers for you to take home. I made a rice and bean casserole last night, and we hardly ate any of it."

Before he could protest, she began pulling food from the fridge and empty containers from the container drawer.

"I think Charlie's about ready to start trying some rice cereal," she said. "She's ahead of the curve, that's for sure. I can pick some up for you next time I get groceries."

When Tad didn't respond, Anita turned around to look at him. He was peering at Charlie's face, his expression inscrutable but tinged with an undercurrent of anguish.

She shut the fridge. "Are you okay?"

He flinched, as if he'd forgotten she was there. His eyes never left his daughter. "I don't know."

"You don't know if you're okay?"

"I don't know what to do. About Charlie."

Anita stepped closer. "I'll help you. She's so smart, I don't think she'll have any trouble learning to eat solid food."

"No. Not that."

The look of torment in his eyes made Anita's gut twist. What if something was wrong with Charlie?

The leftovers were forgotten as she tried to speak gently. "What is it, Tad?"

He hung his head. "I heard . . . I mean, someone told me that . . ."

Anita waited.

Tad let out a long breath. "That I'm not Charlie's dad."

Anita gasped. How could that be? She'd been there when Jenna dropped the baby off. She'd marveled at how Charlie had Tad's nose. She'd seen Charlie make expressions that reminded her so much of Tad that she'd been transported back to when Holly was still around and Tad was a baby.

"Have you talked to Jenna about it?"

Tad's face pinched in misery. "No. I'm afraid to ask."

Compassion swept over her. What this poor boy must be suffering. He must have so many questions, and not knowing was often harder than knowing.

She moved closer and touched his elbow. "What can I do to help?"

His head jerked up. "What should I do?"

That was a question and a half. She didn't want to rush an answer, but she could feel Tad's desperation.

"Jenna entrusted Charlie to you. I think that means something, no matter what you heard. You shouldn't work yourself up or make any decisions until you have all the facts. You need to talk to Jenna."

"She doesn't exactly pick up on the first ring when I call. What am I supposed to do while I'm waiting for her to decide to talk to me?"

"What you've been doing since Charlie first came. Love her and take care of her, and we'll help however we can."

Tad stared at the top of Charlie's head and when he spoke there was a catch in his voice. "Even if she's not mine?"

"Right now, she is."

"But Maddie didn't show up today. I know you don't want to take Charlie with you to the Coalition."

"I think it might be time for me to take a break from the Coalition, anyway. I can always go back someday. It's not going anywhere."

"Don't they need you?"

Anita put a hand on Charlie's back. "They'll be fine without me for a little while. Right now, Charlie needs me more."

Tad's eyes were wide. "Are you sure?"

"Of course." She smiled, her heart so full of love for the baby she thought it might explode. "She's my only grandchild, after all."

He wiped his eyes with his sleeve and sniffed. "Granny Anita. We could call you Granita."

Anita laughed, but Bud's face flashed in her mind, and seriousness quickly replaced her amusement. It was fun to think of Charlie as her granddaughter, but Bud really was Charlie's grandpa—she wanted to believe that—and he might not get the chance to see her again for a very long time. Her spirit stirred with the sense Tad needed to talk to Bud.

"You should go see your dad."

Charlie laid her head on Tad's shoulder, and he leaned his cheek against her curly hair. "I got nothing to say to him."

"Maybe he has something to say to you."

Tad kept his voice low but there was a bite in it. "He hasn't had anything to say to me for years, except for what a screwup I am."

"I know you probably don't remember, but he wasn't always like that. He used to love playing with you and your brother. I think the old Bud's still in there somewhere."

Tad hesitated. "I don't know."

"I think Charlie was starting to bring him out."

Tad's face transformed as he gazed down at Charlie, and Anita couldn't help but add, "That's what she does, isn't it? She brings out the best in people."

He rocked back and forth slowly as the baby snuggled deeper into his shoulder. "Yeah." His voice held equal traces of pride, wonder, and agony. "She does."

There was a lot more Anita could say about what Bud used to be like—about the kind of man she knew he could be—but she turned back to the task of filling containers with food for Tad to take home and spoke over her shoulder. "Every time you take a bite of this casserole, remember . . ."

Tad took a deep breath. "I'll remember you're praying for me."

forty-seven

The drive from Grady to Larkspur, where Bud had been transferred to the county jail, took fifty-two minutes, and Tad had squandered all fifty-two with thoughts of Jenna, Maddie, and Charlie rather than using them to prepare himself to face his father. Now here he was, in the parking lot, kicking himself. What was he supposed to say to Bud? Would his dad even be glad to see him?

Probably not.

He grumbled as he slid out of the Ford and slammed the door. He couldn't sit around and waste time. Anita was already doing him a big favor by taking Charlie on a Saturday, so he needed to get back to the ranch as soon as possible. She already had her hands full with ranch guests and Sam.

Tad's gut twisted at the thought of Sam. He'd avoided Tad all week. He'd moped around every day, and Tad hadn't even seen him kick a rock. The thought of Sam never kicking rocks again caused a pile of rocks to settle on Tad's heart.

He'd considered asking Maddie to babysit today instead of Anita. He'd considered a lot of things. In the end, however, he'd decided not to reach out to Maddie—or Jenna, for that matter. He didn't know what to say to either of them.

He reached the front door and hesitated. Why was he even here? He should be glad he no longer had Bud looking over his shoulder all the time, criticizing and complaining. He should be glad he had the house to himself. That's what he'd wanted all this time, wasn't it? Yet somehow Bud's absence the past week had left a gaping hole in Tad's life.

He went through the necessary procedures to enter the visitation room, with Anita's words about praying running through his mind. It was almost like he could feel her praying for him this very moment. As he sat at a table to wait, whispered words slipped out of his mouth.

"God, will You help me?"

His neck muscles tensed as he glanced around to see if any of the other visitors had heard him, but they were all lost in their own worlds of worry and nervous anticipation. He added "please" under his breath and braced himself as a buzz sounded and the door unlocked.

A handful of prisoners filed in. Some ran to their waiting family members and hugged them tight. Others shuffled, shamefaced, to the table where their visitors waited and hung their heads as they sat across from them. Bud stood near the door and stared at Tad with sharp and unreadable eyes. Tad did not stand up or wave or smile and wondered again what he was doing here. He could be with Charlie. He could be taking Sam out to lunch at Sloppy Joe's to try to cheer him up. He could be doing a million other things.

Finally, Bud walked over and stood beside the table. "What're you doing here?"

Tad fought the urge to bolt out of the room and never come back, but he couldn't escape the fact it could've been him stuck in this place. "Hey."

Bud huffed and sat down, a scowl on his face. "Where's Charlie?"

Tad shrugged. "Anita's got her."

A long minute of silence passed, then another. Tad scoured his mind for something to say.

"Any news about Pine?" he finally asked.

"They don't tell me anything." Bud looked like he wanted to spit. "But it doesn't matter. They're never gonna pin anything on him. He made sure of that."

Tad leaned forward as a flicker of heat flamed in his chest. "So he's just going to find someone else to do his dirty work? The chief'll be watching that old shed."

Bud raised a hand. "He won't go near Come Around Ranch again. He's got plenty of other places."

"He can't get away with this. Did you tell them everything you know? Even if you don't have any proof, maybe if you tell them about—"

"No. I've got nothing more to say about it."

Tad frowned. It wasn't fair that Matthew Pine wouldn't get what he had coming to him. Why had his dad ever joined up with that man in the first place?

"You could make a deal or something. You could get a shorter sentence."

Bud looked away and didn't respond.

Tad kicked the table leg. "Charlie misses you."

Bud flinched. "She's better off without me around."

"I don't know how much longer *she'll* be around."

Bud narrowed his eyes. "What're you talking about?"

Tad pictured his daughter's face—he still thought of her as his, he couldn't help it—and his stomach clenched. "It's just . . ."

He wiped a hand over his face, and the story spilled out. About what Maddie had heard. About Charlie's curls. About his greatest fear. As he spoke, he pictured Charlie looking up at him with those wide, trusting eyes of hers, and he remembered how for a minute there he'd thought maybe he could be something more. Because she seemed to believe it. But who was he kidding?

When he'd finished explaining, he was met with silence. He didn't look up. Couldn't meet his father's eye.

Bud pounded a fist on the table. "You're a real idiot."

"Really, Dad?" Tad looked up now, fire in his eyes. "You think I don't know that? You've been telling me my whole life."

Bud blinked. "No. You're an idiot if you plan to give up on Charlie. She's the only good thing you got going."

Tad swallowed. "But Scooter—"

"To hell with Scooter. He's an even bigger idiot than you are, and Charlie looks nothing like him."

"But her hair . . ."

"Who cares about her hair? Your brother had dark hair when he was a baby, and then it turned blond. Don't you think I recognize my own granddaughter when I see her?"

Tad didn't know what to think. All he knew was the idea of Scooter holding Charlie, touching her cheek, made a sharp and jagged piece of flint ricochet through his rib cage.

Tad picked at a crack in the table, his mind racing.

Bud lowered his voice. "You can't give up on Charlie. No matter what. I don't want to be in here for nothing."

❦ ❧ ❦

Tad peeked in on his daughter, then quietly shut the door. She was sound asleep. He tiptoed down the hall and onto the front porch. Now that Bud wasn't around to be irritated by her crying at night, he could move Charlie into a different bedroom. He could create a proper nursery for her. But at some point, his dad would be back. And Tad couldn't get the single-wide trailer with the big yard out of his mind. He wanted his own place.

He sat on the top step and pulled out a cigarette. He stared at it for a long time before setting it down and tapping his phone. After leaving the jail earlier, he'd texted Jenna that they needed to talk. He'd said it was urgent. She'd responded that he could call her tonight after eight.

It was 8:01.

The phone rang five times, and Tad's stomach lurched. Nothing in his life had prepared him for a moment like this.

There was a click. "Hey, Tad."

"Hey." He jiggled his knee and glanced at the cigarette on the step, his fingers itching to pick it up.

"What's so urgent?" Jenna asked. "Is Charlie okay?"

She sounded different than the last time. Steadier. Less frantic.

Tad took a deep breath. Let it out slowly. "Did you tell Lexi that Scooter is Charlie's dad?"

Silence. Inescapable, agonizing silence.

Then.

"Yes."

Tad's head jerked back like he'd been slapped. No. Not his Charlie.

The feel of his heart breaking was like his body being sliced in two, falling away on either side, never to be whole again.

"But I don't know for sure," Jenna continued, her voice strained.

He blinked. Forced himself to breathe. He sat up straight, every sense on high alert. "What's that supposed to mean? Why would you say it then?"

"I'm not sure if it's you or him, okay? I couldn't let him think . . ."

Her words dropped off, and Tad jumped to his feet. He bounded down the steps and paced the front yard. How could she do this? How could she tell him he was Charlie's father when she didn't even know?

"I'm sorry." There were tears in Jenna's voice. "I didn't know what to do. I knew he wouldn't want her, and I was afraid he might hurt her. But they caught him, you know. I heard he's going to be in jail for a really long time, so I thought maybe . . ."

Tad stopped pacing and froze. "Maybe what?"

"I could come back."

This time the silence was on his end, and his body shook as his mind sorted through what he had heard. A lump formed in his throat. He opened his mouth and forced the words out.

"You want to take Charlie away."

"No. I just want to see her."

A hot summer breeze blew over the sweat on Tad's forehead. His first thought was that Jenna had no right. She didn't get to drop a baby off with him, not even knowing whose baby it was, and disappear, then decide to show back up one day as if nothing ever happened. What kind of parent would do that? It wouldn't be fair.

His second thought was of what Dan had told him about grace. *"It means we give people chances and love them even when maybe they don't deserve it."* He didn't want to, not one bit, but shouldn't he show grace to Jenna after Dan and Anita had shown it to him? Hadn't he also needed someone to step in for Charlie when he couldn't take care of her?

Was he any better than Jenna?

His third thought was of hope. As Jenna's words sank in deeper and deeper, his heart stopped splitting in half and held tight to hope, the only thing that could stitch it back together. Charlie *might* be Scooter's daughter, but she might not be. That beautiful butterfly might be part of *him*. His honest-to-goodness daughter. He loved her more than he'd ever realized was possible. Didn't that mean something?

"Please," Jenna said. "I miss her so much. I was trying to keep her safe."

"Okay." He looked back at the house, picturing Charlie in her crib, her chubby fists raised above her head, her little tummy rising and falling as she breathed. "When will you come?"

forty-eight

Anita glanced around the corner at the stairs Wednesday morning, though she didn't expect to see Sam. Ever since Curly died, he'd been sleeping in.

"I'm going to make some calls today." She moved close to Dan as he ate his breakfast and kept her voice down. "See if I can find anyplace willing to hire Sam part-time."

Dan cut up the reheated leftover pancakes she'd set out. "Have you talked to Sam about it?"

"I thought it'd be best to check our options first."

Dan gave her a look, and she sighed. Would she ever learn to let Sam have his own life? Be his own person? She'd worked hard to understand what other people needed—Maddie, Tad, Vernon—but she'd been blind to her own son's needs. She'd been so sure she knew what was best. She'd even had the nerve to ask God why He wasn't doing what she thought He should do.

"Okay, you're right," she said. "I'll ask him how he would feel about getting a job when he comes down."

Dan grunted his approval, and Anita took a sip of strong coffee. Charlie would be here soon, and Anita would need all the caffeinated energy she could get.

"Maybe you should call Bill today too." She drummed her fingers against her mug. "I know we haven't made any decisions about the trust yet, but it might be helpful to know what he's thinking."

Dan set his fork down slowly. "You know, I think Bill's a great guy, but this is a big decision. I'm not sure . . ."

Anita's heart squeezed. The hesitation in Dan's voice matched what she'd been feeling in her own spirit. Bill knew Sam well and loved him. He was a godly man and a good friend. But . . .

"He's only been out to the ranch a couple times." Dan leaned his elbows on the table. "I don't think he's ever ridden a horse. I don't know if he can understand how important it is to make sure Sam can continue his ranch life as long as he wants. I can't imagine Sam living in town, but it wouldn't be fair to expect Bill to move out here."

Anita nodded. "And he's never been a parent. He's used to being around kids for a little while and then sending them home."

"I can't help but wonder if there's a better choice." Dan shook his head. "I trust the Lord will make it clear."

Anita stilled as a wild idea skipped into her mind like a rock across the river. "What about Tad?"

Dan held up his hands and made a face. "Whoa, there. I agreed that we could extend his contract for the rest of the year on a trial basis, but you're talking about a whole different ball game. Tad's barely more than a kid himself."

"Him and Sam have known each other their whole lives. And Tad knows the ranch." She allowed her mind to picture it. Charlie could spend her days growing up here while Tad worked, and Tad and Sam would be like partners. Aside from her and Dan, no one knew Sam better than Tad. "At least think about it."

Dan let out a long breath. "This is our son's welfare we're talking about here."

"Believe me." Anita thought about all the food she'd fed Tad over the years. The talks they'd had. The prayers she'd prayed. "I know."

❖ ❖ ❖

The blistering afternoon sun baked the hard dirt. Tad slipped through the corral fence to check the self-filling troughs. They couldn't afford for anything to happen to the horse's water supply on a day like today. TJ left the shade of a cottonwood tree to march over and supervise but kept himself out of reach.

"You got trust issues?" Tad hooked his thumbs in his belt loops and tried to act as if he couldn't care less what the horse did. "Join the club."

TJ stepped closer, and Tad put a hand on his neck. The muscles tensed at Tad's touch.

"Charlie's mom is coming to visit this weekend, what do you think about that?"

TJ tossed his head, and Tad snorted. "Yeah."

As he walked back to the barn, he spied Sam coming around the corner. He was desperate for the kid to talk to him, but, as with TJ, he tried to play it cool.

"Hey, Sam," he called.

Sam scrunched up his face. "Guess what? My mom said I can work in town if I want. I can go two days a week."

Tad hid his surprise. "Oh? Where you gonna work?"

Sam shrugged. Tad wanted to say how sorry he was about

328

Curly. He wanted to hug Sam tight and tell him he never, ever meant for Sam to get caught up in Bud's schemes. He wanted to see the old Sam again, the one who thought everybody was nice and *City Slickers* was real life.

But that Sam was gone.

He was about to ask Sam if he wanted to go to Sloppy Joe's for dinner with him and Charlie after work, but a trail of dust in the distance caught his eye. Someone was coming up the drive. Someone in a red car.

Oh great.

Maddie.

What was she doing here? He glanced at Sam to see if he'd noticed. The kid was frozen, watching the dust cloud grow closer. Tad shook his head. It took guts on Maddie's part to come out here, he'd give her that.

Maddie pulled up slowly and got out of the car as Tad and Sam stared. Tad had done a lot of thinking the last few days about what Maddie had told him—or tried to tell him, anyway, before he'd cut her off and stormed away. She'd said she was sorry, and she'd said, *"I thought if I went along with my dad's plan, I could protect Sam."* Later, once Tad was back home and alone, he'd remembered her words and thought she and he weren't so different. He'd gone along with his dad's demands too. He'd tried to protect Sam.

Maddie approached, and a lot of feelings rolled around in Tad's heart.

She hesitated. "Hi, Sam."

Sam hung his head. "Curly's dead."

"I know. I'm sorry." She turned her eyes on Tad. "You haven't responded to my texts."

He raised one shoulder. "Been busy."

She ran pink fingernails with white tips through her hair. "I'm going away for a while, but I wanted to tell you the trailer's yours, if you're still interested."

Tad's eyebrows shot up. When he lay awake at night, he dreamed about that property and what he could turn it into with some time and labor. The treehouse he would build for Charlie. But it was a pipe dream. His future was uncertain.

Maddie read his face and held up a hand. "Hear me out. The owners are getting old and want to unload the property because it's too much work. They're willing to do a lease-to-own."

Excitement buzzed in Tad's chest, but he tamped it down. What if the Wilsons didn't renew his contract next year? What if he screwed up again?

She pulled a card from her pocket and held it out to him. "Think about it. Here's the number for a Realtor I trust. She's super nice, and she's expecting your call."

Tad reluctantly took the card. "Where are you going?"

Maddie smiled. "To school. At WSU. I've got to get settled in and find a job before classes start next month. I'm leaving tomorrow."

It crossed Tad's mind that tomorrow was the Fourth of July. Independence Day. "That's great."

"Since I'm going to be busy with work and school"—she turned her head toward Sam—"I need someone to take care of Jasper for me. I was hoping . . ."

Sam's eyes widened as Maddie opened the back seat of her car and a gangly golden retriever burst out. He ran three circles around Maddie's legs, then sniffed the air and came to a stop in front of Sam with a big doggy grin on his face.

"Holy huckleberries," Sam said. "He likes it here."

"Of course he does." Maddie sounded wistful. "This is a much better place for him than an apartment in Pullman. Will you look after him for me?"

An inner war played out on Sam's face. Tad could only imagine what a mind like Sam's would make of a situation like this.

"Why don't you show Jasper around the barn while you think about it?" Tad said.

Sam nodded in relief and spun on his heels. Jasper followed without hesitation as Sam lumbered toward the barn.

Maddie watched them go. "I really am sorry. About everything."

Tad didn't feel angry at her anymore. He'd made so many of his own mistakes. "Are you going to come back to visit?"

"I don't know. I need to get away from my parents for a while. And about what I said about Charlie—"

Tad held up a hand. "It's okay. You were trying to help. I needed to know."

"For what it's worth, I don't believe it. Anyone can see she belongs with you."

Tad kept what Jenna had told him and all his doubts, questions, and hopes to himself, but he nodded. "Thanks."

He didn't know what was going to happen, but he knew his world would never be the same again. He knew he wanted to build a life like the Wilsons had. He knew Anita would be praying for him.

"I better go." Maddie peered toward the barn. "Do you think Sam made up his mind yet?"

As she spoke, Sam and Jasper came bounding around the corner, and Sam swung his leg with all his might and kicked a rock. Instead of counting the skips, Sam laughed and laughed as Jasper chased the rock, picked it up in his mouth, and dropped it at Sam's feet.

"Yes." One side of Tad's mouth lifted. "I think he did."

He helped Maddie unload Jasper's bed and food and toys from her car, then stood back to give her space as Anita came out of the house and the two women stood close, talking intently, Charlie in Anita's arms between them. After a few minutes, Anita pulled Maddie into a hug, and Maddie wiped tears from her cheeks as she climbed into the Mazda and drove away.

Tad was surprised to find his mind entertaining the thought that he might actually miss her a little bit, though he quickly reminded himself he only had room in his life for one woman right now, and it wasn't Maddie. He hurried over to Anita and grinned as Charlie caught sight of him coming and squealed.

"Da-da." She reached her arms toward him. "Da-da."

He swallowed hard as he took her from Anita.

Anita smiled. "Did you hear that? No matter what anyone says, she knows who you are."

He buried his nose in Charlie's dark, curly hair and closed his eyes. She smelled like bubble bath and sunshine and applesauce, and he thought his heart might explode from loving her.

No matter what anyone says. He held Charlie closer. It wasn't that simple, he knew. Jenna was coming. Decisions would need to be made. Rumors were flying around Grady, and some people would probably always wonder whether Charlie was his daughter. But he didn't care. His heart belonged to Charlie.

Forever.

forty-nine

"Ready for your big day?" Mom asks and I nod even though I'm not sure how one day could be bigger than any other day. She smiles at me but her forehead is kind of pinched so I don't know what kind of smile it's supposed to be but that's okay because Mom said we don't always have to understand each other to care about each other and be on the same team. I was on a baseball team once.

I clear my breakfast plate and say, "I hope Jasper doesn't miss me too much while I'm at work" and Mom says I shouldn't worry about that because Jasper will be fine. I think Jasper loves me as much as Curly did and maybe more. I miss Curly and I miss Maddie. Maddie said she would visit on Labor Day.

I stand by the mudroom with my boots on hoping Dad will hurry up already because I don't want to be late on my first day but he's still in the bathroom so I watch out the window for Tad because if I can see Charlie before I leave then my day will be better. I wonder if Charlie was happy to see her mom over the weekend.

"Do you think Jenna is nice?" I ask and Mom says she hopes so. Dad's still not ready so I tell Mom about how I decided I'm going to pray for Charlie every day for the rest of my life because she's the best baby there is and Mom says she's praying too that everything will work out.

"Jenna's going to need our love," Mom says and it's a good thing Mom knows so much about that.

"And grace?" I say because I learned about grace at church from Mr. Bill and Mom says yes.

Finally Dad comes out of the bathroom and puts on his boots and kisses Mom and I think maybe Mom's going to kiss me too like I'm a little kid but instead she puts her hands on my shoulders and says "Have a good day, work hard." I'm ready to go and I follow Dad outside and I get in the truck and as we drive to town I realize Mom was right this is a big day.

author's note

Farming and ranching in all its many forms are not for the faint of heart. The agricultural life is filled with high levels of stress and high levels of risk. If you are an ag worker, I know it can sometimes feel like the burden of working the land and producing year after year for your community is too heavy. If you or someone you know is an ag worker in need of mental health resources or support, please visit FarmStress.us or call the Farm Aid Hotline at 1-800-FARM-AID. You are not alone. The ag community stands with you.

discussion questions

1. In the story, Tad learns a lot about grace. Talk about a time you either needed or extended grace.
2. Anita struggled with letting go of control over Sam's life. In what area of your life is God teaching you about letting go?
3. Who was your favorite character and why?
4. Which character do you think changed the most throughout the story?
5. Sam had a special relationship with his dog Curly. Have you ever had a special relationship with an animal? If so, what did they teach you?
6. What are your thoughts on the high levels of stress agriculture workers face? How can you support any ag workers in your life?
7. Which character do you identify with the most and why?
8. How would you respond if a baby unexpectedly appeared in your life?

9. Talk about all the ways Tad's poor relationship with his father impacted his life.

10. The story's conclusion is pretty open-ended. What do you think happens next?

acknowledgments

I'm grateful to everyone at Bethany House, from the people packing books in the warehouse to those making the hard decisions about which books to publish in the future. Because of you, dozens of uplifting and meaningful stories are released into the world each year. Special thanks to the people who worked on this book specifically, especially Rochelle Gloege. You are amazing.

I'm grateful to Kerry Johnson and Emily Conrad for reading my story in its early stages and providing honest and valuable feedback. You both bless me beyond words, and I love you.

I'm grateful to Amanda Reichman and Breakaway Youth Ranch in Cardwell, Montana, for insight and guidance with regard to horses and ranch operations. Any errors or liberties taken in that department should be attributed only to me.

I'm grateful to those who have supported and encouraged me on this journey, especially my husband and my mom. I'm grateful to my awesome agent, Keely Boeving, and all the wonderful readers out there who are willing to give my stories some of their time and attention. I hope to hear from you soon!

I'm grateful to my family: Andy, Michael, Simon, and Patience. More than grateful. I love you all bigger than the Montana sky. And I'm grateful to the God of grace and hope, without whom none of this would matter.

For more from
KATIE POWNER,
read on for an excerpt from

The Wind Blows
in
Sleeping Grass

After years of drifting, fifty-year-old Pete Ryman has settled down with his potbellied pig, Pearl, in the small Montana town of Sleeping Grass—a place he never expected to see again. It's not the life he dreamed of, but there aren't many prospects for a high-school dropout like him.

Elderly widow Wilma Jacobsen carries a burden of guilt over her part in events that led to Pete leaving Sleeping Grass decades ago. Now that he's back, she's been praying for the chance to make things right, but she never expected God's answer to leave her flat on her face—literally—and up to her ears in meddling.

When the younger sister Pete was separated from as a child shows up in Sleeping Grass with her eleven-year-old son, Pete is forced to face a past he buried long ago, and Wilma discovers her long-awaited chance at redemption may come at a higher cost than she's willing to pay.

Available now wherever books are sold.

The garbage truck grumbled to life like a grizzly waking from hibernation. Pete Ryman stepped down, blew out a breath that hung suspended in the frigid air, and turned to the seventy-nine-pound pig at his side.

"I told you, Pearl." Pete tugged on the zipper of his insulated coveralls. "If the truck runs, the route runs."

Pearl grunted. Pete unplugged the block heater as they made their way back to the passenger side, which was on the left in this particular vehicle—a beat-up, hand-me-down Xpeditor that the town of Sleeping Grass had purchased from nearby Shelby when Shelby bought a new Kenworth T370. Pete opened the door and set Pearl's portable pet ramp in place. The floor of the cab was almost four feet off the ground, so once Pearl had grown too big for Pete to lift, the ramp had become a necessity.

He made an exaggerated sweeping gesture toward the ramp. "Your Majesty."

While Pearl pranced up into the truck like the Queen of England's prize swine, Pete puffed out another breath. At zero degrees, his coat stiffened when he walked outside. At ten below, his nostril hairs froze. At twenty below, the early morning seemed to be a still life painting with only the crunch of his boots and slow rise of steam off the creek to prove it wasn't.

It was twenty below.

Once his sidekick was safely in her seat, he folded the ramp and hurried over to the right side of the truck. Pearl sniffed at the makeshift outfit she was wearing and gave him a long-suffering look as he buckled.

"I'm sorry." Pete shivered as he laughed. "It was the best I could do."

Pete had always believed an animal should wear only the covering God gave it. He'd mercilessly teased Windy Ray about the sweaters the old man put on his scruffy little dog. But what kind of protection did a potbellied pig have against a morning like this? He'd shortened the sleeves of an old hoodie with scissors, then tied up the back with a rubber band to keep the sweatshirt from dragging underneath her. She looked . . . well, ridiculous.

A gust of wind rammed the truck, poking frozen fingers through the cracks in the old beast.

"Don't even think of leaving this house without a coat."

The words pelted him like sleet, and he shook his head. For most folks, February was the shortest month of the year. For Pete, it was the longest. In February, the wind carried his mother's voice.

He turned up the radio and glanced over at his partner in crime. "Ready to roll, oh Pearl of great price?"

She stomped the fleece blanket with her front hooves, spun a cumbersome circle like an overweight dog, and nodded before settling in. At least that was how he took it. After nearly three years together, they seemed to have an understanding.

"All right, then."

The Autocar Xpeditor shuddered into drive and rumbled onto Seventh Street. He should've gotten up earlier to let the truck warm up. Even with a knit beanie on, he could feel the cold seeping through the bald spot on the back of his head. It would be an hour before the cab was comfortable. In the meantime, he and Pearl would tough it out.

Lights were starting to come on in some of the houses,

and Pete could see inside the windows that weren't covered by curtains. Mrs. Baker sat at her kitchen table, scooping the guts from half a grapefruit one spoonful at a time. Everett O'Malley sat in front of a giant flat-screen TV that flashed and flickered. Did that man ever sleep?

Pete knew their names because they left him Christmas cards. A handful of folks around here did that, even though he kept to himself and interacted with others as little as possible. One lady even left a neatly wrapped tray of homemade caramels every Christmas and a gift certificate to The Hog House in Shelby on the first day of every summer. She must not know about Pearl. She never signed the card.

Pete routinely caught glimpses of the private lives unfolding in Sleeping Grass, but folks rarely paid any attention to him. So long as he did his job, the garbage man remained largely unnoticed. He just drove and dumped, drove and dumped—week after week, month after month. Which was fine with Pete. He didn't want to be noticed.

"Hey, Pearl." He turned down his first alley and pulled up to the battered blue garbage bin waiting stoically for him like an old man at the bus stop. "What do you suppose we'd see if we ran the route backward one day? Just flipped it right around?"

She seemed to shrug. He'd be tempted to do it if it wouldn't send everyone into a state of panic and confusion. Folks would surely notice him then.

The hydraulic mast clutched the bin and dumped it effortlessly into the truck's hopper. At the next stop, a shabby-looking baby walker leaned against the bin, so Pete hopped out to grab it. Snake on a rake, it was cold.

This house had already used up their two "hand pickups" for the month, yet Pete never reported anyone if they went over the allotted amount. If the Sleeping Grass Public Works Department could look the other way when he had a potbellied tagalong in his cab, he could handpick a few extra items without complaining.

The walker was filthy—crayon marks covered the tray, and mashed Cheerios were crusted to the seat—but he saw no broken pieces. All four wheels were present and accounted for. No rips in the fabric.

It wasn't easy to wrangle the walker into the cab and over the center console. Thankfully it was collapsible. Pearl snorted irritably when Pete wedged it down in front of her seat, forcing her to reposition.

He quickly shut his door on the cold. "It's not my fault folks insist on throwing away perfectly good stuff."

Pearl snorted again, and Pete huffed. "And where would *you* be if I never rescued anything from the landfill?"

She nudged the chair with her snout.

"That's what I thought."

Pete was nearly two hours into his route when the sun peeked over the frozen prairie. It brought little warmth, but the temperature could rise to zero by noon. Maybe. On days like this, he kept the heat cranked up and recited Robert Frost's "An Old Man's Winter Night" to his unwitting cab companion.

Sleeping Grass was enduring one of the cold snaps common to February in the northern plains of Montana, an area along Highway 2 referred to as the Hi-Line. It had never bothered him when he lived here as a child, but now that he'd returned to the place where so many cold memories lived, the bitter chill weighed him down.

"Oh, February, you most unbearable and endless of months,
cold and dark and empty with no sign of spring.
Why must you breathe your stinging breath
all over everything?"

He liked to recite his own poetry to Pearl, as well. Her expectations for his body of work were, thankfully, not very high.

Pete turned down another alley while repeating the words of his poem in his head. December was cold and dark, too, but there were glimpses through windows of Christmas parties and holiday lights and gingerbread houses. And January's cold and dark were tempered by the promise of new beginnings, the hope of starting over. But February?

February was the reason not everyone made it on the Hi-Line.

He stopped alongside the trash bin belonging to a tiny gray bungalow buttoned up tight against the cold. A wisp of smoke rose from the chimney. He maneuvered the joystick to lower the grabber while peering over the fence. Though run-down and nondescript, this was his favorite house.

The house where *she* lived.

There were never extra items to handpick here, only a bin full of beer cans and tequila bottles, week after week. He was sure those belonged to Jerry, the other resident of the house. He'd often seen Jerry out carousing, and Pete had faced him down twice now when he'd met Pete at the truck to chew him out over letting the lid of the trash bin hit the fence.

Pete had seen the hard set of his jaw and the mean glint in his eye. He'd never seen *her*, though, except for a few brief glances through the window. He'd never met her. Didn't know her name. But he knew it couldn't be Jerry who was responsible for the burgeoning flower beds in the backyard. The picnic table painted yellow with white daisies stenciled across its top. The bird feeders and wind chimes and well-kept crabapple tree with a barn-shaped birdhouse perched in its branches.

She had done all that. And she'd been the only reason Pete hadn't broken Jerry's nose that last time. That and the fact Pete was tired of never lasting more than a couple years at a job before being fired for losing his temper. Tired of having to find a new place to live. This time he was planning to stick it out, if only to watch her backyard stutter to life every spring like a foal finding its legs. He was getting too old for fighting.

There were no flowers now, not in godforsaken February. The picnic table lay under a tarp. But he could picture it all, and he believed the hands that nurtured this oasis must be beautiful hands indeed.

Surely they must be.

The hands that cultivate the seed
Must be beautiful indeed . . .

Pearl grumbled, and Pete blinked, his face warming as he realized how long he must've been staring at the house, hoping to catch a glimpse of her. Daydreaming in rhyme. Boy, was he ever stupid. Stupid!

He saw Pearl looking at him as he quickly drove forward to the next bin. He chuckled. "What are *you* staring at?"

Pearl tolerated him at least. Pearl and Windy Ray were his only friends in Sleeping Grass. He'd feared coming back here would mean running into all kinds of folks from his past, but he hardly remembered anyone. That was what almost forty years of being away did. It made it easier to pretend he had no past here at all. No history.

Except when February rolled around.

about the author

Katie Powner, Christy Award–winning author of *The Wind Blows in Sleeping Grass* and *Where the Blue Sky Begins*, grew up on a dairy farm in the Pacific Northwest but has called Montana home for over twenty years. She is a biological, adoptive, and foster mom who loves Jesus, red shoes, and candy. In addition to writing contemporary fiction, Katie blogs about family in all its many forms and advocates for more families to open their homes to children in need. To learn more, visit her website at KatiePowner.com.

Sign Up for
Katie's Newsletter

Keep up to date with Katie's latest news on book releases and events by signing up for her email list at the link below.

KatiePowner.com